# NOTHING BUT GHOSTS

Also by Judith Hermann

*The Summer House, Later*

# JUDITH HERMANN

# *Nothing But Ghosts*

## STORIES

Translated from the German by
Margot Bettauer Dembo

FOURTH ESTATE • *London* and *New York*

First published in Great Britain in 2005 by
Fourth Estate
A Division of HarperCollins*Publishers*
77–85 Fulham Palace Road
London W6 8JB
www.4thestate.co.uk

1

A catalogue record for this book is
available from the British Library

ISBN 0-00-717455-1

Typeset by Palimpsest Book Production Limited,
Polmont, Stirlingshire
Printed in Great Britain by Clays Ltd, St Ives plc

*for Franz*

*Wouldn't it be nice*
*If we could live here*
*Make this the kind of place*
*Where we belong*

The Beach Boys

# Contents

# Ruth
## (Girlfriends)

Ruth said, 'Promise me that you'll never start anything with him.' I still remember the way she looked when she said it, sitting on the chair by the window, bare legs drawn up to her chest. She had showered and washed her hair, and she was in her underwear, a towel wrapped around her head, her face very open, wide, looking at me intently, more amused than worried. She said, 'Promise me that, OK?' and I looked past her out of the window at the multi-storey car park across the street. It was raining and already getting dark. The car park sign shone blue and beautiful. I said, 'Listen, why should I promise? Of course I won't start anything with him.' Ruth said, 'I know. Promise me anyway,' and I said, 'I promise,' and then I looked at her again; she shouldn't have said that.

I've known Ruth all my life.

She had known Raoul for two or three weeks. He had come to do a guest appearance at the theatre where she had a two-year engagement; he wasn't staying long; perhaps that's why she was in such a hurry. She phoned

1

me in Berlin – we had shared an apartment until she had to move because of her stint at the theatre. We weren't good at dealing with being apart. In fact, she called me every evening. I missed her.

I was sitting in the kitchen, which was empty now except for a small table and a chair, staring at the wall while we talked on the phone. There was a little piece of paper she had tacked up on the wall once: '*Tonight, tonight it's gonna be the night, the night.*' I kept thinking about taking it down, but then I never did. She had phoned as usual and blurted it right out. 'I'm in love,' she said. And then she talked about Raoul, and her voice sounded so happy, she made me feel restless, in a way even nervous, and I had to get up and, still holding the phone, walk through the apartment.

I'd never been interested in her men, nor she in mine. She said, 'He's so tall.' She said all the things you always say, and a few new things too. Being in love this time didn't seem to be different from her other, earlier infatuations. For a week she and Raoul had been tiptoeing around, stealing glances and trying to be near each other. After a party one night, drunk, they had kissed for the first time in the pedestrian mall of the small town. They kissed behind the scenery during the break between scenes and in the canteen after their colleagues had left and the canteen cook had put up the chairs. Raoul had such soft hands, she said. His head was shaved; sometimes he wore glasses – small, bent metal frames that didn't suit his face. He looked strange with them on. She said, 'He's really more *your* type, really, exactly *your* type. You'd faint if you saw him.'

I said, 'What's that supposed to mean, my type?'

And Ruth hesitated, giggled, then said, 'I don't know, maybe physically? A little common maybe?'

He said nice things to her – 'The colour of your eyes is the colour of grass when the wind sweeps through it, reversing the blades to white.' She quoted him reverently; he was also vain, she said (and laughed), like a child in a way. He was playing the part of Caliban in *The Tempest*. Evening after evening, the audience went wild. He was from Munich. His father died a long time ago. Raoul had studied philosophy. Actually, this summer he was going to Ireland, would sleep in his car, would try to write while sitting on the cliffs with a view of the sea. Raoul. Ruth pronounced it *Ra-uhl*.

When I visited Ruth – not because of this new love of hers; I would have gone to see her in any case – she picked me up at the railway station and I saw her before she saw me. She was walking along the platform, looking for me. She wore a long, blue dress, her hair pinned up. Her face glowed, and the physical tension, her walk, the way she held her head and her searching gaze expressed an expectation that could in no way ever be meant for me. Nor did she find me, and eventually I simply walked over and stood in front of her.

She was startled but then she hugged me, kissed me, and said, 'Oh, my dear, my dear.' The new perfume she was wearing smelled of sandalwood and lemons. I took her hands and held them in mine, I looked into her face; her laughter was very familiar.

Ruth had rented a tiny apartment downtown, an American-style apartment, one room, a kitchenette, a bath. There were no curtains at the big windows; the bathroom was the only place you could hide from the drivers who parked their cars in the multi-storey across the way and then stared over at you for minutes at a time, seemingly absent-mindedly. The room was small, one bed, a rack on which to hang up clothes, a table, two chairs, a stereo system. On the windowsill stood a photo I had given her as a goodbye present, the view from our apartment in Berlin. On the table, a silver ashtray from Morocco, and tucked into the frame of the mirror over the bathroom sink a passport picture of me.

There must have been a moment when I was alone in the apartment – Ruth at the theatre or shopping with Raoul – and I remember that I sat on the chair by the window, on Ruth's chair, smoking a cigarette and exposing myself to the eyes of the people in the multi-storey; the neon sign flickered, the room was unfamiliar, the stairwell on the other side of the apartment door dark and quiet.

Ruth doesn't look anything like me. Everything about her is the opposite of me. All the places she's round and soft and big, I'm skinny and bony and small. My hair is short and dark; hers is very long and light, curly and bouncy. Her face is beautiful, quite simple, and everything is in proportion – her eyes, her nose, her mouth, all in symmetry. The first time I saw her she was wearing a pair of huge sunglasses and even before she took them off I knew what the colour of her eyes would be – green.

I intended to stay three days, go on to Paris, and then return to Berlin. Back then I would often travel to foreign cities, stay for an aimless, dogged week and leave again. While we were still at the railway station, Ruth said, 'Stay a little longer, won't you?'

It was a small town and easy to get your bearings in.

## Ruth (Girlfriends)

The pedestrian zone was right behind the station; the theatre was on the market square; and the church steeple was always visible above the roofs. Taking my suitcase Ruth regarded me closely; she said she was worried that I might become cynical – disparaging and arrogant about the pedestrian zone, the Tchibo coffee bar, the department store, the hotel in the market square – this place where she'd be living for the next two years. I had to laugh; I was far from becoming cynical; I envied her these two years in a small town, without really being able to explain why.

We sat down in an Italian café, ordered strawberry ice cream with whipped cream, coffee and water; I lit a cigarette and turned my face up to the late summer sun. I thought, 'I could feel more carefree in a small town.' The waiter brought two small coffeepots, dishes of ice cream, glasses, and looked at Ruth, enthralled; she didn't notice. Me, he ignored. Ruth was restless; didn't finish her ice cream, ordered another coffee, kept glancing up and down the pedestrian zone, a rushed, hurried, searching glance at the people there, back to my face, and away again.

Then she smiled. 'It's awful, awful, awful,' she said, looking not at all unhappy. 'You have to tell me what you think of him, all right?' she said. 'You have to be honest.' And I said, 'Ruth –' and she said, very serious, 'It's important to me.' Things had become more difficult with Raoul last week; there was a fight, a stupid misunderstanding, all in the past now, and yet . . . Evidently there was some sort of ex-wife in Munich with whom he had long telephone conversations while Ruth was in the room; from time to time he withdrew, didn't keep dates, or arrived late, was sometimes untalkative, sullen and then again euphoric, impatient, intoxicated with Ruth's beauty.

She wasn't sure what he wanted from her; she said, 'Maybe he only wants to go to bed with me.' Up to that point he hadn't yet done that. And there were these rumours. Someone said he had a reputation and it wasn't the best. Actually something like that wouldn't rattle Ruth. Still, she said, 'I don't want to become his trophy, you know?' looking at me so innocently and openly that I was almost ashamed, ashamed for myself, for Raoul, for the rest of the world. I said, 'Ruth, that's silly, you're not a trophy. Nobody is going to betray you, and nobody wants to prey on you; that much I know.' I meant it sincerely, and for the moment Ruth looked comforted and reassured. She took my hand and said, 'And you? How are you?'

As always, I evaded the question and, as always, she allowed me to be evasive, and then we sat there like that, sleepy in the afternoon light, feeling close. Towards seven o'clock Ruth had to go to the theatre, and I went with her.

Ruth, sleeping. When we shared our first apartment – how many years ago? was it five, ten? – we slept in one bed. Often we went to bed at the same time, lay next to each other, face to face, Ruth's eyes dark and shiny in the night; she would whisper half-sentences, hum softly, then I would fall asleep. I could never have gone to sleep like that with a man; I don't know whether Ruth could. Her sleep was deep and sound, heavy and motionless. She always lay on her back, her long hair fanned out around her head, her face relaxed, like a portrait. She breathed quietly and slowly. I always woke up before she did and then I lay there, my head supported on my hand, watching her. I remember that once, during one of our

6

rare arguments, I threatened to cut off her hair while she slept. I don't want to believe that I could ever have said something like that, but I know it's true.

Ruth owned a nightmarishly huge metal alarm clock; its earsplitting ring was the only thing that could actually wake her. The alarm clock stood on her side of the bed, and even though I was always awake first, I never woke her up but let the crazy ringing do it; she emerged from sleep visibly tormented, opened her eyes, hit the 'off' button on the alarm, and immediately groped for the cigarettes she always put next to her side of the bed at night. She would light one, sink back into the pillows, smoke, sigh, and at some point she would say, 'Good morning.' Later, in other apartments and other beds, she gave up smoking in the morning. Maybe because by then we were no longer waking up together.

Ruth was playing the role of Eliante in Molière's *Misanthrope*. I had seen her in many productions while she was an acting student at the academy. As a Viking king in Ibsen's *The Vikings of Heligoland* her small form was wrapped in a bear pelt and her hair arranged like a cloud around her head. She was carried on stage on a sea of lances and bellowed her soul out for two hours. As Lady Macbeth she was suspended head down by silken threads in front of a white wall and made fishlike gliding motions with her hands. But I thought she was strangest as Mariedl in Schwab's *Lady Presidents*, scarcely recognizable in a grey house-cleaning smock, cowering under a table. Ruth was a good actress, a comedienne with great stage presence, very physical, but she was always Ruth to me; I recognized her, her face, her voice, her posture.

Perhaps it was because I was always trying so hard to

7

recognize her – the Ruth who dressed in the morning, slowly, carefully, one item after the other, then looked in the mirror with that special expression intended only for the mirror, and always sideways. The Ruth who drank her coffee holding the cup with both hands and not setting it down till she had emptied it, the way she smoked, made up her eyelashes, smiled into the receiver with her head tilted to one side when she was on the phone.

She had wanted to impersonate me, do a portrait study of me, and she followed me around for three days with a scholarly expression on her face, imitating my movements until I stopped, stood stock still in a corner of the room, and yelled at her to quit it. Later she impersonated her mother with a precision and attention to detail that made me shudder.

The staging of *The Misanthrope* was straightforward and faithful to the original, far removed from the chaotic and improvisational student productions. At first I was bored; then I found it beautiful, perhaps because, for the first time, I saw Ruth as if from afar, unencumbered by pretentious suspensions from steel scaffolding. She was wearing a kind of white children's sailor suit with her hair twisted into a braid; her face was clearly defined, thoughtful and sensible. Perhaps her voice was a little too trembly for Eliante, too cracked, as if she were choking, and not quite authentic: *'That isn't really how love works at all for most people. You find that a man in love always justifies his own choice. His passion makes him blind to all faults and in his eyes everything in the woman he loves is lovable. He counts her defects as perfections or finds flattering names for them.'*

I was disappointed and at the same time relieved not to see her in the role of Célimène, the foolish, vulnerable, loving Célimène. There was sustained applause after each act; but, then, I had expected nothing less in this small town. Ruth took a deep bow, beaming, radiant. She had a new habit of immediately running off stage like a child; in other productions she had gone off hesitantly and reluctantly.

I remained in my seat till the last person in the audience had left the auditorium. The stagehands were beginning to dismantle the sets and the lights were turned off. Dust rained down onto the stage. There were times when I had envied Ruth her talent, her profession, the applause, the possibility of fame. But this envy faded at some point when I realized that I was absolutely unsuited, really quite impossible, for the theatre. I sat in the empty row of seats, leaning forwards, and tried to understand Ruth, to understand what she was doing here, how she worked, what she felt. I couldn't, didn't understand a thing, and then I stood up and went to the theatre canteen. Raoul's performance on the second stage would be finished at about eleven o'clock; Ruth had asked me to wait with her for him.

On the day she moved out of the apartment we shared and left Berlin for this small town, I was in no state to carry even a single box out to the removal van. Her entire family had come to help with the move, her mother, her two sisters, and her brother and his wife. We all had breakfasted together; it was January and the harsh winter sunlight streamed pitilessly through the windows. I had tried to draw out breakfast as long as possible but then it was over, and everybody got up and began to pack Ruth's things, while I sat as if turned to stone in my chair at the table, with the remains of our breakfast. I clutched the arms of the chair; I couldn't move; couldn't even get up.

Ruth's family worked around me; they pushed bureaus, chairs, cartons across the room, carried Ruth's suitcases and boxes, her bed, her bookshelves, her kitchen cupboard, her desk, all of her things, down the three flights of stairs, all the while making it clear how impossible and rude they thought I was. I couldn't help it; I sat there motionless, mute.

The apartment door was wide open, and cold air swept in from time to time. Ruth briefly came over, putting her dirty hand on my cheek; then she left again. When everything was packed, one of her sisters put the breakfast dishes into the last of the removal boxes and managed to get the table outside as well. Eggshells, a jam jar and one coffee cup were left on the floor. I got up. The family disappeared down the stairwell; in the van Ruth's brother blew the horn. Ruth put on her coat; we stood facing each other in the empty hall, then we embraced. She said, 'See you soon.' Or maybe I said it. Then she left. I closed the apartment door behind her and stood there until I was certain they were gone.

For a long time I didn't know what to do with Ruth's room. It stood empty for a month, two months, three. At some point I began using it to watch Super 8 home movies. I would sit on a chair, the projector humming, and on the white wall a child, supposedly me once upon a time, walked across a sand dune. In May or June, I moved my bed into Ruth's room, to the same spot where hers had stood.

The theatre canteen was small, stuffy and filled with cigarette smoke. It had Formica-topped tables, wooden benches, spherical light fixtures and mirrored walls that did nothing to make the room look larger. Instead it seemed smaller in a labyrinthine, chaotic way. The stage-hands were sitting at tables in the rear, the actors in the front. Behind the counter, a fat woman, who was the cook and looked dead tired, drew beer from the tap. Ruth was nowhere to be seen.

I sat down at the only unoccupied table, ordered a cup of coffee and a glass of wine, not sure whether I wanted to wake up or get drunk. I wondered where my suitcase was. Ruth had taken it either into her dressing room or left it with the doorman. Suddenly I wanted to have my things back again, my book, my appointment calendar. I felt insecure sitting at this table, a stranger, someone who had absolutely nothing to do with the theatre. I looked over at the actors; there was no one sitting there who was '*so tall*' with a shaved skull and a face at once childish and manly, and then the canteen door opened and he came in.

I recognized him instantly. It was a two-fold recognition, and it was so unmistakable that impulsively I actually ducked, hunching my shoulders and drawing in my head. I hastily moved my chair out of the circle of light cast by the ceiling lamps, and he walked by me without noticing me and sat down with the actors, who seemed delighted to see him. He took off his jacket without getting up, a suede jacket with a brown fur collar. Touching someone's arm, he laughed, spoke, I could hear his voice distinctly among all the other voices. I tried not to listen; I would rather have seen him first with Ruth, Raoul as Ruth's Raoul. *You have to tell me what you think of him.*

I searched for my cigarettes in my coat pockets; the cigarettes weren't there; they were in my bag, probably in Ruth's dressing room; I felt a brief flash of anger. I wanted to analyse what I was feeling, to examine some particular thought, and a cigarette might have helped. I could still hear his voice and I could see his face in the mirror, an alert, open face; he wasn't wearing his glasses; his look was one of attentive concentration, the dark eyes narrowed; there were remnants of white theatrical make-up at his temples. His profile, on the other hand, was not beautiful, but dull, complacent and ordinary, a protruding chin, a low forehead. He really *was* very tall, his body heavy and massive, and he had coarse hands with which he gesticulated and rubbed his shaved head. I could hear Ruth's voice – *I don't know, physically, maybe a bit common* – I knew what she had meant to say, but that's not what he was. I stared at him. I thought I knew everything there was to know about him and yet nothing at all. I carefully moved my chair back to the table. My breathing was shallow, soft; suddenly I felt at a loss. Then the door opened and Ruth came in.

She came in and saw Raoul immediately. Her eyes went straight to him, and her face took on an expression that was new to me, and then she looked over the heads of the others, across the room until finally she saw me. She made an indecipherable signal with her right hand, stopped at the counter and ordered a beer. She was standing very erect, like someone who thinks she is being watched, but Raoul hadn't even seen her yet. Then she came over to my table, sat down next to me, thirstily drank some beer, put the glass down, and said, 'How was it?' and then, 'Did you see him?' I said clearly, 'By any chance would you have a cigarette?' and she raised her eyebrows, irritated, then smiled and pulled some cigarettes from her pocket.

She was wearing her blue dress again, her hair still in the Eliante hairdo; she looked beautiful, tired; she said, 'It's good that you're here.' And then again, 'Did you see him?' She nodded her head in his direction, and I said, 'No.' She said, 'He's already here, he's sitting over there.' I said, 'Where?' She whispered, 'At the third table on the left in the middle.' I lit my cigarette, repeated to myself the words we had just exchanged – *did you see him, no, did you see him, where* – turned my head and looked over at Raoul, and just then he turned round in our direction.

He looked at Ruth and smiled, and Ruth smiled back while she pressed her leg against mine under the table. I puffed on my cigarette, I said, 'I really liked the play'; I said it again. Raoul got up. It looked as though he wanted to excuse himself from the others, was held back, pulled himself away, came over to our table, slowly, calmly, all the while very clearly presenting his body, his entire person. I looked away, and then I looked back; somehow I felt embarrassed. Raoul sat down, he could have sat next to Ruth, but he took the chair across from us. Ruth introduced me, and we shook hands across the table; I quickly pulled mine back. Under the table Ruth's leg kept pressing against mine. He said, 'Ruth told me a lot about you,' and he smiled; his eyes revealed nothing even though they were fixed directly on mine for a long time. The cook called out his name, 'Raauuul,' like a howl. He got up again and went over to the counter. Ruth said, 'Good Lord,' and then, 'What do you think; quick, tell me,' and I had to laugh and I said, 'Ruth, I met him less than sixty seconds ago.'

He returned with a plate of soup, sat down again, and began to eat, saying nothing. Ruth watched him as though she had never seen anyone eat before, so I watched him too; I had no choice. Actually his eating was quite odd; perhaps he had some particular role in mind, a special way of eating, a Franciscan monk at a wooden table in the refectory of his monastery, a South Tyrolean peasant holding a tin plate on his lap, or something equally absurd. He ate bent forwards over his food in stolid absorption. He slurped and carried his spoon to his mouth and back to the plate with the regularity of a machine, swallowed noisily, and none of us said a word until he had finished. Then he pushed away the empty plate, and for a moment I expected him to emit a loud burp, but the performance was over. He seemed to be a master of brevity. He wiped his mouth with the back of his hand, leaned back, smiled at us, and said, 'Well, how are you?'

The tone of voice in which Ruth said 'All right, thanks' was new to me; it had a note of stiffness and insecurity that I hadn't heard before; she seemed nervous, testy, and there was a strained expression around her mouth. 'How did the performance go?' Raoul asked; actually he was making it easy for her, he asked it pleasantly, showing real interest, and Ruth answered sarcastically, 'As usual, a roaring success.' She made a disparaging face, as though to indicate that the small-town public was an unde-manding one, an attitude I knew was foreign to her. 'I didn't have to give it my all.' With that she finally moved her leg away from mine and looked around the canteen with feigned nonchalance. Raoul smiled, still pleasantly; it seemed that he neither expected this kind of capri-ciousness from her nor found it appropriate. Ruth, however, was sticking to that line, or perhaps she couldn't backtrack; it was as though she wanted to prove some-thing to him.

Raoul simply ignored me; it wasn't rudeness – actually, it was rather pleasant. He was very attentive to Ruth, yet to me he conveyed the vague feeling that this attitude of his was supposed to tell me something about him. He asked her about the simplest things, and she didn't give straight answers but instead became involved in such twisted subtleties that I got up and excused myself because it was becoming unbearable. I went to the toilet, stood in front of the mirror for a while and gazed helplessly at my face. I wondered what Raoul thought of me. Then I went back out and walked up and down the corridor outside the dressing rooms.

The performance by the theatre's resident ballet troupe had just finished; all the performers were rushing to the canteen, fat trumpeters, tipsy violinists, lean, cheerful dancers. I squeezed my way along the wall, took momentary pleasure in the palpable post-performance euphoria that emanated from them and immediately came down to earth again. The neon lighting was harsh and the musicians looked tired and seedy. 'That Mozart shit,' one of the dancers said to a cellist who was dragging his instrument case along behind him as if it were an old suitcase.

When I came back to the canteen, Raoul and Ruth seemed to have calmed down, or at least Ruth had calmed down; she looked more relaxed and her cheeks were flushed. She was leaning across the table, talking insistently to Raoul. When I sat down again, she stopped and leaned back, slightly embarrassed. Both looked at me, and I didn't know what to say; I felt foolish, stared stubbornly at the tabletop. I tried to make Ruth understand that I didn't feel up to this, didn't feel like talking, not ready to help out, at least not now, but she smiled absent-mindedly and blissfully past me, put her hand on mine in an outlandish gesture, and said, 'Would you two like something else to drink?' I said dully, 'A glass of wine, please,' then I pulled my hand away. Raoul said, 'Nothing, thanks.'

Ruth got up to order the wine, and as she passed Raoul, he turned towards her and suddenly grabbed her between the legs from behind – it was the ultimate of obscene gestures. She stopped, the expression on her face did not change a bit; she stood there in his grip and looked into space, he looked at her; no one was watching although they were like a sculpture caught in the beam of a searchlight. They remained there like that for a long time, much too long, then he let her go. Ruth swayed a little, straightened up, walked over to the counter. Raoul turned to me and said, 'I've never seen anything like you in all my life.'

When Ruth is sad she cries. I remember a fight she had with her mother; afterwards she sat huddled by the telephone, inaccessible. I remember a scene on the street at night; she and a friend were having an awful argument, and he hit her, and I remember her stricken, surprised face, how she put her hand up to her cheek, not a theatrical gesture, very genuine. When Ruth was sad for reasons she couldn't or didn't want to talk about, she would sit in the chair at her desk, her hands on the armrests, her feet up on the edge of the seat, her body gone slack and given over entirely to her sadness. How often did I see her like that – twice, three times, maybe four? She would cry without making a sound; I would stand by the door, leaning against the doorframe and say, 'Ruth, is there anything I can do?' but she only shook her head and said nothing. I would push away from the door and walk through the apartment to my room, across the hall, into the kitchen, and back again.

## Ruth (Girlfriends)

When Ruth was this sad, I felt numb. I'd wash three plates, smoke a cigarette at the kitchen window, and read a page in some book, and then I'd go back to her room, and she would still be sitting there like that. At some point, much later, she would come over, give me a brief hug, and say, 'Everything's all right again.' Her helpless, angry, hurt way of crying when we argued was different. As for me, I never cried in front of Ruth.

I stayed with Ruth for four days, one day longer than planned. Ruth had hardly any rehearsals to go to, but there were performances every evening. I had expected that she would want to spend her free time with Raoul and would have understood if she had, but Raoul had little time, and while I was there they saw each other alone only one afternoon. We dawdled over breakfast, walked into town, to the river, and along the riverbank to the outskirts of town and back. We were as close as always. Ruth talked constantly about Raoul, as if she were talking to herself, and I listened without giving her a lot of answers; actually she didn't ask me anything. She said Raoul had withdrawn from her; she could no longer reach him; true, there was a sort of sexual attraction but everything else was baffling. In three weeks his guest appearance here would be over; then he would go to Würzburg for a guest engagement there, then to Munich, but they never talked about the future. 'Maybe,' Ruth said, 'it's already over. Whatever it was. But I'm sad about that, do you understand?' I avoided looking at her.

Back at her apartment, I closed the bathroom door and looked at my face in the mirror, at the passport photo of me wedged into the mirror frame and then again at my face. In the evenings Ruth and I, the actors and Raoul

17

sat together at the Formica-topped tables in the canteen. I drank quite a lot. Every time Ruth got up from the table and disappeared briefly, Raoul looked at me and said very distinctly, 'I miss you.' Nobody except me could hear it. He didn't touch me. That first evening when Ruth went to get the drinks, he had laughed after he said that he hadn't seen anything like me in his entire life. A happy laugh that I returned without giving it a thought. He had said, 'Do you know who you are?' At first I hesitated but then I did reply, 'Yes.' He said, 'Are you the woman I think you are?' and I said, 'I don't know.' And he said, 'Yes. You know.' And then Ruth came back to the table and the words fitted into a precisely measured length of time. Just the right number of words.

When we fell asleep those nights, I turned away from Ruth, my face to the wall. I slept lightly. 'What will you do once you're back in Berlin?' Ruth asked, and I said, 'I'm not sure.' How could I have explained to her that my whole life was suddenly open again, empty, a wide uncharted space? I stood by the window in her apartment looking at the blue neon sign of the multi-storey car park, the reflecting windows of the apartment block behind it. The moon was already up. Ruth said my name, and I turned round. We bought dresses, shoes, coats. I said, 'I would like to stay, but I have to leave tomorrow.'

On my last evening, Ruth had an open rehearsal. Actors, onlookers and musicians sat here and there in the rows of seats; I sat on the stairs; Raoul came and sat next to me for a short while, and I moved away from him. On the stage Ruth looked over at us. We both looked at her; Raoul said, 'You're leaving?' I said, 'Tomorrow.' He said, 'And will we see each other again?' I said, 'Yes, we'll see each other again,' without taking my eyes off Ruth.

He remained sitting there several minutes longer; then he got up and left.

Later on we didn't sit at the same table in the canteen. 'What did you talk about?' Ruth asked. 'About the play,' I answered. She looked exhausted, pale and tense. The afternoon she had spent with Raoul, he had stretched out on the bed in his hotel room and watched television; Ruth had sat on the edge of the bed waiting for him to turn the TV off, but he didn't turn it off. Ruth said, 'I don't know what he wants.' That night we walked through the deserted pedestrian zone, our steps echoing on the pavement; Ruth had tucked her arm into mine; we were drunk and a little tottery; I had to laugh; Ruth's hair brushed gently against my cheek.

The next morning she took me to the railway station; it had turned cold, windy; we hugged each other on the platform; the train was already there, doors open. 'For heaven's sake, what are you going to Paris for?' Ruth said. 'What are you going to do in Paris?' I got on and leaned out of the open compartment window. Ruth was wearing a little black cap under which her hair had disappeared; her face looked stern. She put her hands into her coat pockets and hopped from one foot to the other; she said, 'You haven't told me yet what you think of him.' Her voice sounded no different than usual. The conductor blew his whistle; the doors slammed shut. I took a breath, and then I said, 'I don't think he's right for you.' Ruth said, 'Oh.' I wasn't sure she had really heard me. The train started. Ruth remained standing there; I looked out of the window as long as I could still see her slender figure in the light-coloured coat, the dark spot that was her cap; she didn't wave. Then she was gone.

*     *     *

19

I had never travelled anywhere with Ruth. There was one winter when the temperature dropped far below freezing, and we took the S-Bahn out to the Grunewald and walked across the frozen lake; neither of us was wearing the right kind of shoes. That was our biggest excursion. Every summer we lay on the grass in the park and talked about going to Greece, Italy or Sicily, to the sea, but we never did. She went to Portugal with B. and to Poland with J. and to Italy with F. I flew to New York and London and travelled through Morocco and Spain. We didn't miss each other during those times; maybe we had different expectations and weren't suitable travelling companions.

In Paris I took a room in a small hotel in the north of the city, in the African quarter; for a week I walked through the city from morning to night; it was cold, the Seine was muddy and green; it rained constantly and I was freezing. What in the world was I doing in Paris?

There were long queues outside the Louvre, so I decided to forgo that pleasure and went instead to a small museum on the Rue de Cluny where there was an exhibition of talismans of twelfth-century pilgrims, tiny blackish pendants: a wheel, a Madonna, a frozen teardrop. For a long time I stood before the warmly lit exhibition cases and felt comforted without being able to say by what.

In the Metro it smelled of tobacco, metal and rain-damp coats; people's faces were reserved and beautiful – Black Africans, Chinese, Indians. On my way back to my hotel at night there were men standing in doorways, whispering words in a foreign language behind me.

At midnight, once I was certain I wouldn't be interrupted, I took a shower in the communal bathroom down the hall. I stood on the slippery tiles and let the hot water course over me till my skin became red and wrinkled. I thought about him, his name, and tried to understand – him, myself, Ruth, the difficulty of the situation. I couldn't even have said what it was that was difficult. *I miss you.* I missed him, I kept thinking of him, of someone I didn't know but someone I wanted to visualize. I tried again and again, but couldn't assemble even his face from memory; there were only fragmented details, his eyes, his mouth, a gesture of his left hand – perhaps his voice was what I recalled best.

I tried to write a postcard to Ruth but couldn't get beyond the first two words, 'Dear Ruth . . .' The rain kept falling on the silvery roofs. At night, I lay on the hotel bed smoking a cigarette in the darkness, listening to the reassuring foreign sounds from the street and tried to answer Ruth's question at the railway station, *For heaven's sake what are you going to Paris for?* Aloud, I said, 'Ruth, maybe it's that you keep searching for yourself and can really find yourself over and over again, and that I, on the other hand, want to lose myself, to get away from myself. And I can do that best when I'm travelling and sometimes also when I'm loved.' I would never have spoken to Ruth like that, and I thought it would shock me to hear myself say it out loud, but I wasn't shocked. My voice sounded strange in the dark.

The next morning I had breakfast at the mosque near the Natural History Museum, mint tea and sticky pastry. I was the only one sitting there; the windows were open and rain was getting in, and sparrows flew inside and up to the ceiling and launched themselves from there. I lost all sense of time.

A Black African came up to me at the Place de la

Madeleine; he wanted money for stamps so he could mail his dissertation to the university; the university accepted only dissertations that arrived by mail; he had sent all his money to his family in South Africa. I gave him ten francs; he said, 'Not enough', I gave him twenty, then thirty; he continued to hold out his hand, looking at me as though I should be paying for something quite different. I gave him all the money I had in my trouser pockets, much too much; it was ridiculous. He handed me a piece of paper and a pencil and asked me to write down my address; he'd send me the money as soon as he found work. I wrote down an imaginary address that I immediately forgot, and he put the piece of paper in his pocket and mouthed the question: 'What is your name?' Then he walked off; I watched him go. The expression on his face was dignified and contemptuous; suddenly I knew that I had to leave, that I was no longer safe here.

People were streaming through the Gare du Nord; gypsy women squatted on baggage carts with sleeping children in their laps or draped over their shoulders. The letters on the information board announcing train departures and arrivals fell into a jumble, flashed out the names of cities and far-away places, and then disappeared again. I felt a longing, or perhaps I was running a fever; I couldn't tell which any more. I thought, 'Keep on going, keep on going, go away, as far as possible.'

The Asian woman in the glass ticket booth stared at me. 'Berlin,' I said, 'a ticket for Berlin, please,' and now the feeling in my stomach was clearly fear. I dropped my last coins into a pay phone and dialled Ruth's number. I wanted to say, 'Ruth, I'm taking a train home now, and then something will be decided.' I hoped she would say, 'I know,' and maybe add, 'Get lost,' but she didn't pick up. The answering machine came on, and I held the receiver out into the station concourse, recording the voices, the announcements on the public address system, and the sounds of the moving trains; then I hung up.

Oddly enough, it wasn't me, it was Ruth who had said, 'I'd like to be you.' Not the other way around.

Late that evening, I arrived in Berlin. The apartment was stuffy and still, totally strange to me – whose bed was that? the chair? the books, papers, teacups, the shoes in the hall, whose were they? Ruth's voice on the answering machine, three calls, the first one affectionate and yearning – 'I miss you,' she said; in the background someone seemed to be walking about in the room. In the second call she was short, 'Are you there? Hello? Are you back?' then she hung up. The third time it sounded as though she had been crying; her voice trembled; she said I should call her when I got back, whenever, even in the middle of the night.

I unpacked my suitcase, hung in the wardrobe the things I had bought with Ruth but hadn't worn, not even once, opened all the windows and went to bed. I slept briefly yet soundly. The next morning was windy and grey; I went shopping, then back to the apartment, read a newspaper, did laundry, looked through the mail. And throughout, I watched myself from outside myself, from a distance, from far away, moving about lightly.

In the evening the phone rang. I let it ring four times even though it was right next to me; only then did I pick up the receiver. 'Oh, you're there,' Ruth said. Her voice sounded so close it was as if she were standing beside me. I said, 'I just got back.' She said, 'You don't have to apologize.' I said, 'No, why should I?' Then I had to laugh. Ruth did not laugh. She burst out crying, and I let her cry. I just sat there and looked out of the window – the night sky over the park, no moon, no stars. I imagined Ruth in her room, in the blue light of the car park sign, the silver ashtray on the table, the photo on the windowsill. Ruth's hair, loose, her teary face. I said, 'Ruth, oh Ruth.' She went on crying for quite a while. Then she stopped, blew her nose; we were silent, then she said, 'How was Paris?' I said, 'Nice.' She said, 'It's over, you know. The thing with Raoul, I mean. It's over,' and I said, 'Why?' and she said, 'Why. Good question.'

I thought about the fact that Ruth had never been alone, one affair or relationship or friendship had always merged into the next, and when one love ended, there was always a new one, a greater one, a better one in the wings. It seemed that now she would be alone for the first time. I said, 'Is it worse than usual?' and then Ruth did laugh, softly, and said, 'No. It's the same as always. But in spite of that it's shitty, isn't it?'

They had argued, she said. He had felt hemmed in, almost threatened, she had come on too fast, too close; he wasn't as much in love as she was, basically he wasn't in love at all. Drunk and desperate, she had called him at his hotel one night; she knew he was there, but he didn't answer the phone for an incredibly long time and, when he did, he said only, 'You must be out of your mind,' and then he just hung up.

Now he was avoiding her; in three days he'd be gone for good. She didn't know which was worse – to see him and not be able to be with him or not to see him at all any more. She said, 'Somehow the awful thing is that I think he didn't recognize me for what I am, you know?

He sent me away before I could show him what I'm really like; he didn't let me get close to him, he didn't give me a chance. That's what's so terrible, do you understand?' I said, 'Yes. I understand.' And I really did understand. Only I thought that he *had* recognized her quite well, and maybe she knew that too. Ruth was silent.

Then she sighed and said, 'Actually nothing happened, nothing at all. We kissed a little, we told each other two or three stories; once we walked through town holding hands. That's all there was. But I fell in love in spite of that, and he didn't want me, and that makes me furious. You said he wasn't right for me.' I didn't say anything, and Ruth repeated, 'You said that, didn't you?' I had to laugh, and she said seriously, 'Actually, why wasn't he?' I could have said, because he's the right one for *me*. Under different circumstances Ruth might have laughed at that. I didn't know how to answer her. I said stupidly, 'Maybe he's a size too big for you,' and Ruth asked, understandably nonplussed, 'What's that supposed to mean?'

I got up and walked through the apartment, taking the telephone along – Ruth's room at the end of the hall, dark and wide; I still expected to see her bed there whenever I went in, her desk and the chair on which she sat when she was sad. Now the chair stood next to a window in her apartment in another town. I said, 'Ruth, I don't know either; I don't know him at all; he's good-looking but more than that I can't say, except I had the feeling that you didn't understand each other.' 'Yes. That's possible,' Ruth said simply.

In the hall I leaned against the wall, my knees were giving way; suddenly I had a feeling of utter hopelessness, Raoul far away, his face – now I remembered what it looked like. I wanted to get some information from

Ruth that could prepare me for him; I didn't know how I should phrase it, and what it really was I wanted to know. I said, 'Did you sleep with him?' and instantly felt the blood rush to my face. 'No,' Ruth said and didn't seem to find my question odd. 'No, we didn't. Somehow he didn't want to, or maybe he wanted precisely that; it was strange. At any rate, I didn't sleep with him, and I can't tell you how glad I am about that.'

I was silent, and she was too, or maybe she was listening to my silence, then she said, 'Was that the right answer?' And I laughed, embarrassed. She asked me again about Paris; I told her a little – about the Black African at the Place de la Madeleine, the hotel room, the African markets on the side streets of that section of the city. I thought, I should really have been consoling her, but I didn't know how; also, she didn't seem to want to be consoled. She said, 'I'll call you again tomorrow, all right?' I said, 'Ruth. Take care of yourself.' She said, 'You too,' then we hung up. I drank a glass of wine in the kitchen; the refrigerator hummed. I thought he would call, soon. I was sure he would. Then I went to bed. Very late at night I woke up because the telephone was ringing. It rang three or four times; then it was still. I lay on my back and held my breath.

I could never have explained to Ruth, I couldn't have explained what it was all about for me, how I felt. I never had to explain anything to Ruth; she didn't ask me to, even though there must have been many times when she didn't understand me. She was with me during all those years, in good times and in not-so-good times. Sometimes she asked, 'Why are you doing that?' She didn't expect an answer and I couldn't have given her one. She watched me; she knew me very well; sometimes she imitated me: the way I held my head to the side, smiled, looked away. She knew I had no secrets.

The letter arrived on September 20th, the fifth day after my return from Paris. Somehow Raoul must have got hold of my address at the theatre before he left for Würzburg; he knew that it was Ruth's former address; anyhow, he knew pretty much everything about me from Ruth. He had gone to Würzburg, had probably organized his rehearsal schedule and moved into his new quarters, had spent one evening alone or maybe not, and had addressed an envelope to me the next day and sent it off. He was fast. In the envelope was a second-class ticket to Würzburg for the midday train on September 25th along with a return ticket. Also a piece of paper on which was written only a single sentence: 'It would be nice if you came.' Oddly enough, instead of signing it he had drawn a cartoon-type side view of his face, an unflattering profile.

I put the letter on the table; it looked strange and yet quite ordinary, a narrow white envelope on which my name was written. I had four days to decide, but there was nothing to think over; I knew that I would go. I no longer felt different than usual, no longer borne up by great expectations. I slept a lot, got up late, sat around in the afternoons in the café in front of my house, drinking coffee, reading the newspaper, looking up and down the street, never looking anyone in the eye.

The telephone rang several times; sometimes I picked it up and sometimes not; it was always Ruth, mostly towards evening. She wasn't feeling well, but not really bad either. She was very busy and seemed distracted; in spite of that, she talked a lot about Raoul, lots of questions which she herself answered. Nothing was clarified before his departure; he had left without their having another talk. 'You should be happy that he's gone, that idiot,' the make-up woman had said to her several times. She said, 'I'd like to write to him; do you think I ought to write to him?' and when I didn't reply, she said, 'It's probably useless, completely useless, I know.'

As we were talking on the phone, I leaned out of the window so she could hear the street noises, the traffic at the intersection, fragments of the conversations of people sitting outside the cafés. Ruth used to like that; now she whispered, 'Stop it, it's making me homesick.' Talking to her on the phone wasn't hard. During the phone conversation we had just before I took the train to Würzburg, we didn't talk about Raoul at all; I didn't ask about him, and Ruth didn't mention him. It was as though he had never existed. She told me she had had a call from a theatre in Hamburg; she'd probably get out of her contract and move again; she seemed happy and excited about that. She said, 'Then we'll be much nearer each other again.'

We talked a long time; I was drinking wine, was drunk by the time we finished and feeling melancholy. I said, and I meant it, 'Ruth, I miss you very much,' and she said, 'Yes, me too.' Then we hung up.

I went to bed but couldn't sleep; the street was noisy and full of people until late into the night. I lay there listening with a single absurd picture in my head – Raoul carrying me through a dark, unfamiliar apartment, through a hallway and many rooms, till he finally put me down on a bed, gently, as though I were a child. The morning of September 25th, I stood in front of my wardrobe, uncertain; I didn't know how long I would be staying – one night, a few days, for ever? I didn't know what he wanted, and actually I didn't know what I wanted either. Finally, I took nothing except my toothbrush, a book and a nightgown. I turned off the telephone answering machine, locked the apartment door, and took a bus to the railway station, much too early.

What else is there to say about Ruth and me; what else can there be? We kissed each other once, just once, at night in a bar. Actually it was only to get rid of someone who wouldn't leave Ruth alone. Ruth leaned over and kissed me on the lips, deeply and tenderly; she tasted of chewing gum, wine and cigarette smoke, and her tongue was peculiarly sweet. It was a beautiful kiss, and I remember that I was surprised and I thought, 'So that's what it's like to kiss Ruth.' I thought we would feel embarrassed afterwards, but we didn't, nor did we talk any more about it. Ruth's admirer disappeared without saying another word.

When we were younger, Ruth was more effusive and exuberant; she drank a lot and loved to dance on top of bars and tables. I liked that and urged her on, 'Go do it, Ruth, dance on the table!' Without further ado, she would push aside glasses, kick the ashtrays off the table with her high-heeled shoes, and then she'd dance provocatively. Not until much later would she rebuff me, getting angry sometimes, saying, 'I'm not living a vicarious life or whatever for you.' We wore the same clothes, long skirts, coats with fur collars, pearl necklaces – but we never looked alike. Someone said, 'You're like two lovebirds, like those little yellow canaries; you always sit there the same way and move your heads back and forth in the same rhythm.' We liked that comparison.

29

Sometimes when someone asked us a question, we answered simultaneously, saying exactly the same thing. But we rarely read the same books, and we never cried together over anything. Our future, which in the beginning didn't exist and which later became more like a space to which we had to accommodate ourselves, was a shared one – Ruth and I. Ruth was not afraid to say it: 'We won't ever part.'

I often looked at her, trying to imagine what she'd be like when she got old; I never could. She is most beautiful when she laughs. When she just sits there and doesn't speak, I don't know what she is thinking. Her eyebrows are plucked into thin silvery sickles; her hands are very small. There were moments when she clearly was not listening to me as I told her something. No photo exists of the two of us together. Did I really know Ruth?

The trip from Berlin to Würzburg took six hours, and I was happy during those six hours. I read and I slept, and woven into that light sleep were momentary dreams: Ruth on a staircase, looking for me, mute; Raoul at a table in the theatre canteen, alone, a stranger; my empty room in the Berlin apartment, sunlight on the wooden floor; the voice of the train conductor, 'We will be arriving in Braunschweig in a few minutes'; Ruth whispering; my legs asleep; Raoul standing in the rain under the awning of a hotel. I woke up again, my face swollen and hot.

I went to the buffet car to smoke a cigarette; people sat hunched over their beer glasses, silent; the landscape outside the tinted windows hilly and green, the fields already harvested, small birds perched on the swinging telephone wires, forming a long, dark chain. The train rolled on and on, measuring the time, the distances, getting closer, inescapably, and I wished myself back at home, and further back into an earlier time, a before, and at the same time I was so impatient that my stomach, my head, my limbs ached. Ruth, I thought, Ruth, I would so much like to tell you about all this.

I returned to my seat, walking along the corridor, past all those faces looking at me. I read and then couldn't read any longer and stared out of the window and got so tired that my hands shook and my knees became weak. Another hour to Würzburg, half an hour, twenty minutes, soon. The street lamps went on in the suburbs, there were lights in the apartment blocks, small, bright windows in the dusk. Perhaps that kind of life? That table under that lamp in that room with that view of the garden, faded asters and flowerbeds covered with branches for the winter, a children's swing, a concrete terrace. What is going on, I thought, what is going on . . . This yearning of mine was both terrible and inane.

The train was slowing down, and that was vaguely comforting. I got up, took my little bag, my coat, my hot face; I thought, 'Raoul, I'm dreadfully sad.' Then the train stopped, coming to a standstill with a single resolute jolt. Würzburg's main terminal, 6.22 p.m. I joined the long line of passengers waiting to get off, step by step by step; no one detained me, and then I was on the platform, walking towards the exit. And when at last I spotted Raoul, I knew instantaneously and with hopeless certainty that I had made a mistake.

He was standing at the end of the tracks leaning against a board listing the train schedules; he had on a coat I had never seen him in at the theatre, was wearing his glasses; he looked a bit arrogant and bored, arms crossed over his chest, shoulders raised. He stood there looking like someone who's meeting someone coming in on a train, waiting, in expectation, perhaps impatient; he stood there like all the others, and he was not afraid. I walked towards him and I could see that he was not afraid; he might have been unsure and nervous, but the fear that had me shaking, this fear he didn't have.

When he saw me, his bored expression changed in seconds to one that was joyful, convincingly happy and at the same time incredulous; he came towards me in two or three quick strides, and before I could have warded him off he drew me close and held me in a tight embrace. I didn't know what to do with my hands, my arms, my face. I embraced him too, we stood there like that; he smelled of shaving lotion, his cheek was soft, the frames of his glasses pressed slightly against my temple; it was almost preposterous to feel him so suddenly, only now. He held me for a long time before letting me go. He said, 'How wonderful, how wonderful that you really came.' I didn't know what to say, and he took my hand and pulled me along behind him through the station concourse. He said we'd get something to eat; he had reserved a table in a Chinese place; he was hungry, was I hungry? I wasn't hungry.

In the square outside the station we got into his car, a small red Alfa Romeo; I had never before been in an Alfa Romeo, and I wanted to tell him so, but then it seemed silly and I didn't say anything. He started the engine, drove off at breakneck speed, looked at me, shook his head, kept bursting into laughter, seemed to find something inordinately amusing. Did you have a good trip? How was the weather in Berlin? Heard anything from Ruth? I didn't answer the last question, nor the first two either, really.

He parked four blocks away in a no-waiting zone. The Chinese restaurant where he had reserved a table was totally empty except for the Chinese family behind the counter staring at us unwaveringly and eerily, till one of them came to our table and handed us a much-fingered menu. Raoul ordered appetizers and a main course; I wanted a salad, if anything at all; I felt ill; my stomach was in a knot. 'Jasmine tea, please,' I said to the unfriendly face of the waiter.

We sat across from each other and looked at each other; nothing else seemed possible. Actually, I thought, I had come to Würzburg just to look at him, the way you want to look at a person you've decided to love. Raoul was good at that, he endured my gaze and I his; his eyes were large, wide open, they seemed to be brown, amber tinted, in their corners a smile that would not go away. We looked at each other and that took all the strength I had, until the waiter finally stepped in, putting the jasmine tea, the appetizers and my salad on the table. I looked away from Raoul's eyes in which there was no longer any light, no remoteness, and no promise, and I resolved not to look at him like that again; it wouldn't change anything.

Raoul ate, not the way he had in the canteen, but like a normal man; he used chopsticks, skilfully dissecting the vegetables, the fish, talking from time to time in a matter-of-fact way that took my breath away. Actually, during those four days with Ruth, he and I hadn't talked at all, saying only disjointed words with an absolute meaning-lessness that seemed to intoxicate him as much as me. He had said 'I miss you' into the face of a total stranger, into a utopia, in the hope that the sentence would reach its destination and then dissolve into nothing or everything.

33

That's how it had been, and now he was sitting across from me, eating Chinese noodles and intermittently taking small sips of beer, smiling at me and talking about the Musil production, his colleagues and disagreements at the theatre. And I nodded obediently and said, 'Aha,' and, 'No, really?' What had I expected? Something different? Nothing at all? And what now? How were we supposed to go on from here? I pressed my hands together under the table; they were cold and damp. My heart was pounding; I felt ill; I thought of Ruth, of Ruth.

'Did you tell her that you were coming here?' Raoul asked. I shook my head and he looked at me expectantly. It seemed as if he wanted to talk about it, as though my betrayal of Ruth on his account excited him, made him happy, so that he wanted to savour it a little longer, but at least I didn't do him this favour. I shook my head again, and he shrugged and turned back to his food; he enjoyed eating; I could see that.

We sat at that table in this restaurant for maybe two hours, and in all that time not another customer came in. It was as though the world outside had gone under and only we were left – he and I and the Chinese family, who after they had served us had again withdrawn behind the counter. Sometimes I could hear the shuffling of their feet. Raoul talked a lot in those two hours; I talked very little. Sometimes he interrupted himself to stare at me, but before there was a chance that we would again gaze at each other like lovers, or before he could ask me anything else, I would ask him a question.

I asked him about his father, his childhood, Ireland, his ex-wife, and he liked being questioned and replied readily. Once when he told a friend about the premature death of his father, the friend had said to him, 'Lucky you,' and he had punched his friend right in the kisser. Today he regretted it, and he now understood what his friend had meant, that his father's early death had given him a certain strength, invulnerability and maturity. No one at the theatre really knew him for what he was because he wasn't actually an actor but only an imposter, a loner, and he wasn't going to stay in the theatre much longer; what he really wanted to do was to write stories, plays, poems, to reveal himself.

He said, 'I want to reveal myself.' As for his ex-wife in Munich and their child, that was a difficult relationship and it was impossible to end it completely; they had been together too long for that. And the light in Ireland was terrific, the wide expanses, the colour of the meadows when the wind blew through them and reversed the blades of grass to white – it was the same phrase he had used weeks before to describe the colour of Ruth's eyes. But that no longer surprised me.

Finally he thought he had revealed enough of himself. Each answer had been an anecdote that was intended to dovetail with the other anecdotes, forming a picture of the man he was. He seemed to think that it was enough for a start. I had shown him my lovely silence, my mouth, my hands, my head tilted to the side. The back of my neck hurt.

He waved to the waiter, who brought the bill and two little porcelain cups of rice brandy. At the bottom of the cup you could see a naked woman, her legs spread. She disappeared as soon as I had drunk the brandy. He paid, refusing to take my money, nodded to the Chinese family, who didn't move; then we left. It was already dark outside and windy. We got back into his little car. He said, 'Shall we drive home, OK?' Perhaps the wording was intended to console me.

We drove through the dead city, terribly fast, then he slowed down, turned into a side street, parked the car in front of a small house that stood between two large villas. Instead of a hotel room, the theatre had made this place available to him – there were two rooms, kitchen, bath and a garden. He said he preferred this to a hotel room, he was fed up with his unsettled existence. We climbed out of the car. Staggering a bit, I held on to the garden fence and took a deep breath. I wanted to just stand still for a while in this dark garden. But he immediately unlocked the door, pulled me into the house, put on the light, set my bag on the floor, went to get wine from the kitchen, and pushed a chair over. 'Sit,' he said, 'sit down. There's something I have to do, but we'll have something to drink first, OK?'

I sat down, took off my coat and lit a cigarette. The room was tiny and low ceilinged: a table, two chairs and a desk on which were the things he said he always took along with him – two or three books, a small brass elephant, a Pelikan fountain pen, and a large grey rock. A small narrow stairway led from this room to the upper floor, presumably to the bedroom. I sat there and watched as he walked across the room, unpacked his bag, sorted through the scripts on the desk, lost in thought or maybe not.

He poured wine for me and for himself too. I drank some immediately; in a terrible way nothing mattered any more. There was nothing. There were no words for our relationship, no silence and no closeness, not even a feeling of shock about the other person; even my fear was gone, the picture I had, all the images, Raoul in the rain, Raoul carrying me to his bed – none of his actions affected me any more. A tall, heavy man walking across a room

36

in which a lamp casts a golden cone of light on a wooden table. The cigarette tasted rough and bitter and good. I drank my wine and refilled the glass, and he sat down at the table for a short while, talked a bit, and then he said, 'Let's go to bed.'

I brushed my teeth in front of the bathroom mirror and washed my face till it was rosy and soft, drops of water on my eyelashes, water on my temples, then I put on my nightgown and, placing my hands on the tiled bathroom wall for support, I took a deep breath. I climbed the narrow staircase and went into the tiny bedroom. Raoul was already in bed, apparently naked, lying on his stomach. He moved aside and held up the blanket. I crept under it and turned to him immediately; he would misunderstand, I knew that, but there was no other way than to touch him right away, to embrace him, to clutch him tightly.

His body was surprisingly soft and warm, a lot of skin, a lot of strange surfaces, unfamiliar – what an immense imposition. I touched him, and he immediately misunderstood, misjudging my queasiness, my fear and my shock. I said, 'I don't want to,' and he said, 'Why not?' and I said, 'I don't know.' That was true; I really didn't know why, I only knew that I didn't want to. And then he said, 'But sooner or later we'd do it anyway.' He was right, wasn't he? I lay under the cool blanket. It was dark. He had turned out the light. His face was indiscernible in the dark. He said, 'But sooner or later we'd do it anyway,' and I said, 'Yes,' to his indiscernible face, 'of course we would.'

The knowledge that he was right, the understanding of the logical consistency and at the same time its impossibility filled me with an unexpected, crazy cheerfulness. He didn't say, 'See?' But he thought it, and while he did what he was eventually going to do anyway, I lay there and couldn't help laughing, softly and violently, not wanting to stop, and he laughed too, but differently, and I held on to the edge of the bed and thought of Ruth. The way she came into the kitchen in the morning, making herself coffee and sitting down at the table with me and reading the little piece of paper on which she had written what she had to do that day: go to the post office, the supermarket, the chemist, call H. and D., get a present for M., pay the telephone bill. And then it was over and yet it wasn't, and finally it was, and we rolled apart, he turned round, his back like a wide landscape. Then I fell asleep.

The next morning I was awakened by the ringing of the alarm clock. It must have been very early; the light in the room was still grey; my left hand had gone to sleep, and my shoulders hurt. I was instantly awake, at once tense, on my guard. Next to me Raoul groaned, threw back the covers, turned off the alarm and got up; his naked body was heavy and massive and in the dusky light seemed strangely blurred. He began to get dressed, in an awkward way, then he suddenly turned round to look at me as though it had just occurred to him that I was there – that there was someone else lying in his bed.

When he saw I was awake, he smiled at me and said, 'I have to memorize a script now, and the rehearsal begins at nine; you can sleep a little longer.' I said, 'How late is it?' He said, 'A little before seven.' Our voices were rough and scratchy. He opened the little dormer window; cold morning air came into the room, the dampness almost palpable. When he reached the stairs, he turned round once more and came back, stopped at the doorway and said, 'When does your train leave?'

I think he dealt me this blow quite intentionally, but I was awake and alert enough not to look taken aback or hurt or surprised. I had no idea when my train left; I didn't think there was a train back. I said, pleasantly, 'Eight forty-two,' and he said just as pleasantly, 'That means I can still take you to the station.' Then he disappeared; I heard him in the kitchen putting water on to boil, the refrigerator door opened and shut; he briefly went out into the garden; he turned on the radio.

I sat on the edge of the bed, put my bare feet next to each other on the floor, pressed my knees together, placed my hands on my hips and arched my back. Fleetingly I thought about the expression *pulling yourself together.* Then I got dressed and went downstairs. Raoul was sitting at the desk reading softly to himself and rocking his upper body back and forth. Without turning to look at me, he said, 'There's coffee and some fruit in the kitchen. Unfortunately, I don't have any real breakfast stuff here.'

I took a tangerine from the kitchen table, poured coffee into a mug. 'It's seven thirty,' the radio announcer's voice said. I didn't know where to go; I didn't want to disturb him – there were no chairs in the kitchen, and going back to bed was out of the question; so I went out into the garden.

The garden extended down to the street, a narrow rectangle of unmowed lawn, two fruit trees, neglected flower borders, a rubbish bin, an old bicycle, and on the lawn in front of the garden fence a swing suspended from a carpet rod. The grass was dark and damp from the night, and rustling sounds came from the piles of leaves under the fruit trees. By now it was light; the sky was clear and a watery blue. I walked down the length of the garden path and back again; then I sat down on the swing.

The coffee was hot and strong; I would have liked to drink it the way Ruth always drank coffee – in one single long gulp – but my stomach rebelled. I swung back and forth a little. I knew that Raoul could see me through the window, and I was afraid that by swinging, indeed by sitting on the swing, I might present a certain image, like some poster, a metaphor, but by then it didn't matter to me.

The street was quiet – one-family houses, one next to the other, expensive cars parked at the kerb under nearly bare linden trees. There was hardly anyone in sight, but now I could hear voices in the distance, children's voices coming closer, and then I saw them – kids on the other side of the street on their way to school with colourful satchels on their backs, gym bags, trainers tied together by the laces and hung over their shoulders. I could see the wide driveway into the schoolyard, paper cutouts pasted on the window panes, the school clock on the gable. The children walked past the garden; they didn't notice me. I watched them. They came by in small groups, some by themselves, slower and still sleepy-eyed, lost in thought, others holding hands and talking to each other in loud and eager voices. 'Wait for me! Wait for me!' one kid yelled to another and then ran off, his school bag bouncing on his back.

I peeled my tangerine and watched them. A sweet fruity aroma rose from the tangerine; it rattled me. Raoul sitting in the house, reading Musil. He was working, he was awake. Things could have been different, but this way was all right too. I ate the tangerine section by section; the school bell rang and even the slow kids started running, all in a jumble, bumping into each other or grabbing for the hand of a friend; none of them looked at

me. I made the swing go a little faster. The school bell
rang again, then stopped suddenly as though it had been
cut off.

The front door opened and Raoul called my name; I
turned towards him. Perhaps I still wished for something
to happen, one last time, but not really. He said, 'We
have to leave now,' and I got up and went back into the
house, set my coffee mug on the kitchen table, the
tangerine peel next to it, and put on my coat. We got
into his car and drove off. Traffic was already heavy on
the main roads, and at the traffic lights people were
waiting to cross the street on their way to work, the office,
the factory; I felt relieved, as though a burden had been
lifted from my heart. I think we didn't say much; he
seemed to be in a bad mood; he said he did not know
his lines, that on the whole the rehearsals were awful; he
sounded as if he were talking to himself.

At the railway station he double-parked the car, saying,
'I can't go to the train with you; I'm going to be late
anyway.' And I said quite candidly, 'It doesn't matter.'
We embraced in the car, quickly, cursorily; he kissed my
cheek, then I got out. I walked into the station without
turning round; I could hear him rev the engine and drive
off. The train for Berlin was scheduled to leave at 9.04.
I got on and took a seat next to a window, opened my
book, and read till we got to the Berlin-Zoo Station.
Afterwards I couldn't remember a single line I had read.

Later I thought I should have listened to him more carefully. I don't know if that would have changed anything,
if I would have made a different decision. Nevertheless,
I should have listened to him properly. He had said, 'Are
you the one I think you are?' and I had understood

something totally different from what he had intended. He had recognized me in spite of that. What he had actually said was, 'Are you a traitor for whom nothing counts, and who can't be expected to keep a promise?' He had asked, 'Would you betray Ruth for me?' I had said, 'Yes.'

I see Ruth sitting across from me, naked, her legs drawn up to her chest, her face, a towel wrapped around her wet hair; she says, 'Promise me.' She shouldn't have said it. I never told Ruth, 'Ruth, I had to know; it had nothing to do with you.' And I never told her about the kids going to school, their faces, the smell of the tangerine, about that morning. When we were still living together, we had a habit of writing little notes to each other whenever one of us went anywhere without the other. Whenever I came home after having been out without Ruth, there would be a note on the kitchen table if she was already asleep, a short, tender message, sometimes more, sometimes just a few words. Ruth never forgot. I happened to find one of these notes today, a bookmark in a book, the paper a little crumpled, folded up, Ruth's large, flowing handwriting: 'My dear, Are you well? It's been a long day for me and I'm going to bed now – 10 o'clock – my feet are rubbed raw from the damned new shoes. I went shopping, fruit, milk and wine, that was all the money there was. A. phoned and asked where you were and I said, She's out looking under every paving stone for a message. Maybe I shouldn't have said that? Good night, till tomorrow. Kisses, R.'

[Translator's note: the excerpt quoted is from Molière, *The Misanthrope and Other Plays: A New Selection*, translated by John Wood and David Coward, Penguin Books, 2000, p. 114.]

# Cold-Blue

The package arrives early in the morning. There's postage due because Jonas didn't put on enough stamps. It is addressed to both of them, to Jonina and Magnus. Magnus is sleeping. Jonina sits down on the white sofa by the window. It is still dark and she has to turn on the light. She doesn't hesitate, not even for a moment. Maybe she acts as if she were hesitating, but she isn't. She wouldn't think of waiting for Magnus to get up. The package is rectangular and flat; it feels a bit heavy, there's a 'handle with care' sticker on it, and the wrapping paper is sloppily secured with sticky tape. Amazing that it arrived in one piece. She rips open the paper and pulls out a framed photograph, very painstakingly framed, the photo surrounded by a green mount, and an enclosed card, nothing else: 'The photo comes a little late, but we've been thinking of you constantly. The beautiful blue hour, eleven o'clock in the morning of December 3rd, much too short. Regards – see you soon. Jonas.' The phrase *a little late* might be considered amusing; it was exactly a year ago; that's not a little. It might be a little

43

for Jonas. She doesn't want to think about the phrase *see you soon*.

In the photo, the moon is suspended above the road that leads to the Old Althing. The sky is a glowing, diaphanous blue, everything else is white; the road is white, the mountains are white, blanketed in deep snow. Magnus, Irene and Jonina are walking towards the camera. Magnus in the middle; he is blurry, his face unrecognizable. Jonina is on his right, Irene on his left. The distance between Jonina and Magnus is greater than the distance between Irene and Magnus. Irene is laughing; she walks straight ahead. Jonina seems to want to walk out of picture towards the right but is looking directly into the camera. Jonas was standing in the middle of the road, his camera mounted on a tripod. Afraid that the light would change, he had yelled at them – 'Now!' Jonina remembers how he looked just then, his woollen hat pulled down over his eyes, the sheepskin jacket open, swearing at the cold, delighted and enthusiastic.

It's not that Jonina has forgotten that beautiful, much-too-short, blue hour. She hasn't forgotten it. She remembers it exactly, and if she wants to she can recall everything else too, each detail of those seven days. The Soviet star on Jonas's belt buckle, the ring on Irene's left hand – a moonstone in an oval setting – blueberry-flavoured Absolut vodka in a large frosty bottle. Coffee with sugar but no milk for Magnus in a snack bar on the Ring Road going north, the weather forecast on the third day they were together. Sunna's childish drawing of two pugnacious snowmen and the colour of Jonas's eyes – green, dark green with a thin yellow band encircling the iris. She hasn't forgotten any of it. She just hasn't been thinking about it any more. Thinking about it only induces a feeling of heaviness and weariness. And now she holds the photo in her hand early in the morning – nine o'clock, it's not even light outside – and again she remembers everything. She can't decide whether she wants to remember or not, but she can't help it – everything comes back to her.

She recalls how she and Magnus were driving down the Barugata in their car; Irene and Jonas stayed behind, waving to them from the side of the road. 'That's that,' Magnus had said, and Jonina wanted to say, 'Stop, let me out. Let me out,' but didn't say anything. And they turned a corner and Irene and Jonas were gone, had vanished, once and for all. That was that.

She could hang the photo on the wall above the table, on the shiny grey unblemished wall and surprise Magnus with it when he got up. She could hammer a nail into the unmarred surface of the freshly painted wall and hang the photo on it. It is a beautiful photo. They'll have to hang pictures in the apartment anyway. They'll have to acquire things; there's got to be some disorder and some dirt in this unlived-in cleanliness, otherwise she won't be able to cope. But not this photo. Anything, but not this photo, not Jonas's beautiful glimpse of this one, much-too-brief, blue hour.

Irene and Jonas were coming to Iceland for the very first time in late November. Magnus had known for a month they would be coming, but he doesn't tell Jonina till fairly late: 'I'm expecting visitors from Berlin tomorrow.' Jonina doesn't ask him why he waited so long to tell her. It will be disconcerting for him; visitors from the past are always disconcerting. On the other hand, she is rather curious.

She has known Magnus for two and a half years. She

had never seen him before that, and for Iceland that's unusual, but that's the way it was. They didn't attend the same school; they were not distantly related; they hadn't by coincidence gone to the same rock concert. They saw each other for the first time in 1999. Later they discover that Bjarni, the father of Jonina's daughter, Sunna, had been Magnus's best friend at school. They discover this long after all contact between Jonina and Bjarni was broken off. Magnus grew up on the west coast and Jonina on the east coast. When he was twenty, Magnus went to Berlin. Jonina went to Vienna. Magnus studied psychology. Jonina studied literature. Twelve years later, they returned to Iceland at about the same time. In the end all Icelanders come back to Iceland, almost all. They study or work abroad and live there ten, twelve or fifteen years, and then it's enough, and they come back. Almost all of them.

Jonina has never been to Berlin. She doesn't know what that city in which Magnus lived for twelve years looks like. She can't imagine what he looked like in those years, what he was like, what he did, can't imagine him speaking German and spending his days with German girls.

When they first met, they talked a lot about those days abroad, how it felt to be a foreigner, and about the happiness and hardships experienced. They talked about it as if it were something that happened a long time ago and in no way affected the present. They never speak German with each other, not even for fun. They don't even give it a try. A different Magnus and a different Jonina.

But she loves the story about Magnus's first days in Berlin and the story about his departure. Perhaps she loves these two stories because they form a frame for the time before she knew Magnus; they enclose it and put an end to it.

Magnus was living in a one-room apartment in a rear building in Berlin-Neukölln. It is the winter of 1986 and colder in Berlin than it ever gets in Iceland, 20° below zero. His apartment has a tile stove but Magnus doesn't know how to work it. All he has is a mattress, nothing else. When he comes home from the Institute, he lies down on the mattress with his clothes on, covers himself with a quilt, and smokes and reads. He has no curtains. His room faces the rear courtyard. Everyone else has curtains; he knows that they can see him lying in bed, smoking, alone – he doesn't care. Around midnight he goes to a bar, annoying everyone there with his childish German, and stays till they throw him out. He knows some other Icelanders in Berlin, and he gets together with them, but he didn't go there because of them. He'd love to meet someone, a foreign girl, just not a psychology student. But it doesn't work; he remains alone. And then one day when he comes home, there's a letter lying on the floor in the hall, dropped through the letterbox, a small, white, folded piece of paper. He takes the paper to bed, lights a cigarette, unfolds it and reads: 'Hey, old man, I can see you, man. You're pretty much alone and you lie around in your bed all evening and every weekend reading, and you really seem to be all alone, and I thought, maybe you could just drop in sometime. Side wing, fourth floor, left. Slick Chick.' That's all. Jonina loves this story. She loves it when Magnus mimics the Berlin accent: 'Hey, old man, I can see you, man.' And even though that was just what he had been wishing for, to meet someone by chance, he finds it impossible to simply drop in on someone who addresses him with 'Hey, old man'. He never went to see Slick Chick; he doesn't even know what she looked like. He says that sometimes he regrets it.

And then during his last days in Berlin, twelve years later – by then he had met lots of girls but didn't yet know that these would be his last days there – he suddenly lost everything. He lost his apartment key, his money and his watch, he was fired from his job, hung out in bars with some guys he met, and had the feeling his whole life was coming apart, for no reason, inexplicably, out of the blue. He seemed to be falling and falling and there was nothing to check his fall. And then with the last of his money he bought himself the most beautiful suit he had ever owned, a pair of sunglasses, new shoes, and for two days and two nights he made the rounds of all the taverns and pubs in town. Early the third morning, at seven, he was standing at Hjalmar and Irene's door in Schöneberg saying, 'I've got to get some sleep. Would you please let me sleep here?' And Hjalmar and Irene put him in their bed, closed the curtains and turned off the light. Magnus slept for two days, then he got up, said goodbye, broke into his own apartment, packed his things, left Berlin and returned to Reykjavík.

'Oh, Magnus,' Jonina says and claps her hands when he tells her this story, 'oh, Magnus, what a lovely story about your departure.' Magnus hasn't been back to Berlin since. He doesn't keep in touch with the friends from those days any more. Jonina telephones a girlfriend in Vienna twice a year, that's all. The past is shut as tightly as a clamshell. And then Magnus says, 'Irene is coming to Iceland, and she's bringing someone. I don't know him; at any rate it isn't Hjalmar and he's not an Icelander.'

Irene. What a solid, compact, cold name. 'Were you living with her?' Jonina asks. It's really the first thing she wants to know, and Magnus laughs a little defensive laugh. 'No, never. She was with Hjalmar for a pretty long time; they didn't break up till after I left Berlin.'

Irene is giving a slide lecture in Reykjavík about German architecture. Hjalmar gave her the phone number of another Icelander, in Japan, he in turn directed her to someone in California, and in California she was given Magnus's phone number. She calls him and says, 'Excuse me, Magnus. We haven't been in touch for a long time. But I'm coming to Reykjavík soon and I thought we could get together.'

'Are you looking forward to it?' Jonina says. 'In a way, yes,' Magnus replies. 'Of course I'm looking forward to it. It could turn out to be very nice. It could also misfire completely. I don't know.' You can't know about anything, Jonina thinks. Dear Magnus, you can't know about anything at all, and you always have to be prepared for the worst, and for the best too.

That year the snow came unusually early. In mid-November it is already four feet deep outside Reykjavík; the Ring Road has to be cleared daily; many of the roads leading into the interior of the island are closed; villages cut off from the outside world. In other countries the airports would be shut down in weather like this; not in Iceland. The planes of Iceland Air land even on iced-over runways. Irene and Jonas arrived at Keflavík airport at the end of November, in a snowstorm with gale-force winds and below-freezing temperatures. Jonas will keep talking about it for the entire ten days of their stay.

Magnus doesn't pick them up at the airport, although he has the time, but the first evening after their arrival in Reykjavík he goes to hear Irene's slide talk. He really is interested in architecture. Jonina is driving to her parents' summerhouse in Olurfsbudir with Sunna. 'Ask them if they want to come to Olurfsbudir. Ask them if they'd like to drive out there,' Jonina says. 'Are you sure?' Magnus asks. Jonina looks at him, annoyed. Of course she's sure.

She's been with Magnus for two years now. She is thirty-five and has a six-year-old daughter who has no contact with her father any more. She met Magnus at a dinner at the house of some friends – he was described to her as someone she would surely be interested in, a psychologist, refined, a little odd, reserved and a bit mixed up, but good-looking; the description proved correct. Once they separated for four months, but now they're together again.

She can't stand it when Magnus asks if she's sure. If she weren't sure, she wouldn't have said anything. She wouldn't have invited Irene and Jonas – total strangers to her – if she weren't sure that it would work out well. Or maybe not well. Why should it always work out well? They would either get along or they wouldn't, whichever. She says, 'I'd like to meet Irene, and it would be nice for Irene to get out of Reykjavík, so ask her,' and then she drives off.

She has packed snowsuits, food, wine and packets of cigarettes into the boot of the car and has driven off with Sunna to Olurfsbudir. A cluster of small summerhouses on the west coast, six miles from the ocean – seventeen summerhouses on a hillside in the middle of the heath. Grassy hummocks, moss, dwarf shrubs, and on the horizon, very far away, the mountains. That is all. The summerhouses are simple low, log cabins, each with two small bedrooms, an eat-in kitchen, a terrace and a pool you can fill with hot-spring water.

Jonina's favourite time to be in Olurfsbudir is winter when the snow has covered the heath and everything is white all the way to the blue mountains. It gets light at eleven o'clock and dark again at four. It is silent, vast and godforsaken – black herds of Iceland horses and the steam rising from the pool, the only things moving. And the light changes from minute to minute, fog, walls of fog, the sun, a sudden view of the mountains, the sky splitting open and drawing shut again with threatening, blue-black clouds, then again fog and no more light at all.

Jonina finds driving to Olurfsbudir soothing; it calms her nerves, her whole body and also her heart. She longs to sit on the sofa by the window in the wooden house, to stare out at the grassy hummocks and not think of anything. Even after all these years she still finds it purifying. She was afraid that Magnus wouldn't know how to deal with Olurfsbudir when she took him out there for the first time, that he would think it all too monotonous, too quiet, but her fears were unfounded. Magnus enjoyed Olurfsbudir. On his first visit there, he took a small leather suitcase the contents of which Jonina inspected while he was in the bathroom. Three ironed shirts, three pairs of trousers, a perfect travelling case with shoe polish, brushes, polishing cloths, another case just as perfect containing sewing things, and a CD by Nick Cave. Jonina stood before the suitcase staring at its contents, at its touching and disquieting contents; then she snapped it shut again.

Magnus calls late that night. Sunna is already asleep. The other summerhouses are unoccupied in the wintertime. He says, 'Well then, we'll come tomorrow; they would very much like to come too.' 'What are they like?'

Jonina asks. 'What's the guy like and how did it go with Irene?' Magnus laughs softly. Jonina feels a wave of affection; she suddenly feels very sorry for him; or rather, she would like to touch him now. It must really be awful – meeting again after such a long time. He says, 'It was good. No, really, it was good. She gave a fine lecture and afterwards we went out to eat. It wasn't difficult; actually it was the way it used to be,' and Jonina says, 'Then come. Don't get here too late. It is very beautiful out here.'

Jonina folds the wrapping paper around the photo again; her breathing is shallow and quiet; her heart is pounding; she is afraid that Magnus might wake up any moment. He doesn't. He is sleeping his sound, childlike sleep behind the white bedroom door. In the kitchen Sunna pours cornflakes into a bowl; the sound seems incredibly loud to Jonina. She gets up and walks over to the hall cupboard and puts the package under the boxes that contain her old school exercise books, her photographs and letters. She's got to find another place for it, maybe get it out of the apartment entirely, or maybe she ought simply to show it to Magnus. She isn't sure. 'What are you doing,' Sunna calls from the kitchen; it's not a question, it's a statement; she sounds suspicious and grown up. 'Nothing,' Jonina says. 'I'm only putting things away.' She has to laugh.

She, Magnus and Sunna moved into this apartment four weeks ago. When Irene and Jonas arrived in November, a year before, they had just bought it. They had been looking for a long time and then finally found it, a small five-room apartment in the old harbour district of Reykjavík, with trees outside the windows and plasterwork on the ceiling. They were both very busy at work – and so they planned to renovate in January and move in February. They began the renovation in March, painted the walls, enlarged one of the doorways, put in new windows, and everything was actually finished, but then Magnus pulled up a floorboard, then a second and a third and decided to lay new parquet floors.

At that point Jonina opted out. She simply let go. She let him do the renovating by himself, and he took the entire apartment apart and couldn't finish, he simply couldn't finish, and in dismay Jonina concluded that concealed behind his reserve, his quiet and absent-minded manner, there was an absolute mania for perfection.

For months after that she no longer went to the apartment. She just couldn't stand it. She couldn't bear to see the awful mess – the destruction of things that had really been quite all right, and Magnus still thinking of new ways to make more changes. Summer came, and finally autumn, and in October he forced her to come and look at the result. They stood facing each other in the empty living room where the sunlight fell on the shining parquet floor and the walls gleamed. The plasterwork on the ceiling was accentuated by white paint, the doorways leading from one room to the next were wide and high. The windows had received a third coat of paint, and a huge silvery refrigerator hummed in the kitchen. Sunna's room. Your room. The dining room. Our room. Magnus took off his glasses; he looked ill. He said, 'I still have to lay tiles in the bath,' and Jonina said, 'Either I move in tomorrow or not at all, ever. Take my word for it. Tomorrow or not at all,' and then he gave in.

In the kitchen, Sunna, wise beyond her years, says as if she were talking to herself, 'There's nothing to put away

here,' and she's right. Magnus didn't have any things, and
Jonina had sold her own furniture. In all the rooms except
Sunna's there was only what was absolutely essential.
Perhaps Magnus thought this was the way it ought to be.
This was how an apartment for the three of them should
look. It had to be empty so that it could then be filled
with their new, shared life. Maybe, in his awkward and
insecure way, he had visualized it like that. But so far
nothing has been added.

Jonina had sensed their friends' astonishment, their
embarrassed politeness: 'What a wonderful apartment,
such a lovely location. But it's rather bare, isn't it? You
ought to hang some pictures, some photos, anything.'

'Could it be that Magnus worked on the renovation
for such a long time because he wasn't actually sure?'
Jonina's sister had asked hesitantly. And Jonina had said,
'Could be. But I'm not sure either, and we still have time,
all the time in the world.' It was reassuring. Her sister's
conjecture reassured her. It was good to know that
Magnus was afraid of living with her, of the decision and
its outcome; she is afraid too.

She shuts the cupboard door, goes to join Sunna in the
kitchen and sits down at the table with her. The tap is
dripping. Sunna is silent. Jonina gets up to turn it off.
Then she sits down again. Sunna eating her cornflakes
from a lemon-yellow bowl, sleepily, slowly. The cornflakes crackle in her small, closed mouth. She gazes
intently at her mother. It's not yet light outside.

In Olurfsbudir, Jonina and Sunna spend the afternoon –
the last hours before it gets totally dark again at five
o'clock – on the terrace. Jonina is sitting in a garden chair
in the snow; Sunna is in the pool. Jonina has set the water

temperature at 40°C; whenever the water gets too cold, more hot water flows in automatically. The pool is made of turquoise-coloured plastic. The water glitters; the snow around the edge of the pool has melted, but deep drifts of it cover the terrace. Sunna is sitting in the blue water, naked; her cheeks are quite red, her eyes sparkle, an intense and disturbing turquoise. They don't talk much; in general Sunna doesn't talk much. The cold is a dry cold and there is no wind. The plain is white and smooth like a desert; the snow has covered the tough perennial grass. The Iceland horses are standing up to their bellies in snow, not moving. To keep Sunna from saying anything, Jonina doesn't smoke; Sunna hates smoking.

Jonina can see Magnus's car while it is still far off, maybe miles away, but in the clear air she can already see Magnus. He is driving slowly; his car doesn't do well in snow, but he refuses to buy a Jeep. He says he isn't the type for a Jeep, and he's right. The car approaches at a tediously slow pace and stops at the foot of the hill on which the house stands. Jonina doesn't move. Sunna doesn't either, only the water ripples softly. Then the engine is switched off; it is quiet; the car doors remain closed. For one terrible moment, Jonina thinks it isn't Magnus sitting in the car but someone else, someone she doesn't know.

Then the car doors open, and Magnus gets out, Irene and Jonas get out. Jonina stands up. Magnus calls her name with exaggerated relief in his voice. She goes to meet them; they seem rooted to the spot, unable to move, just stand there, looking at the landscape, overwhelmed. Or they are only pretending to be overwhelmed? Jonina is always ready to assume the latter.

Had she known what Irene looked like, she wouldn't

have had to ask Magnus whether he had ever lived with her. She is too small. Too soft. Physically not enough of a presence for Magnus, who feels drawn to women who simply ignore his shyness, his tenseness and his absent-mindedness, and who win him over without his being aware of it. Maybe that's how Jonina had done it. Or maybe she simply touched him, took him home with her and persuaded him to stay; she isn't sure; she can't remember exactly how it happened.

Irene looks shy and absent-minded like Magnus. She isn't really short, but she isn't tall either. Her face is tense, serious, intellectual, with girlish features. A young woman you would notice in the university library only because she's already there when you arrive and is still there when you leave. Jonina knows and likes the type from her time in Vienna. The hand Irene now extends to her is cool, the handshake quite firm. She's wearing an inappropriate denim coat lined with swan-white artificial fur. The artificial fur looks good on her, but the coat won't keep her warm for more than ten minutes. Jonas is wearing a similar jacket of brown suede, also lined, a hippie jacket for a wintry Woodstock; naturally he's wearing it unbuttoned. His jeans are tattered, his green woollen hat is pulled far down over his eyes. He has slung an army backpack over one shoulder; apparently he didn't want to put it into the boot of the car. He doesn't offer to shake hands with Jonina, but says, 'Hey.' Maybe that's supposed to be Icelandic, but it sounds more American. 'Hey,' Jonina says in exactly the same tone of voice. He looks sexual. That's the first word that occurs to Jonina for him; he looks sexual, and Irene looks pale. Magnus puts his left hand on the back of Jonina's neck and gives her an awkward kiss on the lips. She's told him often enough not to do that; he doesn't have to openly demonstrate that they're together. She can do without it; he seems not to believe her.

Jonas says, 'Far out.' He says it in German, *abgefahren*, pronouncing it '*ab-ge-fahrn*' in a dark scratchy voice, and shakes his head. 'Original, like on the moon.'

'What's far out? What do you mean by "far out"?' Jonina asks in German. It feels odd to be speaking German, and Magnus's German sounds weird to her ear.

Jonas shakes his head, looks at her for the first time; his eyes are green, dark green, a narrow yellow band around the irises. Maybe he's trying to find an answer, but doesn't say anything, merely stamps his feet on the snow a few times in his military boots. Irene's expression is unfathomable; she lights a cigarette as if she thought she had to endure something for a long time yet.

Jonina takes a key out of her jacket pocket and hands it to Magnus. She says, first in Icelandic and then in German, 'Show them their house.' She points a short way up the slope where there's an identical house for Irene and Jonas. 'I've turned on the heat; you have to explain to them how the pool works.' 'Poool,' Jonas says dreamily. Up on the terrace, Sunna emerges from the water and stands naked in the snow.

Outside the kitchen window the sky is now turning blue, the same deep blue that drove Jonas out of his mind every morning last year. Sunna pushes her bowl of cornflakes away, annoyed and tired, and says, 'I'm leaving now.' She has been attending school for four months and seems to be moving further and further away from Jonina. In the hall she laces up her boots, slips into her coat, and puts on her fur hat; she looks like an Eskimo, her eyes squeezed into slits. She comes into the kitchen again and kisses Jonina affectionately, then she slams the door shut behind her. The school is at the end of the street. Sometimes Jonina wishes it were further away so that she could take Sunna there, say goodbye to her at the school gate, and watch her until she disappears behind the big door. But Sunna doesn't want to be taken to school. 'Shall I take you?' 'No. I'll go by myself.'

Jonina continues to sit at the kitchen table and gazes across the hall into the big room – our room – the white sofa in front of the window, a bunch of gladioli in a large green vase on the floor, on the windowsill a brass candlestick; that's all. She really should wake up Magnus; he has to go to work in an hour. She doesn't get up. She could put some small stones on the windowsill, the flat polished stones from the beach at Dyrhólaey, abraded till they're flat as paper, black and almost soft. Or some shells. Suddenly she feels close to tears, feels an unusual theatrical impulse to put her hands up to her face and burst into tears; it's silly. She doesn't even know why she should be crying.

She remembers the morning a year and a half ago when she woke up next to Magnus, in his apartment, in the bachelor room with the tiny window and the stone floor and his permanently clammy bed and the piles of books all around the bed, wine glasses, ashtrays. It seems that here in the new apartment Magnus wanted to put an end to that clutter once and for all. She woke up, watched Magnus sleeping for a long time; then she got dressed without waking him, and went home. Later, when he called, she didn't pick up the phone. She couldn't have explained why, not to anyone, and least of all to herself. Magnus didn't call again, quite as if he had known. And four months later, she was standing outside his door again, chastened and determined, once and for all. He let her in, said, 'That was that,' and they didn't talk about it, not ever again.

All the lights go on in the house across the street and then go out again. The sky gets lighter, someone walks down the stairs and slams the front door of the apartment block; further away a car drives off, the refrigerator hums softly. The odd simultaneity of the sounds, the concentration on an elusive something. Last year, after a night of drinking, Jonas had said, 'I feel like sitting in a dark cellar and watching black and white cartoon films.' Jonina found that he was often able to say things like that, things she immediately understood. Focused sentences, even though he was never focused, at least not focused on the outside world, on the things around him, the emotional and physical state of others. It was as if he were autistic, given up entirely to his own happiness or unhappiness. I'd like to be like that too now and then, Jonina thinks; I felt that way back then and then forgot about it, and the photo brought it all back – I want to be like that too sometimes.

Irene and Jonas stay in their house. Magnus comes back after he's taken them up. They'll be down for supper. Jonina knows that all the houses in Olurfsbudir are alike, and it makes her uneasy – identical furnishings, the same view of the mountains, the snow and the oncoming darkness – the thought that Irene and Jonas are moving about in front of the same backdrop as she and Magnus and Sunna. The same setting but a different conversation. What are they talking about up there, if they're talking at all?

Sunna is lying on the bed in their bedroom, watching a children's film on the portable TV. Magnus is sitting on the sofa, reading. He reads all the time. Every conversation with him is always a conversation between two paragraphs of the book he's immersed in at the moment. Jonina has given up trying to break him of that habit. She knows she should start to cook, yet doesn't feel the slightest urge to do so. She says, 'Say something.'

'Like what?' Magnus asks amiably, not looking up from his book; he goes on reading.

'What are they like, tell me what they're like; for example, what sort of relationship do they have.' Only for example.

'They don't live together,' Magnus says slowly, finishes reading a sentence, then looks at Jonina. 'Is that what you wanted to know? They're not living together; they both seem to be stuck in tragic relationships. On the way here, Irene talked with someone on her mobile phone and then hung up, furious. And last night Jonas talked of nothing but the woman who's just left him. They don't live together, but Irene says Jonas is her best friend. Has been for years. They've known each other for a relatively long time; they must have met shortly after I left Berlin or while I was still there – I have no idea. I didn't know all of Irene's friends.' He closes the book halfway, leaving his index finger between the pages.

'That's what Irene says,' Jonina remarks. 'And what does Jonas say?'

'Jonas says nothing,' Magnus replies with irritation. 'She talked to me because she knows me. Because she was giving me some personal information. He wasn't there when she told me. And he doesn't know me at all; why should he say to me, "Irene is my best friend"?'

Magnus is right. He puts away his book and lights a cigarette, inhales deeply, puffs the smoke out; then he sighs. The conversation bores him. 'And don't you think they're a peculiar couple? So very different from each other, at least at first glance?' Jonina says, pushing the glass door open and shutting it again, trying to recall what it was she wanted to do just now.

'Best friends are always different from each other,' Magnus replied in a funny didactic tone. 'Because they are different, they can be friends, right? Otherwise, what would be the sense in being friends? And you yourself said it – different at first glance. At first glance.'

'I'm probably mistaken,' Jonina says, perplexed. She empties the refrigerator, and then puts the things back again. Maybe they ought to grill something. Cook some fish, maybe soup. She has no idea what. She also realizes that they haven't been together with other people for a long time. They're mostly by themselves. She and Magnus and Sunna. They work a lot. Are tired in the evenings. Don't drink as much as they used to. She says, 'You cook. I can't cook. I don't feel like cooking.' And Magnus says, 'In a minute, OK? I just want to finish this page, and then I'll cook for us all.'

Towards evening, she goes up to the other house to get Irene and Jonas. It has begun to snow again. The cabin is quiet and dark; Jonina is afraid of finding them naked in the pool, but the pool is empty. She steps up on the terrace; the glass door is open. For a moment Jonina can't see anything; then she makes out Irene and Jonas on the sofa. Irene is sitting and Jonas is lying on his back, his head in her lap. 'Hello,' Irene says. Jonas sits up, not at all embarrassed, and turns on the light. Irene says matter-of-factly, 'With the room dark, you can see the outside better. And we were in the pool for hours. It is beautiful here, Jonina.' She has a way of pronouncing Jonina's name in a childish, trusting way that sounds strange to Jonina. Jonina puts her hands in her trouser pockets and doesn't know what to say. On the table are cigarettes, a bottle of vodka but no glasses, a camera, several rolls of film, three books, a bunch of keys, a hairbrush and an ashtray. Jonina feels a compulsive desire to pick up all these objects and examine them.

The door to the bedroom on the right is open, the door to the other bedroom is closed. Irene follows Jonina's glance and says, 'We'll sleep in that room; it has the more beautiful view.' 'Yes,' Jonina says, 'I also prefer to sleep in the front.' Jonas ties his shoes with vigorous, jerky movements, and says, 'I've always wanted to have a bedroom like that, a room with a window that's at the same level as the bed and has a view of the countryside, a room just like that, and now here it is, it is simply *here*.' He laughs, and casually looks up at Jonina. It doesn't seem to matter to him whether she understands him or not. She says, 'Well, supper is ready,' then she turns and goes out. She doesn't regret having invited them; she doesn't regret it at all.

They come fifteen minutes later, kick the snow off their shoes on the house wall, hang up their coats in the hall, and sit down at the table. Magnus has made fish with lime and sprigs of rosemary. Sunna eats a potato and gazes uninterruptedly and with her mouth slightly open at Jonas, who speaks English with her. She says not a word and at eleven o'clock she just goes off to bed.

When Jonina looks in on her later, she is already asleep, still dressed, lying on her side, her left hand pressed to her ear. Something or other was too noisy for her. Maybe it was Jonas in the kitchen talking very loud, very fast and excitedly; intermittently pounding the table or Irene's knee with the flat of his hand, and now and then throwing back his head and simply letting out a shout. Listening to him is nice, but strenuous too; it makes Jonina uneasy. Sometimes she can't understand anything he is saying; maybe it has to do with the language, maybe it's something else.

He talks about the snowstorm as they were landing, the bus trip through the darkness to Reykjavík, the snow in the streets melting immediately because the streets were heated. Their first night in the city apartment with a view of the frozen lake; Irene had already gone to bed, and he, Jonas, was sitting in the kitchen looking out at the night-time city and not being able to grasp it. Couldn't grasp what? Iceland. *Rey-kja-vík*. The snow. Jonas had a remarkable way of randomly emphasizing some word, illogically and vehemently. Maybe this is what attracts Jonina, this selfish dynamic energy.

Irene is silent. Apparently she has made up her mind simply to show Jonas to Jonina and Magnus. To exhibit him like a rare specimen, to let them decide whether they want to get involved with him or not. She doesn't interrupt him; she rarely joins in. She listens to him, quite often laughing at what he says. She smokes funny non-tobacco cigarettes made of herbs and drinks one glass of water after the other.

'What was it that you did in those days in Berlin, you and Magnus?' Jonina asks and is suddenly afraid to hear the answer. But Irene only lifts her glass symbolically and says, 'We drank. What else can you do with Icelanders? We drank together and passed the nights together, saying goodbye in the early dawn; that's all, actually, nothing else.' Magnus says nothing but eventually whispers, 'Actually, nothing else'; it sounds like an absurd echo.

Jonina says, 'Has Magnus changed?' And Irene hesitates a moment, looks at Magnus – that is, she only pretends to, she doesn't really look at him; then she says, 'No, he hasn't.' What else was she supposed to say?

Jonina feels as though she knows these people. Not specifically Jonas and Irene, but their type, the way they perceive things – spoiled, detached, yet capable of enthusiasm.

'I mean, we're sitting here *at the end of the earth*, aren't we? This *is* the end of the earth here,' Jonas says. 'All this snow and the cold and the mountains, and this *total* far-out solitude, and we're sitting around in the middle of it, talking and eating *fabulous* things and drinking schnapps and wine, and things are going well – just imagine it. Irene. Have you grasped that already, have you? You already understand all that; it's all clear to you. It *is clear* to you what's happening here.' Irene suddenly looks quite distracted, then she laughs, twists the ring on her left hand but doesn't answer him.

Magnus is in bed lying on his back, asleep. The quilt is pulled up over his shoulders. He's breathing quietly and regularly, almost inaudibly. Sometimes at night Jonina reaches over to his stomach to feel his breathing; she can barely hear him. She sits down on the edge of the bed and looks at him. This is forbidden; she does it anyway. Sometimes she can see his real face. The best time for that is when he's not wearing his glasses and his hair is wet, right after he comes out of the pool or the shower and his hair is plastered close to his head, revealing the shape of his skull and his face. She can see how dangerous he really is. Is that the right word? His real expression isn't open, but friendly; his face is narrow and boyish, clean cut and beautiful, there is nothing striking about it. His mouth is perhaps a little too childish, his eyes behind the glasses are very small, often squinting, an absent-minded, inattentive look. But sometimes she can see that his face is actually cold, an aggressive, challenging, determined and cold face; she can see it when he comes out of the water and when he is sleeping. She doesn't know whether he wants to hide this coldness. The coldness neither repels nor attracts her. It is the coldness of a stranger, the coldness of someone she could spend a hundred thousand years with and yet never get to know. *This is an ice-cold fact, a cold-blue fact.* Irene had liked this Icelandic expression very much. Jonina whispers, 'There is mail from Berlin,' then she wakes Magnus up.

It's amazing, but because of Irene and Jonas's visit, Jonina sees Iceland differently now. She can see it briefly through the eyes of a stranger, although she used to think this was impossible. She has been working as a tourist guide ever since she came back to Iceland from Vienna. In the summer she takes tourists through the highlands for weeks at a time, and in the winter she takes charge of the day tours that go by bus to the Geysir, to Gullfoss, the largest waterfall in Europe, to the volcano Mount Hekla, and the hot springs in Landmannalaugar. She works for a Frenchman named Philippe whose organization offers all sorts of tourist tours, tours on horseback, on foot, or by bus, and in special cases by propeller-driven planes that fly as far as Greenland. Philippe himself hasn't been to the Geysir, not even once; he hates Iceland; he hates the cold, the long winters and the feeling of being at the end of the earth.

He keeps telling Jonina the story of Descartes, who came to the Swedish court to teach Queen Christina philosophy at seven o'clock in the morning, and who after a few weeks there died of pneumonia. As he tells the story, he gives her a meaningful look. But he's making an incredible amount of money on these tours, and he says, 'Once I've earned enough money, I'm out of here. I'll be back in France in no time, and you'll have to see how you're going to manage here on this dark and gloomy, horrible nothing of an ice-cold island.' He says this daily.

Jonina can't imagine that he'll ever have enough money. She figures that Philippe will die in Iceland and that's actually how he wants it to be, except that he isn't Descartes and so it will take a bit longer. She doesn't like her work, but she does it anyway. Philippe pays her well, and she has enough time for herself and for Sunna. She doesn't work in the spring, and in the darkest part of winter, from December to February, there's nothing to do either.

In the summer, when the long light nights begin, she takes groups of tourists through the highlands. She goes on three-week hikes with fifteen people – Americans, Frenchmen, Italians and Germans, whose names she rarely remembers – and as soon as they say goodbye to her in Reykjavík she forgets them. There's a saying among the tour guides, 'All love affairs stop in Reykjavík.' Jonina has never had an affair with any of these tourists, and she doesn't open any of the letters they continue to send her even weeks after the end of their vacations; she throws them away unread.

On the tours the Americans always ask in which

direction the river flows and where in the sky the sun rises. The Italians are constantly cold, feel uncomfortable in the barren rock and gravel moraines and the lava fields, visibly yearning for a sign of ancient human civilization. The French are very fussy, quickly develop blisters on their feet, and spit out the dried fish in disgust as soon as Jonina's back is turned. The Germans would much rather go off by themselves but don't have the nerve; the large size of the group puts them in a bad mood and, confronted by natural wonders, they are prey to unbearable bouts of melancholy.

Jonina never talks about her tours in any other way, and it isn't exaggeration on her part; this is how she sees it. She certainly is one of the least popular of the tour guides, but Philippe keeps rehiring her. He thinks she hates Iceland as much as he does, but that isn't true. She is at home in Iceland, and that means that she doesn't think about it. Nowhere else in the world does she sleep as well as in a tent at the edge of the high plateau, rolled up in a sleeping bag on the hard earth. She can hike for hours, finding the right rhythm, walk and look around and become completely silent. She likes the reduction of her thinking to the essentials on these trips; the need to concentrate on her compass, on the signposts made of piled-up lava rocks, on indications of a possible snowstorm, and otherwise nothing. What she doesn't like are conversations about Iceland. The bewildered enthusiasm, the struggling for words, the therapeutic effect the landscape seems to have on the tourists. She doesn't want to talk about Iceland and she doesn't want to have to explain how she can bear living here. The tourists love Iceland, but they wouldn't want to live here. They could never live here. How is Jonina supposed to understand this attitude? If the tourists don't bother her, she is peaceful and shows them what she knows. She doesn't keep anything from them, doesn't keep any place secret. She just can't participate in their enthusiasm. She can't see the island the way tourists see it. She cannot let herself be emotionally affected. But with Irene and Jonas's visit, this has changed for the very first time.

The next morning, Jonina is on the terrace of the summer-house. She stands in the snow, watching the narrow band of light above the mountains getting lighter and wider. She wonders how Jonas sees it. She is interested in knowing how Jonas sees all this; for some reason she would like to understand that. Perhaps it's because at the moment she isn't a guide, but Jonina, a private person. And Magnus and Sunna and Magnus's friend Irene and Irene's best friend, Jonas. What does daybreak at eleven o'clock in the morning as seen from the terrace of the house in Olurfsbudir look like to Jonas? He stands there, naked and pale and wet from the pool, stands there in the snow and shouts, 'Can you believe this!'

They drive to Eyrarbakki and Stokkseyri, to the sea and to the steep bluff at Snæfellsnes and to the black beaches at Dyrhólaey and Vík, to the Geysir, and to the frozen waterfall, Gullfoss. For the first time in a long while, Jonina again feels like going on these excursions. She wants to elicit from Irene and Jonas precisely those reactions she tries to avoid on her guided tours – a burst of stunned amazement. They walk over the hummocky meadows near Olurfsbudir, through snow that no one has gone through before them. 'Look at that,' Jonas says, 'not a single track.' Not quite, one small track, a fox, a snow goose. The sky is as watery white as the land.

Magnus is pulling Sunna through the snow on a sled. Wearing a red ski suit, she lies on her back motionless, as if unconscious. Now and then she makes a slight, vague grimace. 'The little valley we're coming to now,' Magnus tells Irene and Jonas in a voice that reminds Jonina of her own tour-guide voice, 'this valley is a magic place. You can hear the sound made by two waterfalls, one on the right and one on the left, like a stereo effect.'

During the first months of their relationship, Jonina and Magnus often came here in August and during the light nights. She is strangely moved to hear Magnus speaking about it this way. 'A stereo effect.' Jonas, as always, is only half listening, and then says, 'All places in Iceland are magic, aren't they?'

Irene, wrapped in her fake-fur coat, is exhausted enough to simply give up the cool reserve she has been showing, standing like a statue at the edge of the cliff at Snæfellsnes looking down at the sea. With extended arms she drops on her back into the snow. *Look, an angel.*

Sunna, erect and serious, is looking into Jonas's camera. *'Just right,'* Jonas says, 'exactly right, Sunna; stay like that, stay like that, *please* stay just like that.' At the very last moment, she turns away. Jonas keeps taking pictures. He considers it important for them to know that he is a professional photographer, not a tourist taking pictures. Jonina asks Irene whether he works for an agency in Berlin, has he published books of his photographs, does he have shows. Irene says coolly, 'None of that.' 'But still, he takes beautiful photographs, doesn't he?' Jonina asks, surprised. 'Yes, he takes beautiful photographs,' Irene says.

Jonas has brought along an impressively large camera

that he has to set up in the most complicated way and with an enormous expenditure of time before he can take a picture. It seems to Jonina that taking pictures like that clashes with Jonas's nature and his quick temperament, but someone had suggested it, and Irene astutely calls it a 'therapeutic measure'.

Magnus is driving; Jonina sits beside him and in the wing mirror she watches Jonas, Sunna and Irene in the back seat. Jonas has to open a can of beer because he can't bear sitting in the back and not driving himself. Inadvertently, Sunna has put her left hand on his knee. The sun stands above the white mountains; the sky over the fjord is black; small, rotund, brown horses in the snow. Grass, reeds, sedge, a sandbar, ravens and wild geese. Jonas stares out of the window, his face cradled in one hand, like a sullen child. Then he says, 'We're driving past all sorts of paintings, and you have no eye for it at all.' Ten minutes later he shouts, 'Stop! *Stop!*'

Magnus steps on the brake; the car skids, then comes to a stop. Jonas gets out, runs back two hundred yards, and photographs two Iceland horses in the fog. Jonina and Irene get out too and light cigarettes. Jonas comes back and says, 'Get back in. Drive on.' It's all too much for him; he is overwrought, ecstatic; the light is changing too fast, and each impression is too short, wiped out, superseded by the next – the harbour of Arnarstapi, the sea, the three cliffs have already vanished in the fog. The sun is going down, falling through all the colour variations.

Jonas always running. Jonina never sees him just walking, doing something slowly. He runs, waves his arms about wildly, stamps his foot, goes into raptures, and Jonina is completely captivated, so are Irene and Magnus, even Sunna gets caught up in it. All four slip and stumble along behind him, behind his contagious excitement. Jonina wonders, How long can this go on, when will Magnus have had enough? When will I get fed up? They say little to each other on these excursions. They stay close together, stand next to one another at Gullfoss, at the black beach, at the sea caves. It is a coincidence and a shared mood, but they seem to get along well. They seem to expect the same thing from the snow and the cold, and, when all is said and done, from this senseless look at the wonders of nature. 'This wipes me out,' Irene says several times, 'all this really wipes me out.'

In Eyrarbakki they park the car at the dike in front of the school. They eat their ice-cold sandwiches, drink tea from the Thermos, and wait for Sunna, who is curled up on Jonina's lap, to wake up. When Sunna wakes up, they get out. In front of the school, children and grown-ups – excited, red-cheeked and exuberant – are making snowmen of all sizes. Jonina walks up on the dike with Magnus, Irene and Sunna. She wants to see the ocean, the beach. She is impatient, temporarily exhausted by Jonas. He doesn't follow them. When they get to the top of the dike – the sea is black, the beach is black, on the horizon the sky is black, the sun tiny and orange – Jonina turns round and looks back.

Jonas has set up the tripod, is standing bent over the camera; the children and grown-ups are posing next to their snowmen, motionless, smiling. It is still, only the wind whistles. Jonas raises his hand; Jonina sees exactly the photograph he is taking. The moment is already frozen in this almost old-fashioned, posed, motionless scene. She can hear the camera shutter click; then Jonas straightens up, calls out something; the children and grown-ups relax from their frozen poses, wave briefly, and bow. Jonas folds up the tripod. Finished. Jonina walks along the dike, straight ahead, trudging through the knee-deep snow. Gulls sail above the water, the green stones overgrown with algae, and the spray metallic.

In the afternoon they drive back overland, and on, to the Geysir. They stand next to each other at the old sleeping geyser, which hurls its destructive gigantic jet of hot water into the air once every hundred years. 'When was the last eruption?' Jonas asks, markedly casual; he is uneasy and for a change does not want to take any pictures. 'A hundred years ago,' Magnus says. 'We're expecting the next eruption any moment.' And Jonas turns round and walks back to the car. The others don't move. Irene says, 'Well, if that should happen and I'm standing here at exactly the moment when these jets erupt, then I'll gladly surrender.' Jonina makes no reply even though she feels the same way. She thinks about the peculiar expression, *sich ergeben*, to surrender oneself. The surface of the water remains still, smooth, unmoving, a dull mirror that reflects nothing.

'We could drive to Thingvellir tomorrow, to the lake and to the site of the Old Althing,' Magnus says, like a child unusually full of anticipation. He is pleased at the joke he has allowed himself to play on Jonas, and doesn't seem to share the anxiety Jonina feels. Something is happening between them – Sunna is watching them, aware – something is not quite right; they are not on firm ground. Jonina feels she is being too cocky, not careful enough, maybe even too happy. It's been such a long time since she was last outdoors with Magnus and Sunna, so long since she's spent time with people who might almost be friends. She would like to give herself up to these five

72

days they are spending in Olurfsbudir together, and she does, but still she feels as though she is being held back by a quiet, warning voice. Something is happening between Irene and Jonas, and between Jonina and Irene, between Irene and Magnus. Nothing spectacular, not something that might change anything; they are all far from a change, much further than they would really like to be. And still, something is happening.

Magnus showers for twenty minutes, then he has breakfast – as always, one cup of coffee, one slice of bread, one soft-boiled egg cooked with an eye on the second hand of the clock. He takes a bite of the bread, then a spoonful of egg. He takes a sip of coffee, then another bite of bread, and throughout all this he reads the paper. He smokes one cigarette by the window, then he's finished with the paper too. He makes green tea with water cooled to 67°C, fills a Thermos with it, turns off the radio that's been playing only for him, says to himself, 'Go ahead, start,' and goes to work. Every morning. Each and every morning the same ritual. Not that it's bad, it just amazes Jonina.

Every morning it amazes her to see how these rituals mesh – her own, Magnus's and Sunna's – how they mesh because they have decided to spend their lives together, as long as it works out. Sometimes she feels it won't be possible – her shoes next to Magnus's shoes, next to Sunna's shoes under the coat rack in the hall where her jacket hangs next to Magnus's coat. Have you seen my key? You put it on the table in the dining room. It's not there. Then look in your coat pocket . . . Actually it does seem possible. Anything else does not seem possible. They stand together next to the kitchen cabinets, Jonina pours ground coffee into the coffee maker; she always simply pours some in, whereas Magnus measures it out, spoonful by spoonful. Magnus lifts his egg out of the boiling water and cools it off under the tap. Their hands cross as he reaches over to turn off the tap and she turns it on again to rinse out the coffeepot. He opens the kitchen cabinet and takes out a plate, a cup, their elbows collide, the refrigerator door slams shut with that soft, smacking, rubbery sound. Magnus turns on the radio, the classical station, two measures of Schubert and a totally senseless transition to Ravel. Schubert is seven points ahead of Ravel, Sarrasate is hopelessly left behind. The coffee maker gurgles quietly.

Jonina sits down across the table from Magnus, where Sunna usually sits. She lights a cigarette and briefly passes the lighter flame under the filter. 'Why do you always do that?' Irene had asked her a year ago. To which Jonina had replied, 'Because I heard somewhere that it burns up the glass-dust particles in the filter,' and both of them suddenly burst into uncontrollable laughter. After that, Irene always burned her filter too. Jonina wonders whether she still does it. Magnus cuts his egg open with his spoon. If Jonina ever eats an egg, she cuts the top off with a knife; actually that's the only reason she ever eats an egg. Magnus carefully and inconspicuously pulls the newspaper that's lying on the table over to his plate.

As he is beginning to read the lead article, Jonina says, 'Do you still remember the story you told Irene and Jonas last year? The story with the sheep?' The way she said it sounds funny, and she has to laugh. Magnus doesn't laugh. She knows that he doesn't talk in the morning, that it's an effort for him to engage in conversation at the breakfast table. But she would like to talk to him right now, this very moment. He doesn't laugh, but he repeats her funny phrasing, drawing it out, thoughtfully, his eyes still fixed on a headline in the paper – 'The story with the sheep.'

'Yes, exactly,' Jonina says. 'You know the one I mean, the story where you and your uncle and Oddur took the sheep to be mated, that story. Would you tell it to me again?' Magnus refuses to be annoyed. That's the nice thing about him, the thing that Jonina really loves. It is hard to upset him, to upset his equanimity, you can't rattle him; he rarely imputes anything bad to people. He is polite, decent and serious; he knows how to listen; if you ask him a question, he answers it; if you ask him something in the morning at breakfast, he will answer too. He would never say, 'I'm tired, I don't want to talk right now; I'd rather read.' And of course this tempts her, too. There is something stubborn, something stoic and inflexible about him; his politeness is an armour that's almost impossible to pierce.

Magnus puts his hand over the headline as though he wanted to protect it, and says, 'How did you happen to think of that?' And Jonina says truthfully, 'I thought of Irene when I was burning the filter of my cigarette, remembering that Irene always did it too. I was thinking of that one evening in Olurfsbudir and then I remembered the story, and now I'd like to hear it again.' It's a game they often play, although not as often as they used to. Going back over a string of thoughts, the amazing combination of associations, memories, the flash of an idea. Magnus could ask, Which evening; there were a lot of evenings in Olurfsbudir. Which evening do you mean? And Jonina would tell him which evening she meant – the last one. But he doesn't ask. Completely at a loss, he says, 'Am I supposed to tell you the story again, now?' and Jonina says, 'Now.' She wonders whether her voice sounds cruel.

Magnus looks up from his paper, looks directly at Jonina; for a moment his face has a guarded expression, then he says – as though he were talking to Sunna – 'All right then. I was sixteen or seventeen back then, it was winter, February, the time when they take the ewes to be covered. The snow was pretty deep, and my uncle had to take his ewe to a ram in another village. I went along with him, and Oddur, my best friend, came too. Actually we didn't really want to. We were in a bad mood – but, Jonina, you know all that, I've told it to you a thousand times already. We loaded the ewe into the Jeep and drove off. It was sometime in the afternoon, but it was already dark. The snow was so deep that it took us more than two hours to drive from our village to the other one; normally you could have driven there in twenty minutes. I sat in the back with the sheep; Oddur sat with my uncle up front. We drove very slowly. Now and then we'd get stuck in the snow and we'd have to shovel ourselves out. The stars came out above us.' Magnus goes over to the coffee maker and pours himself a second cup of coffee, doesn't even notice he's doing it. He sits down again, looks at Jonina, and continues, 'When we arrived in the village, the ewe was taken to the ram; we waited in the farmer's kitchen and drank schnapps to warm up. The ram mounted the ewe, and when he was finished, the ewe was loaded into the Jeep again, and we drove home. We had taken the open bottle of schnapps with us and drank it driving home through the snow. The moon had come up, and we could see all the stars, the entire Milky Way; we talked a little and then fell silent, and it was very beautiful to be in the Jeep with the ewe on the country road, all alone in the world. That's all.'

And if only we could communicate like that, Jonina

thinks. If we could communicate like that, exactly that way. He tells a story, and I listen to him, and then we look at each other, and we know exactly what it's all about. We know without having to say it.

'Was that the one?' Magnus asks.

In Olurfsbudir a year ago, the last evening they were spending with Irene and Jonas, he had told the story at the kitchen table, late at night. Jonina had looked at him and had the feeling her heart was bursting with love and sadness. He really didn't think he could tell it, and then he did start telling it, and at the end he asked, 'Do you understand that?' doubtful and unsure. 'Is that understandable?' A story without a point, a story that's about nothing and yet about everything. 'Well, I understand it,' Jonas had said without even a second's hesitation. 'I understand it, and Irene understands it too.'

'I just wanted to hear it again,' Jonina says softly, leans across the table and briefly and firmly puts her hand on the back of his neck. 'I'd better go now,' Magnus says. He says it as though there's a possibility he might not go; but that possibility does not exist. He looks regretfully at his newspaper, sticks it into his briefcase, smokes a cigarette by the open window. Today Jonina makes the tea for his Thermos. She watches him. He is smoking but he isn't reading, he's looking out the window; moves his right hand over the smooth paint of the windowsill, checking it out.

When he leaves, she watches him through the window; the smoke of his cigarette still hangs in the air; she sees him walking down the street, his briefcase clamped under his arm, his hands in his jacket pockets. His shoulders are raised, and she would really like to know what he's thinking about right now. She leans forward and calls after him – Icelandic windows can't be opened wide; you can only tilt them a bit – she calls after him through the narrow crack through which cold air is blowing in. She yells, 'Magnus, do you still remember how I fell in love with Jonas?' He doesn't stop, keeps going, doesn't turn around to look at her.

In the evening, when they come back from their excursions, they separate for a while. Irene and Jonas disappear into their summerhouse. Usually Jonina can hear them in the pool: Jonas's gleeful, high-pitched laughter and Irene's soothing voice. It sounds as if Jonas has jumped into the pool, and then afterwards, throwing himself into the snow, he squeals like a girl. They're apart for an hour or two, then they meet for supper at Jonina's house.

Jonina is waiting for that. The time she is alone with Magnus and Sunna and can hear Irene and Jonas up there seems endless to her. She becomes tired, gets a headache, she can't talk to Magnus, she is impatient with Sunna, restless and irritated. And then she hears them coming down, Jonas's non-stop exclamations of wonderment at the snow, the solitude, the thousands of things you have to wear to walk those fifty yards between the two houses. 'You should see the way you *look*, Irene! You look like an enormous, stuffed rag doll, far out, *extremely* far out.' She hears them coming, and she has to pull herself together to keep from running to meet them, from ripping open the door, and dragging them in.

Magnus is cooking; Jonas is talking in children's English with Sunna; Irene sits down on the sofa and stares out of the window as if she were watching television. They may not talk much on their excursions, sit silently in the car, and stroll along without saying a word, but in the evening they talk, all at the same time, almost shouting. Irene and Jonas try to express the way they feel about Iceland. Jonina is familiar with this. On her tours the tourists sit around in the tents every evening, talking. Jonina never listens to them, but she listens to Irene and Jonas. They've each reached the end of a relationship back in Berlin. They don't talk about that, but they hint at it, and they see Iceland as a kind of miracle that will heal their broken hearts.

Irene repeats an expression she read in the travel guide, a description of Iceland that dates back to the year 325 BC, *Ultima Thule*, the most distant land of the far north. 'And that's just how I feel here,' she says, 'away from everything, in the most distant land.'

'And therefore *the closest*,' Jonas shouts.

The expression is completely new to Jonina, and she doesn't know how to deal with all this. She thinks – as usual – that it's ridiculous, childish and naïve. But she doesn't try to restrain Irene and Jonas. And she is really touched by their enthusiasm, is swept up in it and is convinced by it, for a little while. For the first time she has the feeling that she lives in a country in which smoking volcanoes and spewing water lead to an answer to all questions, an answer you can't decipher and which is nevertheless sufficient.

'What would we show Jonina if she came to visit us in Berlin? What places would show her how we live?' Jonas asks, and provides his own answer, 'Café Burger? The Luxusbar? The Oderquelle?' Irene stops him. She says, 'Magnus, if you wanted to show Jonina the way you lived in Berlin, what would you show her?' Magnus ponders this for quite a while, then he shakes his head and doesn't say anything. 'The Kumpelnest,' Irene says. 'We'd have to take Jonina to the Kumpelnest at five in the morning and stand there with her on the corner of Pohlstrasse and Potsdamer and tell her, This is the spot where, totally plastered, we used to hail a taxi. That would be the only thing we could show her, and it would still be true. That's what it was like. It makes me really sad.'

Jonas, who can't bear it when people talk about things that happened when he wasn't around, lifts his glass and says, 'Well, then, we'll see each other in Valhalla.' Magnus asks, 'What's Valhalla?' And Irene says, 'I don't know exactly, but I think Valhalla is the Vikings' hereafter. Their Paradise, a huge hall with a long table where you sit with those you love and where you drink and drink till the end of time.' 'Exactly,' Jonas says. 'That's exactly what Valhalla is, and when you're having a *drink* together here, you can safely clink your glasses to that over and over again.'

'And what kind of friendship do you have?' Jonina asks; she is relaxed enough to ask the question. Jonas is about to answer, but then a sleepy-eyed Sunna is suddenly standing in the kitchen, and Jonina is glad to take her back to bed, glad for an excuse to leave the table. When she comes back, Jonas and Irene are outside by the pool. Magnus is sitting at the table by himself, calm and composed, his hands on his knees; he is looking at the four beer cans he has emptied, lined up in front of him. He's going to drink one more, no more and no less. Then a glass of wine maybe.

Jonina fell in love with him for precisely this. She fell in love with this puzzling, stubborn attitude, and now she wants him to stop. She wants to shake him and push him, she wants him to confront Jonas, wants him to pit his own strength against Jonas's strength and presence, wants him to stand his ground and show himself, but he is far from doing that. He isn't confused by any of this. Jonas doesn't confuse him, Irene doesn't, and Jonina hasn't for a long time. After they leave he will clean off the table, turn off the light, and go to sleep. He has a clear conscience, Jonina thinks, and I haven't.

Irene and Jonas come back into the kitchen. Sunna still isn't asleep by midnight, so Jonina goes into the pool with her again. 'Look, the moon,' Sunna cries. The moon is surrounded by a corona in all the colours of the rainbow. They sit in the hot water, and snow falls on their heads, melts on the surface of the water. Jonina looks through the window into the kitchen; Jonas is talking; Irene gives him a light push with her left hand; for a long time Jonas laughs about something.

Magnus opens the first bottle of wine, sets out four glasses. The view through the window is quite nice. Jonina climbs out of the water, dries herself and gets dressed. Jonas could look out, but it doesn't even occur to him to do that. Sunna rubs herself with snow till her skin is red and glowing; later she sits for a while on Jonina's lap at the table, takes a tiny sip of wine and then goes to her room.

At some point Irene says, 'I'm going to bed now.' Jonas gets up, swaying. It takes them a long time to put on their sweaters, coats and shoes; then they stand a while longer on the terrace, looking out into the night. Jonas demonstrates how his head will explode, imagining what it will be like returning to Berlin and being asked, 'Well, how was it?' He says, 'I hope nobody will ask us how it was.' They say, 'Good night,' then they leave.

'Aren't you tired?' Magnus says. 'No,' Jonina replies.
'I'm going to stay out here a little longer.' She puts on
her ski jacket, takes a cigarette, her last one, and sits
down on a garden chair by the pool. The view across the
snowy landscape is a view she doesn't comprehend; she
can't turn her eyes away from it, but the view is not the
only thing she would like to understand. Jonas and Irene
are already asleep; Sunna is sleeping; Magnus is falling
asleep. What yardstick should one use to take the measure
of this, the end of the earth? And how far away is the
horizon, and is it always and everywhere the same
distance away? And what about Magnus, standing on the
corner of Pohlstrasse and Potsdamer at five o'clock in the
morning – what did he look like then, and where was
*she* during those years?

It is still; in the stillness a sheet of snow slides off the
roof; in the distance she can hear the Iceland horses; the
digital pool gauge drops soundlessly to zero.

Jonina goes into the kitchen, washes the breakfast dishes,
dries them and puts them away in the cupboard. She
stands at the window, looks out into the street. A gentle
rain has begun to fall. She has another hour, then she
should drive to Philippe's and pick up fifteen orange rain
jackets from the office, choose the bus and the driver she
likes best, make the rounds of the hotels, collecting the
tourists, and then drive with them to Hveragerdi and
Selfoss – Iceland's most successful garden centre, where
there are greenhouses heated by geothermal installations,
a hot-springs area in the middle of the village, a modern
Lutheran church with a beautiful altarpiece, and Iceland's
only horticultural school. It's the most boring tour they
offer. At this time of year the tourists come from Sweden,

Denmark and Germany. Sprightly retired folk who don't want to go hiking any more and who take in the sights through the tinted panoramic windows of the bus. There's nothing wrong with that.

Jonina turns away from the kitchen window; she doesn't have the slightest desire to go on this tour. She goes into the living room, moves the vase of gladioli from the left side of the sofa to the right and back again. She thinks of Magnus. She wishes he were here, were sitting here reading and smoking, being with her without saying anything. But he isn't here. He's sitting at his desk in the Centre for Social Education; there is no photograph on his desk, no stone, no shell – 'I work there, Jonina, I don't need all that stuff.' He listens to young people who have been abused, beaten, or thrown out by their parents. He listens to them with this quiet, inward face that allows them to say even the worst things with total confidence and trust.

Jonina regrets the way she said goodbye to Magnus half an hour ago. She regrets having called after him that foolish question even though she knows that questions like that just roll off his back. He doesn't hear them. He doesn't even want to know the answer. He firmly believes that what is, is, and what is supposed to happen will happen; he doesn't stand in anyone's way and makes no decisions. That's how it is. And that's that.

She goes to Sunna's room and opens the door. Sunna's is the only room in this apartment that's bearable. A child's room full of clutter, full of clothes and toys and little lamps on which fairytale princesses drive in coaches through a blue universe. Sunna's favourite colour is yellow, and so everything is yellow, the sheets and curtains, the rug, her wardrobe and the desktop. There's a piece of paper on the floor on which Sunna has written in big, crooked letters, 'for magnus'; underneath that, drawn in pencil, is a cat. Jonina takes the picture to the kitchen; she looks for a drawing pin, finds one, and resolutely pins the picture up above the kitchen table. Then she sits down and gazes at it: 'for magnus'. The cat has disproportionately long whiskers, three legs and a sickle-shaped, extravagant head.

Jonina falls in love with Jonas on December 3rd, shortly before eleven o'clock in the morning on the road that leads to the site of the Old Althing. That's how it was. That time of year it gets light between ten and eleven o'clock, and during this hour the sky turns blue, a bright, deep, tremendous blue that seems to reconcile the entire world; it lasts for ten minutes, then wanes and fades away. The sky becomes light and the sun rises.

December 3rd on the road to the Old Althing the sky turns blue at 10.42, slowly, gradually as if it had all the time in the world, but Jonina knows it will pass quickly, be over soon; Jonas knows it too. In the desolate snowy landscape high up in the mountains there stands a small white church, all by itself, brightly illuminated; there is no road or path that leads up to it. They drive past this church on the unpaved road; Jonas, condemned to passivity in the back seat, steps on an invisible brake, shouts, 'Stop!' Magnus obediently steps on the brake; it's become a ritual by now. They all get out, only Sunna stays in her seat. Jonas pulls his tripod and camera out of the car, runs into the snow; the others remain standing next to the car and watch him. They wait. Magnus clears his throat and says, 'One could envy Jonas for always being able to simply take a photo of these things. All he needs are his camera, his heart and a little luck, that's all.' Irene is surprised, looks at him sideways.

Jonas photographs the church in the snow; it's a photograph Jonina knows nobody will believe. The sky is still blue. Jonas comes back. He asks them to line up and walk towards him in a row, the three of them next to each other. He yells at them, 'Faster, hurry, c'mon, faster,' slides towards them, presses the light meter roughly against Irene's cheek. He slides back to the tripod, his arms extended for balance, the road an ice rink, Jonina's breath frozen; Irene says, 'Jonas attacks his photographs like an enemy; I like that.' And that's all.

It is 10.47, and in that moment Jonina fell in love with Jonas as he slid back to his tripod with his arms spread. How is that possible? It's absurd to ask; it is the way it is, as though a useless layer of skin flaked off Jonas, and beneath it the man Jonina wanted to love became visible. The feeling Jonina has for Magnus submerges and emerges again, floating over to Jonas, light as a feather, unmistakably and painlessly – that's the most terrible aspect of all this – absolutely painlessly. Jonas yells, 'Now!' and they walk towards him, next to each other.

Later Jonina doesn't ever want to have to look at that photo because she knows that it would be a dead giveaway. Above them, the moon is clear and bright. The distance between her and Magnus is greater than the distance between Magnus and Irene. Magnus himself is going to be blurry, he's walking too fast. And Jonina's face, her own face, seems to be downright enraptured; she no longer has control of her expression. Irene is laughing. Magnus walks stiffly straight ahead. Jonina looks into the camera, looks into Jonas's eyes as much as she can, Jonas presses the shutter release, says,

'Thanks,' folds up the tripod, packs up the camera, gets into the car. 'We can drive on.' Jonina's knees are trembling.

Half an hour later, the sky is white and the sun hazy, a sharp wind is blowing across the plain, they get stuck in a sinkhole in the snow shortly before they arrive at the site of the Old Althing. The car won't move forwards or back, there's a hard-as-rock sheet of packed snow under the tyres. 'Dammit, why don't you buy a Jeep?' Jonina says to Magnus in a fury. Magnus doesn't answer. They stand around the car, helpless.

Then three of them push while Magnus steps on the accelerator. Dirty snow sprays up into their faces. The car doesn't budge. Sunna simply walks off into the snow-covered lava fields. Magnus gets out again, puts his hands on his hips and looks intently towards the mountains, as though that could help. Then he takes his mobile phone out of his jacket pocket and tries to reach the Snow Removal Service. 'Why are you calling them?' Jonina asks. 'What use is that?' 'Maybe they're going to clear the road today and can pull us out,' Magnus says with irritation. Irene stands in the snow, her arms crossed over her chest, as usual. She seems to have no idea what to do. Jonas says, 'Rubbish,' and rummages around in the boot until he finds a rod and an ice scraper. Then he lies down on his back in the snow, slides under the car and starts breaking chunks of snow off the tyres. Jonina says, 'Give me the rod.' He's not really paying any attention to her but kicks the rod over to her. Jonina goes to the other side of the car, crawls under it as far as she can go and breaks up the snow with the rod.

For half an hour they lie under the car while Irene and Magnus simply stand there and gingerly push a little snow aside with the toes of their boots. Magnus has given up trying to call the Snow Removal Service. Jonina and Jonas are under the car, sometimes lying head to head, breathing heavily, laughing now and again, pushing the snow off by hand and with the rod and the ice scraper. And then the tyres are clear of snow, and Magnus gets behind the wheel, steps on the accelerator, the car slithers forward and with a heavy jolt comes out of the sinkhole.

Jonina calls Sunna, who by now is far away and takes her time getting back to the car; when she finally does, she gives Jonina an odd look. They all pile in; Magnus turns the car round and drives back. The road is too snowed up for them to continue in the same direction. Jonina is sitting in the front seat next to Magnus. The heater blows hot air into her face. Her trousers, her jacket, her hair are wet. She is freezing. Her knees are still trembling, her hands too, and now she knows that was all there was. This absurd closeness to Jonas under the greasy car, their heavy breathing while they pushed together against the snow. That was all, and under the circumstances it will have to have been enough.

The tower clock of the Catholic Church on Lækjargata strikes eleven times, softly and far away. Jonina gets up and goes over to the telephone. She'd like to phone Magnus. She phones Philippe. He picks up at once, makes his French telephone response, *ouiah*, a funny sound. Jonina sees him sitting in his huge loft – incredibly large by Icelandic standards – near the Laugavegur, looking down at the rain-wet street, longing for the streets of Paris yet having his reasons for staying here in Reykjavík, in Iceland, at the end of the earth. He makes the sound once again, more indignantly. Jonina says, 'It's me, Jonina.'

'Ah, my dear,' Philippe replies, and laughs to himself; he always laughs when she phones him, laughs as if he knew something about her. Jonina takes a breath and says, 'I can't come to work. I mean, I can't do the tour today. You have to get someone else; there's still enough time.' She listens. If Philippe were to say, 'There isn't anybody who can take over for you today,' she'd give in immediately. But Philippe says nothing. He is silent. In the background the pieces of a glass mobile are clinking against each other; he is smoking, blowing the cigarette smoke directly into the receiver. 'Oh well, I wouldn't want to do it either,' he finally says. 'I really wouldn't want to go through all this hot-springs humbug and sulphur-spring-water gibberish, and especially not with those Swedes, Danes and Norwegians in their sheep's wool sweaters. You know I hate Norwegians.' 'Yes,' Jonina says, 'I know.' They both laugh a little. Jonina is about to say, 'Philippe, can I ask you a question?' but Philippe beats her to it and says, 'Take care. Somebody else will do it, the tour, that is. And if not – I don't give a shit. I'll call you again,' then he simply hangs up. Jonina stands around in the hall holding the receiver, then she hangs up too.

She puts on her boots and jacket, in a hurry now, turns off all the lights, checks the coffee maker one last time, the stove, then slams the door shut behind her and runs down the stairs. She gets into the car and drives out of the city, onto the Ring Road that leads northwest to Olurfsbudir.

On their last evening in Olurfsbudir, Irene, Magnus, Jonas and Jonina are so drunk they can't focus or walk a straight line. They've drunk all the wine and the beer as well; there's one last swig left in the vodka bottle. It's late, three or four o'clock in the morning. They'll drive back to Reykjavík the following day; Irene and Jonas are going to spend another night in town and then fly back to Berlin. At the kitchen table, Jonas tosses a coin into the air, fish or numeral, leave or stay. The coin drops, the fish side is up. They will leave. 'But we'll come back, Jonina and Magnus, we'll come again,' Jonas says, slurring his words. Jonina says nothing.

The last evening was beautiful; it was as beautiful as all the evenings in Olurfsbudir with Irene and Jonas had been, and now it was over. Magnus gets up and weaves his way to bed. Jonina takes Irene and Jonas out on the terrace. Jonas awkwardly puts on his shoes; Irene has taken the vodka bottle and put it into her jacket pocket. With an impenetrable expression she stares into the snow that is coming down so heavily it is like a wall. They embrace. Jonina embraces Irene, who smells like soap; she embraces Jonas, who smells like the sheep's wool of his Woodstock jacket. She embraces him no differently from how she embraced Irene, and then she turns round, goes into the house, and pulls the glass door shut behind her.

She gets into bed and lies down next to Magnus, the same kind of bed Irene and Jonas will be sleeping in, in the house a little higher up the hill. Magnus is already asleep; his breathing is unusually loud. Jonina lights a cigarette. She really likes to smoke one last cigarette before going to sleep, but she seldom does because it displeases Magnus. Now he won't notice. She lies on her back, looking out of the window, which is at exactly the same height as the bed. The windowsill is narrow; on it are Magnus's watch, his glasses and his book.

The landscape outside the window is bright and white

in the light of the full moon; there is a single street lamp, the only one in Olurfsbudir, and standing under it in the vertically falling snowflakes are Irene and Jonas, arguing. They're stumbling around, shouting at each other. Jonina can't make out what they are saying, but she distinctly hears them shouting at each other. Irene's coat seems suddenly to be much too large; her trousers are tucked into her winter boots. She looks heavy and big. She looks like a very inebriated and, oddly enough, very old Greenland woman. Jonina sits up, takes a drag on her cigarette, and squints so as to see better; she's actually so drunk she's seeing double.

The scene under the street lamp has something theatrical about it. Irene puts the vodka bottle to her lips and seems to empty it in one swig, and then she holds up the bottle, shouts something incomprehensible very loud, and hits Jonas over the head. Twice she resolutely slams the empty bottle down on him.

Jonina rolls over and pokes Magnus; she can't believe her eyes. Magnus doesn't move. Jonina turns back to the window; she isn't sure whether to wake him. She whispers, 'Magnus, look!' She would never have believed that Irene, Irene of all people, pale, quiet, so cool as to be almost cold, could be capable of something like this. She whispers, 'Why is she doing that?' Magnus doesn't wake up, but Jonas falls down. He falls into the snow and doesn't move, and Irene simply stands there, and then she walks off, tramping up the hill to their house.

Traffic on the Ring Road is flowing rapidly and smoothly. Jonina leaves Reykjavík behind her, the suburbs, the apartment blocks, the pre-fab buildings, the therapy centre on the outskirts of town where Magnus is sitting at his desk carrying on the third of four conversations today, pouring his fifth cup of tea from his Thermos. 'Go ahead, start,' he says. He always says, 'Go ahead, start.' He says it to Jonina too when he knows that she wants to tell him something and can't find a way to begin. He could, if he were to look out of the window just now and make a slight effort, see her car driving by on the Ring Road, and he could see the tiny dot that is her head, his Jonina, wearing a woollen hat and slippery gloves, smoking, and as always driving too fast.

She glances towards the therapy centre and then drives past. She doesn't take the Hvalfjördur tunnel, even though that would mean shortening the trip by thirty miles. She drives around the fjord on a deserted macadam road that no one has used since the tunnel was built.

Irene had thought the tunnel was eerie. Irene thought the fences constructed by the Icelanders in the deep fjord to keep submarines from entering were eerie. Irene thought the beach caves were eerie and also the lunar landscape around the glacier on Snæfellsnes. Suddenly Jonina has the absurd feeling that she misses Irene. She drives around the fjord once and continues in the direction of Borgarnes, where Magnus was born. It's still raining, lightly but steadily. She stops at the place where Jonas photographed Borgarnes – 'Magnus, I'm taking this photograph *for you*, a beautiful view of your native village' – less than a mile from the bridge that crosses over to Borgarnes. There it lies, silent and pale under a grey sky. Presumably the photo didn't turn out, or Jonas forgot to include it in the package, or the brief blue hour was really more important to him.

She sits in the car and for a while gazes over towards Borgarnes; then she drives on in the direction of Varmalan, turning off the main road and onto the narrow road that leads to Olurfsbudir. The summerhouses look quiet and deserted on the hillside, no cars parked outside their terraces, no steam rising from the pools. Jonina hasn't been here since last winter. She parks at their house, walks past it and up the path to Jonas and Irene's house. She stops in front of the glass door and looks inside. The table is bare, the four chairs neatly pushed in around it. The sofa is covered with a sheet, three empty wine bottles on the counter next to the sink. That's all. Nothing that would give a hint or trigger a memory. Other guests will have spent time here in the course of the year.

Jonina doesn't know whether to go in. She feels she won't be able to bear the smell, the smell of a house that hasn't been occupied for a long time. She gets a garden chair from the shed, sits down by the empty pool, and lights a cigarette. The heath is flat and colourless; in the autumn it is red, gold and ochre; in the winter, before the snows come, it is pale and grey. Iceland horses. Ravens. How far is the horizon, and is this distance always and everywhere in the world the same?

Magnus, Jonina, Irene, Jonas and Sunna leave Olurfsbudir on the afternoon of December 4th. They drive to Irene and Jonas's apartment in Reykjavík; they say goodbye standing next to the car. Sunna is tired and wants to go to bed. Everything has been said. They are too exhausted to sit through another evening together, drinking and trying to understand one another. They shake hands, then they embrace. 'We had a great time with you. Thank you very much,' Irene says. 'Come visit us in Berlin,' Jonas says.

What do you say in farewell? They are embarrassed and sad; you can see that, and so Magnus takes Jonina's hand and says very softly, 'Come.' They get into the car, slam the doors shut, and drive off. They drive down Barugata. Irene and Jonas stand by the kerb, waving. 'That's that,' Magnus says, and Jonina wants to say, 'Stop, let me out. Let me out,' but doesn't say it. They turn the corner, and Irene and Jonas disappear and are gone, once and for all.

Christmas comes and New Year. Arriving home on January 1st, Jonina hears Jonas and Irene's voices on the telephone answering machine. It sounds as if they're at a party. In the background there's loud music and you can barely understand what they're saying. 'Happy New Year,' Jonas says. 'All the best to you, to you and Magnus,' Irene says, and Jonas says, 'We'll come again.' It could be he says something else. She erases the message immediately. Irene and Jonas don't call again. Jonina doesn't call them back. Magnus doesn't either. At some point he says, 'I liked the week with Irene and Jonas.' Then he doesn't say anything more about it. Jonina doesn't either. In March they begin to renovate the apartment, and in April Jonina stops thinking of Jonas. She simply stops; it's not that she even wants to. But she stops anyway; something has come to an end without anything else beginning in its place – a surprising situation for Jonina, one she has never experienced before. She has trouble falling asleep not thinking of Jonas. But she can't think of him any more – there are his hat and his green eyes, his lack of restraint, his bad moods, and his joy, there is . . . what else? – and before anything else occurs to her, she's asleep.

It is cold on the terrace in Olurfsbudir. The wind is blowing down off the mountains, frosty and harsh; in the mountains there's already snow. Jonina sits in the garden chair; she's cold but in spite of that she remains there, just a little longer; she lights another cigarette. She will call Magnus in about half an hour; she'll call from the little telephone booth at the entrance to the summerhouse colony, and she'll say, 'I'm out here, and – I don't know – maybe you'll come out too. Maybe you can pick Sunna up from school and the two of you can drive out and we'll just spend a couple of days here. It's been a long time since we've been here.' She'll say, 'Magnus. That was that, that was then, and everything is all right now. Don't worry.' And Magnus will say, 'I'm not worried, what are you talking about?' She will call him. For sure. Right away.

She never told him that Irene and Jonas had an argument on the last evening here, that Irene had hit Jonas over the head with the vodka bottle, that Jonas had fallen to the ground and just lain there. Neither did she tell Magnus that she had heard Irene and Jonas, every night, from the very first night, night after night. Magnus didn't hear them at all. He had been lying next to her; had been lying motionless next to Jonina and seemed to be sleeping, seemed not to hear it. But you hear things like that whether you want to or not; you hear them especially when there is no wind and snow is falling, making the world silent.

# Acqua Alta

My parents came back from Venice. They came back from Venice unharmed, nothing happened to them. They could have been mugged, robbed or knifed. They might have died from fish poisoning or, at night, slightly tipsy, have fallen from a vaporetto into the brackish water of the lagoon head first and unnoticed, or have had a heart attack and collapsed on the tile floor of their palazzo room. They could have lost their way, could have disappeared in the labyrinthine alleys of the city, never to be found again, could have vanished from the face of the earth, swallowed by the water. Is Venice a dangerous city? Isn't everything more or less dangerous? And if not dangerous, then, nothing. Every day I expect my parents to disappear. But once again they came back from Venice.

When my parents grew old they began to travel again. Oh, they used to go on trips with my sisters and me when we were children and they were young, trips to Sweden, Norway and the French Atlantic coast, but that isn't the kind of travelling I mean. Once we got older and avoided spending time with them, once we could do that, we began to elude them. They stayed home, raised plants on their balcony, and sat there June, July and August, until it finally cooled off again. Then autumn and finally winter would come, and the memories faded – memories of afternoons on the beach with sleeping babies and little kids under beach umbrellas, of picnic baskets and sandcastles. We came and went, slamming the front door shut behind us, and only after we were on the street, already far, far away, would we call back over our shoulders, 'See you tonight, probably late.' We knew without turning round that our mother was waving to us from the balcony.

Once we were really grown up, adult, finally out of the house, and once they were old, that's when they began to travel again, the two of them, without us. They bought themselves these little suitcases on wheels that you pull along behind you, packed them ridiculously full and then dragged the heavy things along, awkward and nervous on their first trip, later skilful and relaxed. The suitcases got lighter too; they took only the essentials. They travelled through Italy, Greece and Spain, leaving in early June and returning at the end of August, tanned, content, their suitcases full of spoiled food my mother had bought in the markets of Spanish, Italian and Greek villages without knowing a single word of the local language. They didn't have much money and bought cheap tickets on crowded trains. They slept in youth hostels and in hotels where rooms went by the hour, and in the evening they would eat bread and herring fillets out of a can, sitting on the edge of some fountain. They looked at churches, museums and palaces, excavations and other historical sites. They would stand in front of ruins of temples and amphitheatres with these books that had transparent images you could slide over the photographs of the ruins to see what they probably hadn't looked like either, more than a thousand years ago. I think my father found that comforting, and my mother was comforted when he was. During all those weeks they would spend one day at the sea, for my mother's sake. She went into the water and jumped up and down in the surf like a child while my father waited patiently in the shade, a quizzical expression on his face, not taking off a single item of clothing – not even his shoes and socks. He had never liked the beach or swimming, but he granted my mother this one day.

They sent us postcards that often arrived months after they themselves had returned and which my father had chosen – plaster casts of people found buried at Pompeii, Franciscan mummies in the catacombs of Palermo and Messina, Bramante's Tempietto in Rome. On the back, my mother's brief sentences: 'The weather is glorious. We've already seen a lot. Papa still hasn't had enough. We miss you and wish you were here.' And my father's indecipherable handwriting, scrawly, dark hieroglyphs, with occasionally some recognizable words: *open-door psychiatry, slate roofs, zinc coffins, ear of Dionysus.*

When they were about to leave on one of these trips, we would take them to the train. We were remarkably cheerful because at last they'd be gone, off and away, leaving us alone in the city, which in their absence always seemed to us at long last strange, at long last beautiful, splendid and unfamiliar, and in which we could now move about differently, free and independent and alone. But when the train took them away, when their waving hands disappeared, leaving us behind on the platform, embar-rassed and exhausted, we were overcome by the most childish sadness – not that we would ever have talked about it. We didn't admit to each other that we were afraid they wouldn't come back, that we had deserted them and let them down, that because of us they might disappear. I'm sure my sisters felt that way too.

Only once did I meet them on one of these trips, or, to be exact, our itineraries crossed; it was more of a coincidence and almost unintentional on my part. It was July, and they had already been gone four weeks; we met in Venice.

That summer I had come to the end of yet another relationship; at least I was in a frame of mind where I didn't want to think and talk about love in any other way than just like that. And I was turning thirty, a birthday I certainly didn't want to spend at home or with friends. I went to Corsica – I can no longer remember why Corsica of all places, and it doesn't seem to have been important either. I rented a tiny room overlooking the harbour of a fishing village. Stairs led directly from my window down to the beach, and at night the waves seemed to wash right up to my room.

For a week I sat around by the sea, immobile, watching the surf, the seagulls, the sunsets. I thought, I don't want to think about anything any more, and after a while I didn't think anything any more, dug my toes into the sand, drank water, smoked Corsican cigarettes, and said only what I had to say to strangers, or nothing at all.

An acquaintance, actually someone I barely knew, had given me my only birthday present to take on this trip. I hesitated for quite some time before taking it along and in the end did so only because it was in fact a present from a stranger. On the morning of my thirtieth birthday, I unwrapped it. I had made some coffee, sliced open a melon, put a small bouquet of beach grass on the table. The present was a book, a copy of the same book I'd bought for this trip, and which I'd read the first couple of days. On the title page was a totally incomprehensible dedication in English: '*You get so alone at times, that it just makes sense.* Best wishes for your birthday, F.' I put the book into a kitchen cabinet, went down to the beach, and sat on the breakwater. It didn't take me long to convince myself that I was unencumbered, free, that is, and that I would enter adulthood invulnerable.

That evening I decided to leave Corsica and join my parents in Venice. I knew that they had arrived there from Rome three days before and would be staying a week, already their third visit to the city. They had suggested we get together in Venice, and at the time I had agreed, as vaguely as possible, not wanting to tie myself down. But I knew they'd be glad to see me there. The next morning I packed my backpack, paid for the room and left. The birthday present was still in the kitchen cabinet; let the next guest wrack his brains about F.'s dedication.

I took the ferry back to the mainland; Bastia, beautiful in chalky colours, vanished in the mist; the seagulls didn't leave the ship till we were on the high seas. Somehow I missed something, maybe detachment from the world. I took the train to Venice by way of Verona, sleeping almost the entire time or staring out of the window, half asleep. Perhaps it was the approaching meeting with my parents that made me feel so tired, but maybe it was everything else too. Only after I arrived in Venice did I feel better.

I remember a postcard my father sent me when my parents took their first trip to Venice. Most of the sentences were, as always, illegible, but here and there I could make out words like *San Simeon Piccolo* and *Chiesa degli Scalzi* and *Lista di Spagna*, as though it had pleased him to write these sonorous Italian words with beautiful penmanship. He must have been describing the railway station, his first view of the churches and the Grand Canal, their arrival in Venice, which he later said was 'like stepping out onto an operatic stage'. I had to think of this comparison when I stepped outside the railway station. Even though I liked it, it annoyed me. The verdigris Church of San Simeon Piccolo and the Carmelite Chiesa degli Scalzi. Gondolas and vaporetti were cruising back and forth on the Grand Canal; the air was a bit humid and the sky pale and dusky, even though it was still early afternoon. The light and the colours; the casualness with which people walked on the bridge over the Grand Canal as though it were an ordinary street might have been disconcerting, but it wasn't.

Before they left, my mother, who always tried to book in advance as many hotels, rail tickets and package sightseeing tours as possible, had written down the address of their Venetian *pensione*. She had said, 'It's right near the station, you can't miss it, really,' as though that would make it somehow easier for me to decide to come to Venice. I unfolded the map of the city she had so thoughtfully given me and immediately felt hot because I've never understood city maps and above all could never refold them properly. My mother had put a little cross over the location of the *pensione* and an exclamation mark next to it. Still, I had to concentrate very hard to find the Lista di Spagna leading off to the left of the railway station.

I shouldered my backpack and set out, past the hitchhikers on the station steps, the souvenir dealers, the tourist traps. The restaurants were lined up one next to the other along the street; in between were shops selling postcards, sunhats and coffee mugs; there was even an amusement park. I walked slowly, peering at the house numbers, looking for my parents; actually I didn't think they'd be in their hotel this time of day, much more likely in a museum, at a market, or in the *Accademia*. Nevertheless at any moment I expected to discover them sitting at a restaurant table, in the doorway of a wine shop, or turning into the shade of a side street.

I was excited now, glad that I could surprise them, but also uneasy – what would they look like, my parents in Venice? It suddenly seemed to me almost unseemly, the matter-of-factness with which they were staying in this city, whether I joined them or not. The street led to a large square, the Campo San Geremia; their *pensione* must be somewhere around here. Cheap *pensioni* are never easy to spot; actually you can scarcely ever find them.

I stopped and shrugged off my backpack. I felt weak. The sun above the dome of the church was dazzling. I thought I saw my parents come scurrying through the heavy portals, ducking behind a group of tourists, hiding under the umbrellas of the café in the square. Suddenly I had the feeling that they weren't here at all, had never arrived in Venice, had vanished earlier, in Rome or Florence, or right at the beginning of their trip at the railway station in Wittenberg, Luther's city. '*Signor et Signorina P.?*' the receptionist at the *pensione* would say questioningly, drawing out the words, raising his eyebrows and shaking his head sympathetically. And what would I do then? Would I take the room they had reserved and lie down on their unused, freshly made, cool bed? I could already see myself standing in a telephone booth phoning Germany, 'They're not here; they're not in Venice. They never even got here.' And my sisters' sleepy, confused voices, 'Wwhaat?' Not horrified, just a bit slow on the uptake.

And then from across the square somebody called to me. I like remembering that moment on the Campo San Geremia when my mother called me by my nickname, rescuing me. I turned around, surprised and confused; she hadn't called me by my real name, but by the one she had used when I was a child; '*Mädchen!*' my mother called across the square. Looking over the heads of the people, I couldn't find her; she called again, her voice coming from high up, and finally I spotted her on the only balcony of a small narrow building directly across from the church. She laughed and waved like crazy, and for a moment she really looked like a Venetian woman, like someone who lived here, at No.1, Campo San Geremia, and was sitting in the shade on her balcony at noon, high above the noise of the crowds in the square.

I picked up my backpack, pushed my way through the tourists, and ran towards her, stopping beneath the balcony. She looked down at me and repeated my name, still very loud. She called down, 'We knew you'd come. We were so sure. We've been waiting for hours!' I tried to calm her. She was beside herself, and people were staring at me. I said, 'Mama, not so loud, OK?' I had to laugh, and she disappeared and came back out on the balcony with my father. Both bent far over the railing. I shouted, 'Can I come up?' And they shook their heads and pointed to the café in the square where I then had to wait a puzzling twenty minutes for them.

Finally they came down. In the meantime, I had drunk two cappuccinos and smoked four cigarettes, my joy having almost worn off. They walked across the square, arguing about something. My mother talking insistently to my father, who was making dismissive gestures and looking nervously up at the sky. And then they entered the café, forgot what the argument was all about, and stopped at my table, almost rapt and ever so happy. Did I look different? Taller, strange? I was tanned but wore my hair the same as always. What did they see when they looked at me – their grown-up child? Or the little one I would forever be as long as they were around? I got up, and we hugged each other.

Another memory – I'm on the telephone with my father, who isn't feeling particularly well. He's depressed, in bad shape. I know from my mother that a couple of times he's said, 'I've come to the end of the line,' in a tone of voice that wouldn't brook any contradiction. He and I are talking on the phone, no mention of his health; we talk about the book he's reading at the moment, Martin Walser's *Breakers*, about a poem quoted in it, about the hostile language of love, and other things, unimportant stuff; then he feels tired and we say goodbye. I say, 'Papa, don't be sad,' and he says, 'Good luck,' and we hang up. I don't know why I'm thinking of that now. I can still hear the sound of his voice as he says, 'Good luck'; I remember that the end of our telephone call seemed cruel to me – no other word comes to mind – or rejecting? All remembering seems sad to me.

In the café on Campo San Geremia in Venice, my mother ordered a prosecco, my father a small glass of wine. The waiter spoke German to us; I considered that humiliating. We sat across from one another, and I no longer remember

103

whether we were looking at each other; probably not. I said, 'How has your trip been up to now?' I asked because I wanted to know and because I didn't want to tell them anything about *my* trip. My mother answered readily; my father ordered a second glass of wine. They had missed the train in Rome; in Padua they found the cheapest *pensione* room in all of Italy, although it was in a brothel; in Milan the taxi driver had cheated them out of 50,000 lire; on the way to Florence, my father felt so ill they had to get off the bus, and he lay down on the street saying he didn't want to go on. The bus simply drove off. My mother always told stories like that about their trips – long, drawn-out, digressive stories making connections with other trips and situations, often ten or more years back.

At some point my father couldn't take it any more; he cut in, added some details and then took over. He talked about the encrustation on the left side of the south entrance of the Milan Cathedral, the Uffizi in Florence, Michelangelo and Leonardo, the heat, and the ruts worn by wagon wheels in the dusty stones of the Via Appia Antica. My mother said, 'There isn't a single restaurant in Italy where you can simply drink a little glass of wine in the evening. You always have to order a five-course dinner with it, and on top of that they bring you white wine when it's red wine you want.' My father looked at her sideways. Uncertainly she said, 'Isn't that true?' And he, both touched and irritated, put his hand on the back of her neck and shook her a little; she smiled, embarrassed. I said, 'It's nice to see you again.'

Every fifteen minutes the waiter would come over, urging us to order something more. The church tower clock struck six times; my father became restless, pulled an advertising brochure from his jacket pocket, and point-edly began to leaf through it; after all, they had sat around on the balcony all afternoon, wasting time waiting for me. My mother said she had wanted with all her heart to watch from the balcony as I walked across the square. The *pensione* where they were staying was certainly cheap, but visits by strangers were absolutely forbidden. I wouldn't even be able to take a look at their room, not to mention stay overnight with them. 'They won't let you in, not even for two minutes,' my father said. 'Besides they're fully booked; we have to look somewhere else for a room for you.' I said, 'I can find a room for myself.' My father said, 'But you don't know your way around; rooms here are incredibly expensive. We'll look together; you have to know how to bargain.' And I said, 'Really, I can do all that myself.' The thought of going from one hotel reception desk to the next and having to listen shame-faced to him, circuitously *bargaining* in his old-fashioned English seemed dreadful to me. 'Well, then forget it,' my father said, instantly insulted, personally hurt. I said, 'Papa, please . . .' He was no longer listening and gestured to the waiter.

'When do you want to leave, to go back home?' my mother asked quite innocently. From the outset I had told them that I would only stay for one night, if at all. 'Tomorrow,' I said. 'I really have to go home, I have things to do.' That was true, but in a way it wasn't. I had things to do, but on the whole it didn't matter at all when I'd get back. I said, 'Tomorrow,' regretting it immediately. Still I was glad because I was following my inclination. My mother did me the favour of not saying another word; she didn't even look sorry.

We paid the ridiculous bill, made a date for eight

o'clock that evening at San Marco Square. Before then
my parents wanted to see Santa Maria della Salute, Santa
Maria Formosa and Santa Maria Gloriosa dei Frari – my
mother, childlike and earnest, reciting all these names.
My father showed me on my map of the city exactly how
I was to get to San Marco Square. I tried hard to look
as if I were concentrating; I felt hot again. He said disap-
provingly, 'Your map is all creased; you have to fold it
up properly,' and, yanking it out of my hands, he folded
it himself. Then we said goodbye. I watched as they
hurriedly, busily, walked away and were quickly swallowed up by the crowd in the square.

I went into the first hotel I saw down the street from
their *pensione*, took a room for one night at a price my
mother would have deemed outrageous, showered briefly,
and lay down on the bed for ten minutes – the window
looked out on a shaft-like rear courtyard, from whose
fathomless depths came a constant eerie pawing and
scratching – and slowly smoked a cigarette. Far away the
church tower clock struck half past seven. I got up again,
only slightly refreshed, dressed and left the hotel. The
receptionist had dozed off behind the counter. Outside,
Venice was really still there – the Lista di Spagna and the
now-cool humid air.

Actually I find travelling difficult. For no reason I get
anxious two or three days before the start of a trip; it all
seems senseless to me, the distance, the foreign places,
the continents no different from what I can see from my
window at home. Four weeks in a strange country. What's
the point, I think, what could possibly be different there,
what good will it do me – in an absurd way, I feel as
though I've already seen it all. It's impossible for me to

106

feel secure and carefree in strange cities; there's nothing
I'd like more than to stay in my hotel room, lock the
door, and not go out at all. Of course I don't stay in my
hotel room; I do go out. Still the feeling of anxiety rarely
leaves me. It was different in Venice. The presence of my
parents seemed to comfort me.

I had immediately forgotten my father's directions, and
from the Lista di Spagna I simply followed the tourists,
who all seemed to have appointments on St Mark's Square
at about this time of day. They were following little
wooden information signs listing the most important
sights, the Piazza San Marco, the Procuratie, the Ponte
dei Sospiri. I followed the tourists, amused and a bit arrogant. Venice seemed unreal to me, a theatrical stage
setting, an impossibility; no real place can be this strange,
this enchanting. I walked across the bridge of the *Canale
Grande* with just that degree of casualness that had
seemed so ridiculous to me on my arrival. The canal was
laundry-water blue, the light now vanishing, the palazzi
along the shore withdrawing into the shadows. Everything
seemed hazy, mild, but perhaps it was only the sound of
the water, the dusk. I turned into the narrow alleys of
San Polo; I felt protected; after all, I wasn't alone.
Somewhere around here, in the next street, behind the
next bridge, were my parents. A remarkable, a pleasant
idea. People were streaming out of all the alleys; it seemed
to me there wasn't a single Venetian among them. The
tourists walked faster and faster; I was almost running,
and then suddenly they all came to a stop and sighed –
the *Rialto Bridge*. I stopped too; I couldn't help myself.
I leaned against the bridge railing; the stones of the
bridge gleamed white, and the light of the street lamps
was reflected as blue and golden stripes in the water. My

arrogance was gone, my scepticism too. I stood there among all the others, helpless and happy, and thought, How beautiful Venice is, and kept thinking it until I realized that the tourist standing next to me had pushed his hand down inside the waistband of my trousers.

The Rialto Bridge was teeming with people; tourists streaming across it right and left. They pressed against the bridge railing and backed away again, and I had been aware that someone on my right wanted to take an especially long and intensive look at the water. But now it dawned on me that it wasn't getting a closer look at the water that concerned him, but getting a forbidden feel of one woman in the anonymous throng – me. The hand that he had slipped into my trousers was cool and amazingly natural, so natural that, for a second, I calmly surrendered myself to its touch before unambiguously pulling away. The hand slid from my skin, indulgently and without regret. I turned round and looked at the tourist's flushed face. But this was no tourist, he was a Venetian, I was sure. At long last, a Venetian. I don't know the precise moment I freed myself from him. I don't know whether he had just begun to busy himself with me, whether I decisively interrupted him or whether he had already finished. I pushed him away and his face lit up; he met my gaze and returned it brazenly for two, three seconds. We looked directly into each other's eyes, presumably this was the high point of his game, the final sweet climax, and before I could raise my hand to slap him across those eyes, he had turned and disappeared into the crowd.

I'd been spared experiences like this up to now. I'm not squeamish, and actually I'm willing to put up with all conceivable fantasies, as long as they don't get too close. The Venetian on the Rialto Bridge had come too close. He *really* had come too close; yet I regained my composure surprisingly fast. He disappeared so quickly that it would have been senseless to run after him. Besides, I wouldn't have known what to do if I had caught up with him. My initial impulse to hit him had given way to confused astonishment. I had the feeling that he had left behind a smell, an unpleasant, sour smell that was more offensive than his touch, and I noticed that I was holding on to the bridge railing with both hands and breathing very rapidly. The rapid breathing seemed like a gift to him, a gift he hadn't earned. I forced myself to breathe more slowly; I tried to smell something else, the water of the lagoon, the evening air, but maybe everything in Venice smelled odd and brackish. Then I pushed myself away from the railing and walked on. My knees were trembling slightly. From time to time I turned round because I had the feeling he had come back and was following me, but either he had vanished, or he was cleverly hiding. By the time I arrived at San Marco Square – ten minutes late – I had almost forgotten him.

I always thought, When my parents get old I'll go on trips with them. Maybe I also thought, When *I* get old I'm going to travel with my parents. I keep forgetting that they're already old or, more precisely, I repress it. I think, We still have time. I lose my sense of time. Each meeting with my parents is burdened with something like restlessness. Don't I have anything better to do than to sit on some balcony with my mother and father talking with them in this muddled, familiar, stupid way? Aren't there other people in whose company I'd be happier? Isn't it just for my parents' sake that I'm sitting here? And yet each leave-taking is accompanied by remorse and sadness – how nice it really is to be with them; how odd and yet how familiar. And wouldn't I always have to come back to them since I now know about all the other things anyway, about all the rest of life. It's rare for us to have an uncomplicated get-together during which I'm not restless, remorseful or sad, not always on the go, and not trying to put something over on them. I can't say why we were able to sit together like that in San Marco Square, a father, a mother and their grown-up child, nothing more and nothing less.

My mother insisted on going to the Caffè Florian even though a mineral water cost 15,000 lire there. She said, 'When you're in Venice, you have to go to the Caffè Florian. Or to the Quadri. Otherwise you haven't been to Venice.' My father remarked that he was under the impression that he had already been in Venice twice before, even though he'd been to neither the Florian nor the Quadri. We assumed, correctly, that behind a dense circle of backpacking tourists we would find the tables of the Florian set out on the piazza. Most were empty. We sat down at a table at the outside edge that had the advantage, my mother felt, of not being exposed to everyone's view. We had to wait a long time to be served and could see a waiter chasing away people who had sat down just to rest a little. To refute any such suspicion he might have about us, at least after the fact, my mother insisted that we shouldn't order the cheapest red wine. My father gave in. The waiter condescendingly placed a little dish of olives on our table. We clinked our glasses of red wine. 'All the best on your birthday, my old child,' my mother said affectionately, nothing more. I was grateful to her for that. 'Yes,' my father said.

Under the arcade the Florian's musicians were playing 'My Way'. The tourists crowded around them, singing along. My mother whispered, 'Americans.' After our musicians had stopped, and 'Moon River' began to waft over from the Caffè Quadri on the other side of the piazza, most of the people moved on, and St Mark's Basilica came into view. My father repositioned his chair in order to get a better view; my mother said, 'I'm going to stay where I am.' I think she thought my father's behaviour was a sort of discourtesy to the Florian. For a long time we said nothing. I kept looking back and forth between the two of them, sometimes following my father's eyes, then again my mother's as she gazed at the lit-up windows of the Quadri. Suddenly and reproachfully she said to my father, 'The child turned thirty yesterday.' My father put on one of his quizzical expressions. 'Sometimes,' she said to me, 'your father doesn't say anything for hours if I don't ask him about something. But you ought to see how he closes his eyes when I say baroque and it isn't baroque. He knows everything and I know nothing.' Her voice sounded almost triumphant. I thought, That's how it is when my parents go on a trip. I thought of Corsica, of the birthday book in the kitchen cabinet in a locked room by the beach, of the man who was gone, of the one who would come along or maybe not; after all, nothing more could happen to me.

Then it grew cool; we paid and left. I was a little tipsy or maybe just relaxed. I linked arms with my parents; they knew where the vaporetto station was, the railway station, the hotel; they were protecting me and – even though they didn't know it – I was protecting them. We

111

took the vaporetto through the city at night, under the arches of bridges, over the water. We sat down near the railing, me in the middle between them. A little girl in a princess costume was standing in a group of people, her dress was white and decorated with roses, her belly distended and her naked arms as thin as sticks; her face was old, serious and beautiful. She was holding a man's hand and seemed a little fearful; her dark eyes wide open. When the boat stopped at the *Accadèmia*, she got off, bending at the knees, dignified and majestic. I thought of the uncomfortable feeling I often have when I'm going somewhere with my parents, a feeling of being conspicuous, looking peculiar, having people watch me and smile at me, *freaks*. Now I waited for this feeling, but it didn't come. My mother kept urging me to look into the open palazzo windows we passed – 'Look at the brocade, the chandelier, the gleaming glasses. It's hard to imagine that people live there.' I knew my father wished she wouldn't keep saying these things; in some way I wished it too, but I knew that this was precisely who my mother was. 'That time when we took a vaporetto through the Venetian night and you had to babble the whole time,' my father would later gently say. At the railway station we got out, regretfully; for a moment longer the ground swayed under my feet.

We walked along the Lista di Spagna to the hotel. It was midnight. I thought of the Piazza San Marco, of the pigeons, and that you could see the square empty only late at night or early in the morning. 'In Venice they have suicide tourism,' my father had once said. 'People who want to commit suicide make a special trip to Venice and then at five o'clock in the morning they put a bullet through their heads on the Piazza San Marco.' 'How eccentric,' my mother had replied. I had asked my father, 'And you?' and he had laughed, briefly, and said, 'Too old.' I visualized the pigeons flying up in the silence following the shot, and then my mother tripped and almost fell. We held on to her. Shocked, I said indignantly, 'Mama!' and to my father, 'You have to take better care of her!' My father said, 'Normally she falls down every two minutes,' and my mother, childishly and flustered, fended off our supportive, reassuring anxious hands.

I briefly showed them my hotel, but kept them from looking at my room and giving the receptionist instructions about me. I brought them back to their *pensione*. 'So, we'll pick you up for breakfast tomorrow at seven thirty,' my father said and immediately disappeared without any further farewells, not even turning round once more in the doorway; he had always found such exits amusing. I kissed my mother and said several times, 'And be careful on the stairs,' suppressing the desire to ask, 'Can't I come with you? Can't I please sneak upstairs and lie down in your bed with you?' Then she left too.

I waited below my parents' window until the light went on; I waited till it went out again twenty minutes later. Then my father carefully stepped out on the balcony, lit a cigarette. He had taken off his glasses; I was sure he couldn't see me. I thought of calling to him, of once more wishing him good night, but then I turned and left. I drank a final glass of wine in the café on the square. In front of the church some Africans had spread out imitations of expensive handbags; they were wearing traditional costumes, looked cold, and as long as I was sitting there didn't sell a single bag. Then I went into the hotel, past the deserted reception desk, to my room where I'd left the bedside lamp on when I went out. The sound of

113

pawing and scratching still came from the rear courtyard, no longer disquieting, but sleep-inducing. I smoked a last cigarette; then I fell asleep.

In the morning the receptionist knocked on my door, insistently calling out several times, '*Mama e Papa.*' It took quite a while till I realized I wasn't dreaming. I jumped out of bed and opened the door. The receptionist, who'd been standing right in front of the door, started back; then he again said, very slowly and deliberately, '*Mama e Papa,*' and pointed outside, turned and disappeared. I packed up my things as quickly as possible. I was afraid of finding my parents engaged in heated negotiations over the price of my room, having somehow pried it out of the hotel porter. But when I got to the reception desk, they were standing there, seemingly immersed in examining a small painting hanging next to the entrance, and didn't notice me. I paid my bill as inconspicuously as possible and watched them. My father was quietly saying something, pointing with his index finger; out of the corner of her eye my mother was looking at the carpets, mouldings, draperies and potted palms. Then she suddenly turned towards me and said without transition, 'The child's up.' I said goodbye to the receptionist with exaggerated politeness; of all the hotel guests, I wanted him to remember us, to remember me, to remember *Mama e Papa* who had stood in front of his little painting, so nice and united, waiting for their sleepy child. But he remained sullen and distant, and then we walked out into the street.

It was just before eight; the light was bright and the sky white; the street was empty and still; children in school uniforms ran across the square in front of the church, disappearing into one of the narrow streets. I hadn't thought there could be a school or children – actually any kind of normal life – in Venice. The souvenir shops were still closed; café waiters were setting up their freshly wiped-off tables and moving chairs into place; young women wearing tight suits and carrying thin briefcases under their arms walked hurriedly across the pavement on high heels. Not a single tourist in sight. Empty gondolas rocked gently at the Stazione Ferrovia Bar Roma. We sat down in a café in front of the railway station and ordered coffee and croissants. I didn't expect my father to talk again after his commentary about the painting in the hotel. And so I spoke with my mother, and we discussed what she called 'practical things': my return ticket, my telephone bill, my sisters, the plants on the balcony of their apartment on Stuttgarter Strasse. 'I hope,' my mother said, 'that your sisters will have watered them at least once; then maybe they'll have survived.' My father smoked and looked at the water, his head lowered. I liked having this kind of conversation with my mother; I also liked the expression *your sisters*; it honoured me in an odd sort of way. We were the first guests in the café; the waiter had placed chairs for us at the table with a flourish and early morning energy; now he brought the coffee for which I had an agreeable craving. Another guest sat down at the table next to ours. I briefly looked up and away again, and then up again, and to the same degree that my face must have displayed horrified recognition, the face of the guest showed the brightest, most joyful surprise. The man who had just sat down ordered an espresso, and apparently sized up the situation at first glance was the Venetian from the Rialto Bridge. He was sitting behind my parents. They couldn't see him. I think they hadn't even noticed that

115

someone had sat down behind them. I don't know whether he realized that these were my parents from a certain familial resemblance or because of the way we sat there together – whatever, he understood the situation. He understood that I was lost and defenceless and that I would put myself at his mercy for my parents' sake.

He was served his espresso, drank it at one go, lit a cigarette and stuck his free hand, the right one, into his trouser pocket. The street was still almost empty; the waiter had disappeared. 'You still have to hand in your university registration certificate,' my mother said, looking stern; my father was again leafing through his little dog-eared advertising brochure. I held on to my coffee cup. How I longed for a cigarette. I would have given anything in the world to be able to smoke now, but not at the same time as the Venetian. The Venetian went on with what he was doing; I crossed my arms over my chest, turned away, pressed my legs together. A vaporetto roared at the landing quay; far away the waiter clattered with his dishes; the coffee tasted bitter; seagulls swooped over the water; the clock in the church tower struck once, twice. 'I'd like to see the Giorgione in the *Accadèmia*,' my father mumbled. My mother asked for the bill, the croissant crumbled between her fingers. When I was a little girl I was given strawberries whenever I had a fever. Somehow my mother was able to buy strawberries at all times of the year and she would cut them up, sugar them and, piece by piece, put them in my mouth. 'You always give too big a tip because you lack confidence and you're too meek and polite,' my father told my mother, and she smiled at me. For some reason, I thought: *Acqua alta – acqua alta*, high water. In the autumn and winter this city is flooded, and some day it will sink into the sea. 'Are you listening?' my father asked. I said, 'Yes, yes, of course I'm listening.' My heart was pounding. The Venetian threw back his head. Soundlessly. At last. He took his hand out of his pocket. Then he paid for his espresso, said 'Grazie' to the waiter, not to me, and left.

Did we go to the *Accadèmia*? Did we see Carpaccio and Tintoretto and Veronese and Titian? St Ursula and St Mark, St Roch, St George? Did I wait with my mother outside the *Accadèmia* for my father, who came out long after we did and looked as though he'd been crying; did we buy postcards as proof of our visit? Did we sit by the water, near Santa Maria della Salute – so beautiful and so white – with our legs dangling over the quay wall? When we got up, I stumbled and my parents grabbed me as though I were an old woman, a gesture that made me furious, I remember that. Walking over bridges, through narrow alleys, over more bridges, along the water, and back. 'We'll buy you some food for your trip,' said my mother, who loves to buy strange foods in strange cities. My father and I waited for her outside a Venetian deli-catessen. She finally came out after what seemed like hours, looking happy. At a news-stand, a short, unwilling, curious glance at the headlines of a German newspaper of the previous day. Gondolas gliding through the water with Japanese tourists, with Americans, lying in them as though dead. 'Would you like to take a ride in a gondola?' I asked my mother. 'Yes,' she said, looking at my father, 'I'd like to, but we can't afford it.' The bells of Santa Maria della Pietà, Santa Maria Assunta, Santa Margherita and Santa Corona. 'The light,' my father said, 'the light; have you noticed something about the light?'

\*     \*     \*

My parents took me to the railway station and waited till the train left. We smoked a cigarette together. They didn't ask, 'Would you like to stay longer?' Had they asked, I would have stayed. They were going to be in Venice three more nights, then perhaps go to Switzerland, maybe to Austria. My father wanted to see the mountains, the Alps. 'I want to hike in the mountains,' he said; my mother rolled her eyes. I kept reading and re-reading the station sign, Stazione Ferroviaria Santa Lucia; I felt heavy-hearted. I said, 'Send postcards, take care of yourselves; come back safe and soon.' As the train began to move, my mother took hold of my father's hand. The doors slammed shut. They waved. I couldn't stop myself from thinking, If this is the last time I am to see them, then let it be like this, hand in hand on the platform of the railway station in Venice on an afternoon in July 1999.

The train was empty. I sat down in a compartment, closed the curtains on the door leading to the corridor, and moved over next to the window. Outside, the lagoon slipped by. I opened the bag my mother had given me. Bread, sheep's cheese, olives, apples, a chocolate Venetian lion. I ate the bread and the cheese and then tried to fall asleep. At some point the train stopped in the middle of a green meadow carpeted with buttercups; it looked German or Austrian, beyond any doubt. The train simply stood there. I opened the window and looked out – far and wide no platform in sight, only this meadow in the evening light in front of mountains that were already dark. A few passengers got off and sat down in the grass. Apparently it would be a while before the train would start up again. It was cool in my compartment but seemed to be quite warm outside; the air shimmered above the meadow. I got off too.

It was quiet and peaceful. Nobody seemed to be upset about the interruption to the journey. At first I was afraid the train would suddenly start up again, too quickly for me to get back on board. There was something risky about walking through the meadow, away from the train, turning back to look at it standing there so still in this landscape. A couple were sitting in the shade of some trees as though for an evening picnic. I had already noticed them at the station in Venice because both were incredibly fat and didn't let go of each other, simply never let go of each other. They had boarded, arm in arm, very awkwardly, had moved through the corridor clinging to each other. Now they sat holding hands, two huge children, under a tree. I walked towards them; they greeted me pleasantly, giving polite and detailed answers to my question about the reason for stopping. We were not far from the Italian border, they said, and somewhere in the mountains a hang glider pilot had crashed into the electric power lines; the damage was being repaired and the train couldn't continue until the power lines were fixed, perhaps in one or two hours. They spoke almost simultaneously, constantly interrupting and lovingly supplementing each other. Now they paused. I wasn't sure whether I ought to say something about the delay or to express regret for the hang glider pilot's crash. I wondered whether he had survived or whether he had inevitably died. I would have liked to ask them, but somehow it seemed improper. I was silent, and they were too.

Then they began to speak again, telling me that they were on their honeymoon and that their wedding had been dogged by bad luck. The priest had had a stroke just before the service, a car full of wedding guests had hit a tree, and the inn where the party was to be held after the ceremony had burned down. But they were fine. I considered it respectful on their part that they didn't mention the hang glider pilot in their recitation of misfortunes, and so I assumed that he was dead, hanging in the power lines with broken wings. I sat with them a while longer under the tree; from time to time we smiled at one another, and they constantly caressed each other. Eventually I stood up and returned to the train. When it was almost dark, the conductors went around asking everyone to climb aboard again; the train would be leaving now. Everybody got up and boarded the train, slowly, almost hesitantly, as if they would gladly have stayed a little longer. The mountains were now black. The doors closed. I went back into my compartment and even after the train started up again, I left the window open a little while longer. The air streaming in was warm.

Only much later, months later, remembering the four hours spent in the dusk in that meadow near our train because of a dead man, I thought that perhaps we had been so still and peaceful and patient in honour of and out of reverence for this dead man. At the time I did not think of my parents. They also came back from Venice once again.

# Nothing But Ghosts

Afterwards Ellen liked to say she had once been to America but couldn't remember it very well. She had driven from the East Coast to the West Coast and back; she had been in California, Utah and Colorado; had seen Iowa, Illinois and Idaho; had gone swimming in the Atlantic and the Pacific, in the Colorado River, the Blue River and in Lake Tahoe. She had gazed up into the sky over Alabama, Mississippi and Missouri. And she no longer remembered anything.

She says, 'I know I was there because of the receipts from the motel rooms and from the diners, as well as the unsent postcards that fall out of my calendar. I know I was there, but there's nothing I can tell you about it. Sure, I was in San Francisco. In Big Sur and in Redwood National Park. But the only place there's anything to tell about is Austin, Nevada. Austin in Nevada and the Hotel International and Buddy. Buddy is the only one there's anything to tell about.' As though the trip had never taken place, as though she and Felix had not been. Not before, and not afterwards, not at all.

\* \* \*

They arrived in Austin late in the afternoon. They had left Delta, Utah, that morning, intending to cross the desert in one day. They'd checked it on the map – 300 miles on Highway 50. And exactly three towns in that desert solitude: Ely, Eureka and Austin. They had three gallons of water in the back of the truck, an extra can of petrol, a carton of cigarettes, three apples and a loaf of white bread. The Ford Ranger pick-up didn't have air conditioning. They had coffee in Ely sitting on a Hollywood swing in front of the petrol station without saying a word. Ellen was perspiring. White light shimmered over the salt lakes, and everything was covered by a layer of sand, her skin and Felix's hair; there was sand in their coffee and sand in her mouth. They sat outside the petrol station in silence for half an hour looking at the desert. Ellen doesn't really remember where they were coming from or where they wanted to go. Probably they wanted to go to the ocean. They stood up at the same time without saying a word; Ellen threw her empty coffee cup and Felix's full one into the dusty rubbish bin, and then they drove on.

Austin came up out of nowhere, but presumably everything in the desert comes out of nowhere. Highway 50, in wearisome monotony, had led past look-alike salt lakes; mountain ranges rose and fell – valley and hill, valley and hill, and always this glittering, searing light.

Now and then, Ellen began to doubt that they were actually driving, moving, making progress. She slept right through Eureka, and when she woke up nothing had changed. She tried to move as little as possible, kept drinking water, smoked too much. Sometimes she looked at Felix's profile, said, 'How can you stand it without sunglasses?' Then the highway had made a sharp turn, descending unexpectedly and precipitously into a canyon. Ellen looked briefly out of the window at the steep drop on her right. In serpentine turns the highway took them down into a valley; then houses appeared, wooden houses, a church, an abandoned petrol station, more houses, ten maybe fifteen, no human being in sight. Soon the desert spread before them again, a level stretch, and on the horizon the next mountain chain.

But Felix turned the truck to the right, into a car park, stopped, letting the engine idle, and said, 'I think I've had enough.'

The engine rattled softly; the wind blew sand against the windscreen, Ellen gazed out at the car park, which seemed to belong to a hotel, an old western-style hotel with a wide wooden porch and an open-work railing. The second-storey windows were boarded up, but a neon Budweiser sign flickered in a dusty window on the first floor. The neon glow seemed incongruous in the daylight. Above the closed saloon door it said in crooked, weathered wooden letters 'Hotel International'. Across the street there was a motel, its 'Vacancy' sign swaying on a flagpole in the wind. Ellen said, 'What do you mean, you've had enough?' She thought her voice actually sounded dull.

Felix rolled down his window, stuck his arm out to test the air, and said, 'I can't drive any further. I just can't drive any more. I'm tired. I want to take a rest, drive on tomorrow maybe. I'd like to lie down for an hour.' He pulled his arm back in and rolled up the window. 'Lie down somewhere where it's really cool. Or do you absolutely want to go on.' He put an audible period at the end of the last sentence.

Ellen said, 'No. I don't know. I don't have to drive on, not absolutely.'

She sat there like that for a while. Felix said nothing more, and so she finally got out, leaving the door of the pick-up open. She knew it would annoy him. As she walked across the street to the motel, she could hear the truck door slamming shut behind her. She knew that Felix had stayed inside, had leaned across the passenger seat and furiously pulled the door shut. Ellen could feel the heat of the asphalt through the soles of her shoes. She spat, feeling the sand crunching between her teeth. She wiped her hands on her trousers and looked up and down the street; there was nothing to see. The motel, like all motels, was a low U-shaped building with direct outside access to the rooms; not a single car in any of the parking spaces in front of the doors. On the window of the office a sign warned people not to get into a fight with Annie.

Ellen pushed the door open with the palm of her hand; inside it was cool and dim, the venetian blinds were down; it smelled of dust and stale lunch. The door closed automatically behind her, and it took Ellen a moment to make out the thin woman behind the reception desk. She had a towel wrapped around her head and strands of wet hair escaping on both sides; Ellen felt an urgent need to wash her own hair, immediately. The woman was putting on nail polish. Ellen cleared her throat and said, 'Are you Annie?' The thin woman screwed the cap back on the nail polish bottle, blew on her nails, put a registration form on the counter, a pencil; then she looked at Ellen. Ellen smiled. 'I suppose one can't spend the night at the Hotel International any more?' she asked.

And Annie – or whoever she was – said, 'No.'

Ellen began to fill out the form, stopping almost at once when she heard a car drive into the car park. She looked through a space between the slats of the venetian blinds that covered the window in the door. The car had parked right in front of the motel. Felix was still sitting in the Ford outside the Hotel International. A very short, very fat woman got out of the car.

Ellen turned back to the desk and carefully wrote her name and Felix's in block letters. She had been doing it for weeks. For weeks she had filled out motel registration forms, had been giving their orders to waitresses in diners, dealt with national park rangers in camping areas while Felix simply waited, waited till she had arranged and organized things. It wasn't because he didn't speak English well; it was because he was denying himself to America, denying himself to Ellen.

The short fat woman stepped into the office wheezing, dragging a suitcase and a bulging, very heavy-looking holdall behind her. She was quite out of breath and leaned for support on the reception desk. Ellen moved aside a little. Annie stood up and sleepily took the towel from around her head; the wet hair fell heavy and straight to her shoulders. The fat woman said, 'We spoke on the phone. Here I am.' And Annie said, 'Yes.' She said everything was ready, and the fat woman asked her something. At first, Ellen wasn't really listening, but then she did listen, dragging out the process of writing the truck's registration number on the form.

The fat woman was about fifty years old, yet her face was firm and rosy like that of a young girl; she had small squinty eyes and pale eyelashes; her equally pale, very thick hair was done in a braid at the end of which was a pink bow. She was wearing a flowered summer dress, bright red children's sandals, and she smelled funny, not bad, but strange, maybe of perspiration and a sweetish deodorant. 'Very old ghosts,' she suddenly said to Ellen.

'Gold miners. A bad sort with no manners.' She blushed fleetingly. 'I'm gonna contact them,' she looked at Ellen, remarkably serious, then she turned back to Annie, whose face showed neither boredom, nor irritation nor anything else. The fat woman said she was going to photograph the ghosts and would send the photos to anyone who wanted them. She also had a portfolio with photographs of other ghosts. She'd be glad to show them now or later, whichever was more convenient. She looked at Ellen again and smiled. Ellen smiled back, even though it was an effort.

Annie said, 'I'd prefer later.' She was looking vainly for something under the counter, and when she casually remarked that she'd unlock the second floor of the Hotel International towards midnight, the fat woman was beside herself with excitement. She took all kinds of unrecognizable stuff out of her holdall, a plastic camera, and finally a large old-fashioned and sturdy tape recorder, which she put on the counter, directly in front of Ellen.

Ellen finished filling in the registration number of the Ford on the form, gave Annie a fifty-dollar bill and received a key from her. The fat woman fiddled with the recording apparatus; it started with a whirring sound and when the whirring changed into another, quite remarkable noise, Ellen said, 'See you later,' and ran across the street where Felix was sitting in the truck, leaning back with his eyes closed. She opened the door on the driver's side and said, 'Did you see the fat woman?'

Felix opened his eyes, 'Which one?' and Ellen said, 'The fat woman who got out of the Chrysler just now. The one who registered at the motel the same time as I did. She's a ghost hunter,' and Felix said, 'Aha.'

\*     \*     \*

Ellen remembers the ghost hunter. Not the same way she remembers Buddy. She didn't see her the way she saw Buddy, later, but she remembers her. She can still see her feet – the skin milky and swollen from the heat – stuck into these little children's sandals. She remembers the colour of Annie's nail polish, a pearly salmon pink, and she can still recall how the heat in the car park in front of the Hotel International descended on her. Felix had said 'Aha' and then nothing else; he refused to be impressed, and for a moment Ellen imagined what it would have been like if – while she was registering inside the motel – he had simply driven off, down the road and into the desert again. Imagined how it would have been if he had just driven off and she had watched him through the space between the slats of the venetian blinds. She would have heard the noise of the engine fading, getting less and less, and then it would have been quiet again. He didn't drive off without her, and all that isn't important, but Ellen still remembers. She sees sharp bright pictures of it in her mind's eye, as if everything in Austin, Nevada, had had a meaning, but it wasn't like that, not entirely.

Felix drove the Ford over to the motel car park and parked it in front of Room 14. The ghost hunter's car stood directly in front of the motel office; the woman herself was not in sight. Ellen unlocked the door; the room was small and clean – a queen-size bed, a TV set, an armchair, a bathroom, an air conditioner. It wasn't just cool, it was ice cold, and Felix switched the air conditioner off. They got their backpacks out of the pick-up; they wouldn't unpack them; they hadn't really unpacked them even once so far. Still, they got them out of the truck and set them in a corner of the room. Felix took off his shoes and stretched out on the bed. He pulled the yellow bedspread over his legs and said he wanted to sleep for a little while – not long, an hour.

Ellen sat down on the edge of the bed and looked at him; he turned on his side and closed his eyes. She got up, looked for cigarettes in her pockets, found a crushed Camel and lit it; then she sat down again on the edge of the bed. She smoked slowly. Felix lay there, motionless; perhaps he was already asleep, perhaps not. His face wasn't relaxed. Ellen looked at the freckles around his eyes; the skin on his nose was peeling. The expression *to love somebody terribly* popped into her head; she thought it several times in succession, *I love you terribly, I love you terribly*. Then the words lost their meaning. She looked out of the window; the road was empty and silent; the shadows were getting longer and the light was turning bluish. The heat seeped steadily and heavily through the open door. The lights were now on in the first-floor windows of the Hotel International; if she squinted she could see a bar behind the windows, a mirror, and perhaps some bottles, the shadow of a moving figure. She finished smoking the cigarette and carefully put it out in the plastic ashtray on the bedside table. She sat there for a long time, her legs crossed, her head supported in one hand, looking at Felix, whose features gradually softened. Or maybe it was just the waning light, turning greyer.

At some point she stood up, undressed and took a shower. In spite of the heat she showered with hot water, washed her hair twice, and stood under the spray for a long time. Then she showered with cold water. Felix was still asleep when she was done; the room had become dark. Ellen dried her hair with a towel, got dressed and stepped outside. She left the door open and walked down the street; even though it was still hot, she felt slightly cold. She tried to imagine what it would be like to get sick here, just a little bit sick, with a temperature of 37.5°C. It led her nowhere.

She walked past a closed petrol station; in the petrol pump there were gaping holes with flaring edges, and out the back, through the skeleton of the little station house, she could see wrecked cars piled on top of each other, disappearing in a sand dune. She passed a grocery store, its dirty window covered from the inside with newspaper; two, three houses that were probably inhabited but which she didn't want to see; and after that the town ended. She walked slowly, hands in her trouser pockets. Behind the last house the ground, covered with a rampant growth of thorny plants, sloped steeply downwards. She followed the road a bit further until she was definitely in the desert and no longer in Austin. Then she sat down on a rock by the side of the road amidst the spiny plants. The rock was warm. She had just missed the sunset; the sun had gone down moments before. The tips of the telephone poles glowed and the mountains were in silhouette. Austin was no longer visible, and the desert, shimmering blue and cold, swallowed the ribbon of highway long before it rose into the hills.

Ellen recalled that somewhere between Ely and Austin she had told Felix how beautiful she thought the desert was because here she was able not to think anything any more. As always – and this time he was right – he had not answered her.

Far out in the desert, two points of light had become detached from the dusk and were growing rapidly larger and brighter. Ellen waited impatiently for the sound of an engine; she was hoping it would be a truck. It was a truck, and as it roared past her, she had to make an effort to

129

keep from jumping up. The trucker looked down at her from high up in his cab and blew his horn, dragging the long, plaintive sound all the way into Austin. Ellen thought of Felix in the motel room, on the bed under the yellow bedspread, sleeping so unprotected with the door open. America was the America of the movies, of psychopaths and serial killers, of the most horrible segments in Stephen King novels; America didn't exist, not really.

She got up and walked on. She didn't go back to Austin, didn't turn back until a pick-up truck slowed down behind her, stopped almost next to her, and she could see the driver – a white man wearing a cowboy hat. He made a gesture with his hand that she didn't understand; in any case, he said he could never allow her to walk around in the desert by herself at night. Really, never. At that instant she turned round and ran back, much too slowly, the way one flees when one is dreaming. She ran along the edge of the road, emptying the pebbles out of her shoes only after she could no longer hear the pick-up behind her. In Austin the lights had gone on in two or three houses; otherwise the town was dark, and the road wound its way into nothingness.

Felix was still lying on the bed. The room was now hot and sticky, and Ellen turned the air conditioner back on. She sat down on the edge of the bed and put her hand on Felix's cheek. His face was quite warm and Ellen said, 'Felix. Don't you ever want to get up again?'

He turned away from her, but opened his eyes and said, 'What's the matter?'

Ellen said, 'It's late. I'm hungry; I'd like to get a drink.' Her voice sounded odd, and she wished that Felix would look at her.

He sat up. He said, 'Where should we go to get a drink?'

And Ellen pointed vaguely and almost apologetically out the window to the lights of the Hotel International. Felix brushed the hair out of his face with both hands and sighed deeply. Then he put on his shoes and said he'd like to smoke a cigarette. She gave him a Camel and a light; their eyes met briefly; Ellen had to laugh and he smiled a little.

Buddy came into the Hotel International quite late. As he arrived, the fat ghost hunter was just in the process of connecting her old-fashioned recording device to countless mysterious antennae and cables and tuning it. Her movements were either confused or had a virtuosity of their own. Her face was sweaty; hectic red spots glowed on her cheeks; her fingernails were bitten down to the quick. She had spread out all her paraphernalia on the pool table and gradually, as though by accident, the various customers – all of them men – sauntered over, each with a beer in one hand. They never came singly.

When they asked questions, it wasn't about ghosts but about the technique. When they tried to touch the apparatus, the ghost hunter clenched her tiny hands into little balls from which her index finger projected like a barb. The men would back off, grin and rub the backs of their necks in surprise. The ghost hunter said coyly and deprecatingly, 'You're thinking of bats. You're probably thinking of bats and the fact that we can't hear their frequencies, but that they can be recorded. However, we're dealing with something else here. Something completely different. Ghosts have their own frequency.'

The ghost hunter had come into the place at about ten o'clock. Felix and Ellen were sitting at the long and massive bar. It was made of dark gleaming wood and went the entire length of the dim room, which had filled up quickly. At some point someone lit a fire in the fireplace in spite of the heat; the jukebox was playing. Not all the people seemed to be from Austin; some had come into town from the desert, from the scattered houses that one guessed were behind the mountain ranges, behind the shimmering light. None of them paid any attention to Felix and Ellen. They had parked their cars any which way in front of the hotel, stepped into the saloon and, keeping their baseball caps and cowboy hats on their heads, said hello to Annie who was standing behind the bar – she seemed to be doing a lot of jobs here in Austin – and then sat down at the scratched wooden tables or at the bar. If they joined anyone, they acted as if they had only been gone for a little while.

Annie, her hair carelessly done up, greeted Ellen and Felix almost pleasantly but without any sign of recognition. Ellen ordered a cup of coffee, a sandwich and potato chips. Felix ordered a beer; he didn't want to eat anything, stubbornly claiming he wasn't hungry; this annoyed Ellen no end. The fat ghost hunter, determined and self-assured, came in lugging her bulging holdall. She still wore her summer dress but had slipped on a sweater. To Annie, whose face now lit up with curiosity or amusement, she said, 'We can start.' She greeted Ellen warmly and, to her embarrassment, gave her a long hug. She didn't want anything to drink, and immediately began to unpack her bag on the pool table, setting out all her things as if she were going on an expedition.

She paid no attention to the looks the others were giving her; actually she hadn't looked around the room at all, and she didn't seem to notice the silence that fell when Buddy came in. The jukebox had just finished playing. A man got up to press the button for a new number, but sat down again without doing anything when he saw Buddy. Buddy didn't say hello to Annie; at any rate, Ellen hadn't noticed anything like that. Annie put a beer on the counter right next to Ellen. Buddy came up to the bar, took the beer, drank noisily, looked towards the pool table, turned away again, drank some more, and looked back at the pool table – this time somewhat longer. It went on like that for a while. Finally he put the beer glass down and pushed it over for a refill. Annie softly said his name – Buddy – and then Buddy walked slowly over to the pool table. Ellen assumed that Felix, sitting next to her, was not paying attention, but apparently he had been observing Buddy as carefully as she. Now he slid off his stool and said, 'I want to see that up close.' Ellen got up and reached for his hand.

Buddy stepped up to the pool table. He casually touched the fat ghost hunter's wrist and then, using both his hands, he pushed all her paraphernalia into one pile. He said, 'No ghost stuff on the pool table. Ghost stuff on the pool table is going to jinx every game.' Lifting up all the equipment, he pressed it against the fat ghost hunter's chest. It took a while before she raised her arms to hold on to the stuff. She looked at Buddy with her tiny burning eyes, but could not withstand his look. He smiled at her pleasantly; she turned away and carried all her stuff over to the other end of the bar, where she started tinkering all over again. For an unreal moment, Ellen had the feeling that they knew each other, that all the people here knew one another, and that the whole thing was a put-up job, a performance, a staged show the meaning of which she didn't understand. And then

133

the group broke up, returning to the bar or to their tables; someone fed the jukebox, and she forgot it again. She looked around for Felix, who had gone to the bar and ordered a beer; he was watching Buddy with a new, an interested, somewhat tense expression.

It didn't happen often that Felix looked at other people like that, open, unguarded, overpowered, so to speak. Ellen would have said, 'It rarely happens that Felix reacts.' He reacted to Buddy, and soon Buddy reacted to Felix and then also to Ellen. Afterwards Ellen felt that Buddy had immediately understood, and yet she couldn't have said exactly what. The customers had started to talk again. The fat ghost hunter plugged her cables into each other. Buddy returned Felix's look without smiling. Felix turned away and Ellen went over to him. He paid no attention to her, leaned over the bar and said to Annie, 'Are there really ghosts in the Hotel International?' Ellen had the distinct feeling that he asked because of Buddy, that he asked so as to show Buddy, who must have heard him, that he could move, could act, could communicate. To attract him? Or to ward him off? He had asked the question seriously without a touch of irony and Annie replied, also without irony, that about one hundred years ago the Hotel International had been moved, beam by beam and piece by piece from Virginia to Austin, Nevada, to the desert, by a gold miner. The ghosts, startled and torn from their refuges and niches, came to Austin with the old hotel, and people were trying to support them a little in their home-less state, that was all – no reason to be afraid of them.

She told the story slowly, and Ellen listened. The fat ghost hunter, who seemed to have finished putting her paraphernalia in order, was listening too, unmoved, almost apathetic. 'Is it creepy up there on the second floor?' Ellen asked, and Annie said, 'No, not really, not really creepy, maybe cosy in a certain way.' And Felix laughed at that, absent-mindedly, a little tipsy.

The fat ghost hunter caught Annie's look, pointed at her watch, cleared her throat, and said, 'Well then.' It was eleven thirty. The little plastic camera hung on a leather strap around her neck. She brushed the hair out of her face with a firm gesture. Annie took a key out of a drawer and slowly came out from behind the bar. It became quiet again – a silence as though someone had struck a glass so that he could say something important.

Out of the corner of one eye, Ellen looked over at Buddy who was standing calmly in the shadows behind the pool table. The fat ghost hunter took out of her bag a headlamp like the ones miners wear and buckled it around her head. Then she slung the recording apparatus, on which the mysterious antennae were swaying to and fro, over one shoulder. Annie went to a door next to the fireplace and unlocked it. The door creaked madly on its hinges, and everyone stared at the ghost hunter, who now shook Annie's hand, suddenly looking touchingly serious. She then marched off stiff-legged and disappeared in the darkness on the other side of the doorway. Annie stood there looking after her, then softly closed the door. Turning to the others, without any change in her expression, she took the ghost hunter's holdall behind the bar, and sat down again on her barstool by the till. It remained very quiet, and she raised her eyebrows as though she were warning the others. Someone pushed his chair back; the billiard balls noisily plopped into the pool table pockets. Buddy came out of the shadows.

\* \* \*

135

Ellen ordered a glass of wine. Felix turned towards her, raised his beer and clinked glasses with her, looking politely into her eyes. She wished he would say something to her, say a few words about the ghost hunter, who by now must be somewhere above them in the darkness of the second floor. She imagined her in her little children's sandals stealing through the hallways, carrying her absurd equipment, no moonlight falling through the boarded-up windows; and behind the doors, in the corners, or elsewhere, the ghosts – what kind of ghosts, how many? But Felix said nothing, and the others also seemed to have forgotten the ghost hunter. Nobody glanced towards the door next to the fireplace or up at the ceiling. The jukebox music was loud; Annie turned the air conditioner up a notch. Ellen asked for ice cubes for her wine, drank, and watched Buddy, thankful to be able to transfer her tense watchfulness from Felix to someone else. Buddy carefully arranged the billiard balls in the triangle, bent over the table, placed the cue against a ball, remained like that, motionless, straightened up again and gave the cue to someone standing behind him.

Buddy talked to a lot of people, dropped money in the jukebox, and pressed a number without looking, tossed off a beer at the bar, and at some point he returned to the pool table. But he didn't play, and Ellen was sorry about that. For some reason she would have liked to see him play. He was still young, maybe thirty, thirty-two years old. He wore a baseball cap; his expression was childlike, straightforward and intelligent. His stomach protruded over his blue jeans, and he looked powerful in a compact way.

Ellen watched him and thought of a conversation she once had with a woman many years ago. Ellen hadn't been much more than a young girl then. She had let herself get involved in a conversation about sexual fantasies and obsessions; not her own sexual fantasies – as far as she could remember there hadn't in fact been any. The woman had told her that sometime she wanted to find out what it would be like to go to bed with a really fat man, the weight of a really fat man, an idea that at the time had made Ellen blush with shame. Now she watched Buddy, and remembered that conversation.

She sensed that Felix was also watching Buddy. He had ordered some mineral water, presumably either afraid he might have to talk with Buddy, or getting ready to. The thing that was attractive about Buddy and to which Felix was reacting – later Ellen had often looked for a word to describe it, finally finding one that she didn't like but that she nevertheless thought fitting – was his dominance. His sureness, something like a visible force and concentration that emanated from him; he was a spokesman, even without saying much. Felix had always reacted to people of this type. Maybe, Ellen thought, because his own dominance was just the opposite, so concealed and restrained.

Buddy, drinking what must have been at least his tenth pint of Budweiser, was staring at the air conditioner. On one of his walks between the bar and the pool table he stopped quite unexpectedly in front of Ellen and Felix. He looked at Ellen, then at Felix and said, 'How about a game?' Felix shrugged and smiled in that shy and youthful way that made Ellen's heart contract every time.

She leaned forward and said, 'I can't play pool, but Felix can; I'm sure he'll play.' She thought, she shouldn't always be speaking for him, butting in, getting things started, but she couldn't help herself.

Buddy shook hands with Ellen, gave his name. Ellen introduced herself and then Felix, pronouncing both names the American way. *Felix and Ellen, Phoenix in Arizona, and for the salad, Thousand Island, please.* 'I hate the way you pronounce the name of that salad dressing,' Felix had said to her two days ago, and Ellen had burst into tears. She thought apologetically, There is no other way, Felix. They won't understand it otherwise.

Felix got up and went towards the pool table; Buddy handed him a cue. Ellen could sense how much Felix longed for home, his apartment, his room, his bed, once and for all to be back home and away from here. Years later, she would think that this entire time with Felix had at least taught her one thing – that you can't force things, least of all something like love. A ridiculous discovery – still, it was consoling.

Buddy put the balls inside the triangle and gave Felix the first shot. Ellen swivelled round on her barstool so she wouldn't have to watch the game. The tension between her shoulder blades and in her stomach lessened. Buddy was taking care of Felix; now she didn't have to do anything, didn't have to make any more effort, or offer anything, or have to compensate for her presence, the terror of this trip, being imprisoned in America for the three months between the two flights of a non-cancellable return air ticket, for being at each other's mercy. She vaguely thought, Maybe it will all turn out all right. Suddenly she was sure that everything would be all right. From time to time, Felix came back to his glass of water on the bar and then ordered another beer. He said, 'You're not watching.'

'Yes, yes, I am watching,'

When Felix went to the toilet, Buddy came over, stood

next to her, and said without any transition, 'He's a silent one, your friend; you picked yourself a silent friend.' He nodded several times in affirmation, and Ellen stared at him, unable to answer him. 'You have to give him time, right?' said Buddy, going back to the pool table to wait for Felix. He then dropped three balls one after the other without a sign of triumph. The jukebox was playing 'Sweet Home Alabama' and 'I Can't Get No Satisfaction'. Unexpectedly the saloon door opened and warm, dry air came in, forcing its way into the cold, air-conditioned room. Ellen pushed the napkin under her wine glass aside, sucked on an ice cube, and lit a cigarette. She tried to concentrate on something, to concentrate on the fact that she was in Austin, in Austin in America in Nevada in the desert, in the middle of the Nevada desert and very far from home. She tried to concentrate on the fact that she was sitting at the bar in the Hotel International while Felix was finally putting down roots on this trip because he was playing pool with Buddy, stubbing out his cigarettes in the plastic ashtray on the edge of the pool table, and signalling to Annie now for another beer. She tried to find in all this some sort of happiness or awareness or meaning, and then she lost track and started thinking of something else.

Ellen no longer remembers how long it was before the ghost hunter came back. An hour, two? She no longer recalls whether she spoke with Felix during that time. Felix and Buddy kept playing pool. Between rounds they stood next to each other at the pool table, leaning on their cues. Felix would say something that made Buddy laugh. Ellen wasn't sure whether she really wanted to know what they were talking about. She warded off the advances of two drunk Texans wearing silly cowboy hats, and had a second glass of wine, inviting Annie to join her. Annie gave her change for a dollar, and she got up and went over to the jukebox. She had to pass between several fully occupied tables and for the first time realized quite clearly that she was the only woman there besides Annie.

She inserted the coins and took a lot of time to pick out 'Blue Moon' by Elvis, 'Light my Fire' by the Doors, and 'I'm so Lonesome' by Hank Williams – and then Felix was standing behind her, saying, 'Don't do that.'

Without turning round she said, 'Why not?'

Felix said, 'Because you don't know whether the others want to listen to the music you want to listen to.'

'Because you're afraid my choices might make me look ridiculous in front of somebody here,' Ellen said.

Felix said irritably, 'Exactly.'

And Ellen said, 'I'm afraid of that too.'

It was true, she was actually afraid of that and had thought it over, but she still wanted to listen to Elvis and Hank Williams and the Doors. She pressed the start button and went back to the bar, without looking at Felix. And Hank Williams sang to himself in his cracked, droning voice, and in the end nobody paid any attention to it. After the Doors had sung – a choice that Ellen regretted in the meantime – Buddy and Felix stopped playing and came over to the bar. Buddy ordered another glass of wine for Ellen and beers for Felix and himself, and said to Ellen, 'He plays well, your friend.' Felix blushed.

Ellen said, 'I know.' Then she didn't know how to go on and was briefly afraid that all three of them would now come to a dead end, that the expectations they had of each other would not be confirmed, that they would have to stand there together in silence. But Buddy pulled over a barstool and began to talk with Felix about their games. They philosophized for quite a while about caroming and the American way of playing pool billiards, and Ellen was able to observe Buddy undisturbed. His dirty blue T-shirt with the name of some university on it, his baseball cap with no inscription, his very large hands, the scabby areas on some of his finger joints, the blue thumbnail, no ring, a narrow Indian band around the left wrist. His belly curving like a globe above his pants, the T-shirt stretching over it, the eagle on his belt buckle disappearing under it. Yet what was so familiar and calming about him remained invisible. Ellen thought, 'calming'.

It didn't seem remarkable when Felix and Buddy suddenly fell silent, and then she simply said, 'Actually we wanted to cross the desert in one day, but for some reason we got stuck here, in the middle of it.' And Buddy said, 'That happens.'

On the whole, it was always Ellen who spoke with other people, asking, talking – not only in America but also back home, and in other places, always. Felix would just sit there, listening, not saying anything. Most of the time he sat leaning back, legs crossed; he would roll a cigarette, turning it around and around for minutes at a time, inspecting it at length, then light it and inhale deeply – a good cigarette, the best in the world. He would let it go out and gaze at it closely before relighting it. He would look up, sometimes at someone else, sometimes at Ellen; he would sit as still as a Buddha, weightless, his back ramrod straight, his shoulders thrown back. Some people were impressed by this silence, this wordless sitting and listening, thinking it wise and enigmatic, deep. Ellen did too.

On good days, Felix would laugh at something that Ellen had said to someone else in his presence, and thereby give her a weak sign of his solidarity, his belonging. On bad days, he wouldn't react at all. At rare moments he would – reserved, distant – say something; sometimes it was intelligent, sometimes completely incomprehensible. He just about never asked any questions. Ellen had never heard him ask anyone anything, least of all herself. The question he asked Annie about the ghosts in the Hotel International had only been a ploy.

Back home, when they went out together at night, she talked a lot, and he said nothing. They would sit down at a table in some bar, as a matter of principle always next to each other; that was Felix's custom. At first Ellen had considered it suspicious because she thought only people who have nothing to say to each other sit side by side. Later she got to like it; it seemed special and intimate. They would be sitting next to each other and Felix would be silent and Ellen would try to endure the silence. Then she would start talking after all and out of sheer helplessness she'd work herself into telling such sentimental, crazy stories that both of them would eventually burst into tears. Felix sitting next to Ellen would simply start to cry, soundlessly. Ellen had to cry too, a little, and could then console him by stroking his face again and again. That was the ritual. Ellen knew that it was like a compulsion, getting him to cry and then being able to console him. A senseless undertaking.

In America, on this trip from the East Coast to the West Coast and back, they had sat like that night after night, in national parks, in motels, in rented cabins on the banks of American rivers, and Ellen had started repeating herself, doing awkward variations on significant things. She couldn't think of anything any more, and actually she didn't want to talk about anything any more either. She had started asking Felix questions, and Felix had refused to answer. They spoke less and less, until Buddy pulled up a barstool and sat down next to them in Austin, Nevada.

He was the first human being in weeks who had spoken with them, who had made Ellen sit up and concentrate, to formulate answers to his simple, purposeful questions. Buddy said, 'What kind of a trip is this you're on?'

And Ellen said, 'Once across America, from the East Coast to the West Coast and back.' A sentence she had wanted to say all this time because it sounded so terrific, only there hadn't been anybody who had wanted to hear it. Buddy said he had never in his life driven from the East Coast to the West Coast and back. To be exact, he said, he'd never been out of Austin, Nevada. The way he said it was too matter-of-fact for Ellen to have reacted with surprise or disbelief. He wanted to know how they lived back home in Germany. It must be 'an unusual life'.

'It's not unusual,' said Ellen. 'A lot of people live like that. They travel and look at the world, and then they come back and work, and after they've earned enough money, they're off again, to somewhere else. Most of them. Most people live like that.' She told about Berlin and about life in Berlin. She tried to describe it, the days and the nights. Everything seemed a bit confusing to her, mixed up and pointless. 'We do this and we do that' – she had the feeling she couldn't describe it properly. Earning money, sometimes doing one thing, sometimes

143

another. To be on the go all night feeling more and more euphoric, and then other nights when they went to bed at ten, tired, worn out, despairing. A group of friends. A kind of family. Open-ended? For ever? She tried to find something that could be compared with life in Austin, Nevada; life the way she imagined it here. She wasn't sure whether there could possibly be anything comparable, but Buddy seemed to understand this too. He wanted to know how they earned a living, their jobs. Ellen pointed at Felix; she wanted him to say the beautiful words describing his work, and Felix did say it, slowly and softly: 'Bicycle mechanic. A bicycle mechanic.'

Buddy thought that was terrific. He said a bicycle mechanic in Austin would have all the town's bicycles repaired in two hours, once and for all. But in the rest of the world you could stay busy with this trade a good long while. Seriously and thoughtfully, he said, 'In China, for example, how would it be if you went to China as a bicycle mechanic?' And Felix's face lit up and then fell again. Ellen wanted to tell Buddy that it could be disastrous to talk to Felix about Utopias, about mere possibilities. Any 'What if' and 'You might' made Felix suddenly grow weary and depressed. Maybe it's only since he's been with me, Ellen thought. She was actually amused at the idea for a moment.

'What are you laughing about?' Buddy wanted to know, and Ellen shook her head.

'I can't say.' She leaned forward and without thinking put one of her hands on Buddy's heavy, round knee. 'Excuse me, I wasn't laughing at you.' She said, 'I'd like to know about your life, what you do in Austin, Nevada.'

And Buddy said, 'The same things you do.'

*    *    *

Years later, Ellen still stops sometimes – while she's washing the dishes, on the stairs with the mail and newspapers under her arm, at the tram stop, or looking at a timetable – and thinks of Buddy in Austin, Nevada, about his life there. She wonders what he might be doing at that very moment. She's sure that he still lives there, that he hasn't left. There would have been no reason for him to leave. She isn't surprised that Buddy unexpectedly comes to mind; it isn't strange to think of him, to think of someone with whom she spent one night in a bar – no more and no less. In an unspectacular way her life seems to be connected with his.

Buddy had taken off his baseball cap in the Hotel International, had put it back on, and had asked Felix to roll him a cigarette. Unimpressed, relaxed, he had watched Felix for quite a while as he rolled the cigarette. He said he was born in Austin thirty-two years ago, went to school there, later to high school in Ely, then briefly to Las Vegas where he worked as a temporary waiter, then back to Austin. His mother still lived here, in the last house on the main street going towards Ely. His father was dead. He himself lived a bit further out in the desert. He had married the girl he fell in love with when he was sixteen years old, but he wasn't any more. He hesitated briefly; they were still together. Some things just aren't that easy to say.

He said he was now working for the state, for the highway maintenance department, and so on. You could call him a construction worker; he repaired the highway and inspected it regularly for damaged stretches and danger spots, that was all. Well-paid work; he could put up with it; he liked being out in the open, in the desert, between the towns. He looked at Ellen and Felix and said, 'You got any kids?'

145

Ellen shook her head. Possibly Felix didn't understand the question. Buddy said, 'Why not?' He had a way of asking questions, a way of speaking – without emphasis, not subtle, not oratorical; he didn't imply anything and didn't dramatize – Ellen found that good.

Ellen said, 'I don't know. I haven't thought about it, I mean, of course I want a child, but not now – I think that's how it is,' and Buddy nodded slowly and ponderously.

He said, 'I have a kid, a son, he's three years old now,' then he looked at Annie, who was sitting on her stool behind the bar and who had been listening, motionless, all this time. Ellen saw him look up and had followed the direction of his eyes, but then at the last moment she didn't look at Annie. Annie laughed; Ellen had no idea about what. She had noticed the hesitation, the short hesitation in his interconnected, calm sentences, and she said, 'The girl you married, is she the mother of your child?'

Buddy answered almost indignantly, 'Of course she is. Who else should it be?'

And Ellen said half playfully, 'Is she beautiful?'

Behind the bar Annie again burst out laughing. Buddy said she had once been beautiful. She had been very beautiful; now she wasn't beautiful any more; she was ugly and fat. He said, 'She is so fat that you can only photograph her from an airplane.' Ellen was no longer sure he was serious. He said she had lost her beauty once and for all, and maybe this kind of life was responsible for that, life in Austin, or life in general; whatever, he still loved her, if only because she was the mother of his son. He said, 'I love her because she is the mother of my son.' And the sentence lay there between them for a long time until Ellen turned to Annie and asked for another glass of wine.

\*     \*     \*

'You set your heart too much on what's been said, on sentences, on possible meanings,' Felix had once said to her. After Austin? Before Austin? Ellen is no longer sure. In any case, she didn't contradict him. She still remembers that Buddy's sentence seemed dangerous to her because it contained a question, unspoken. But the look Buddy gave Annie seemed even more disquieting. She thought, I'd die if Felix ever looked at me that way. Annie slid the glass of wine towards her, filled to the brim with ice cubes. The bar had emptied. On the dark street outside the saloon door, drivers were starting their cars, whirling up dust. Only a few people still sat at some of the tables. Annie switched off the light over the pool table. Buddy raised his beer bottle and clinked it against Ellen's wine glass, 'To your trip and a safe return home. To you.' Felix had finally finished rolling the cigarette for Buddy and handed it to him. Annie came over to them behind the bar, gave Buddy a light, and stayed there, leaning over with half-closed eyes. Buddy inhaled in the cautious, surprised way of people who smoke a cigarette once a year, then he gently blew out the smoke. He said, 'If you don't have a child, then you don't know, for instance, what it's like to buy him a pair of little blue Nike sneakers.' He gave a short laugh and shook his head.

Ellen said, 'What's it like?'

And Buddy looked past her out into the street, squeezed his eyes shut, and said, 'Well, it's like this – it's hard to describe, but it's nice. These sneakers are so small and tiny and perfect, a perfect copy of a real sneaker.' He looked at Felix and said, 'Right?' Felix nodded. 'You buy these tiny sneakers, blue and yellow with sturdy laces and cushioned soles in a perfect little shoe box, and you take them home to your kid and put them on for him, and he runs off in them. He simply runs off in them. That's all.'

147

He took another drag on the cigarette, then he gave it back to Felix, who took it and went on smoking it. Buddy leaned back and was going to say something – Ellen was sure something completely different – and then the door next to the fireplace very slowly creaked open, and the fat ghost hunter stepped out.

'There's amazingly little time,' Ellen said to Felix afterwards, 'amazingly little time for things, for such moments, and sometimes I'm glad it's like that. It keeps me from losing control. From saying idiotic things. It keeps me from yielding, from total surrender.' Felix didn't really let her know whether or not he understood.

The fat ghost hunter came into the room as though she had been waiting on the other side of the door. She looked no different than she had – how many? – hours ago; her hair wasn't messed up and her skirt wasn't torn, but she was covered with dust and cobwebs, and there was something solemn in her face, something at the same time sad and triumphant.

She walked across the room towards the bar with dignity, made a slight bow, and with an exhausted, satisfied and conclusive gesture she put her recording equipment down on top of the bar. Without asking, Annie poured her a glass of whiskey, which she drank in one long draught. Buddy brought over another barstool and slid his over to Ellen, making room between himself and Felix.

The ghost hunter pulled the plastic camera attached to the leather strap over her head and handed it to Annie, who carefully, as though it were made of glass, put it down next to her on the bar. Then she sat down on the high stool like a fat, dressed-up child, drank another whiskey and started hiccuping. Ellen had to laugh, and

148

the ghost hunter gave her a friendly nod. They sat like that for quite a while, quietly, next to one another; all the other customers had left; the air conditioner droned, and water dripped into the sink. Annie leaned her head on her hands, you couldn't see her face. The fat ghost hunter smiled. She pointed to her holdall, and Buddy pulled it over and handed it to her. She took a well-worn album out of the bag.

She said, 'I'll show it to you if you like,' then, not waiting for an answer, she opened the album. Ellen, Felix and Buddy bent over it, Annie looking over Buddy's shoulder. There were colour photos, postcard-size colour photos; and though they were in plastic covers, they were wrinkled. They showed living rooms, stairways and cellars in dim half-light, and on each photo you could see in some corner a silvery stripe, a little shimmer, the reflection of a lamp or an out-of-focus head in a double exposure. There were intimate looks into bedrooms, wardrobes and kitchens, and Ellen would normally have said, 'Those were simply defects caused by the film processing. Double exposures, reflections, dust on the lens, nothing more,' but that night in the bar of the Hotel International she didn't think so. She believed the fat ghost hunter, the seriousness and the conviction with which she pointed to the photos, unintentionally always covering precisely the crucial elements with her index finger.

Ellen looked at the ghost hunter from the side, her bright red, glowing cheeks, the strands of colourless hair falling over her sweaty forehead, the little beads of perspiration on her nostrils and her upper lip. The smell she had exuded in the afternoon seemed to have become stronger and was now mixed with something else, with dust and wood and ghosts – Ellen thought resolutely –

with whatever it was that ghosts smelled of. She had to laugh at that. She had the clear sensation that she was happy just then, very happy, feeling very light. Buddy returned her laughter, gently and softly, and the fat ghost hunter said, 'Yes, well, I really liked this one; you like some more, and some you like less.' She nodded and pointed with her index finger at a photograph in her lap, staring at it as if remembering something.

Then she raised her head and looking at Annie she said, 'Those ghosts up there –' she pointed briefly towards the ceiling and everybody looked up, 'those ghosts up there can't come to terms with life.' She cleared her throat exaggeratedly and went on, 'I have to come back, in any case – if possible. Is it possible?'

'Of course it's possible,' Annie said reassuringly. 'I'm quite sure.' She exchanged a serious look with Buddy. Buddy got up and rubbed his face with his left hand; he finished his beer and began to put up the chairs.

Over his shoulder he said, 'Time to go home, time to go to sleep.' Annie wiped down the top of the bar, rinsed the last glasses, and turned off the air conditioner. Ellen drank her wine slowly; she felt tired and peaceful; she knew she still had some time. The fat ghost hunter rocked back and forth on her barstool, lost in thought, humming a tranquil melody. Felix rolled himself a last cigarette. Whatever Ellen had tried to concentrate her thoughts on hours before was here, sharp-edged, crystalline, fragile and clear. The fat ghost hunter pointed to her plastic camera and said, 'There's one last picture left on the film, the very last one. Does anyone want to have their picture taken?' And Buddy said, 'If you're going to take one, then take it of all of us.'

\*      \*      \*

The street outside the Hotel International was still and dark, except for the neon light of the Budweiser advertisement; the sky was deep blue and wide and full of stars. 'How warm it is,' Felix said, speaking mostly to himself. The warmth was dry and dusty. Annie locked the saloon door. The fat ghost hunter set her camera on a post – the same post they used to hitch horses to in the old days, Ellen thought – and peered awkwardly through the viewfinder, all the while mumbling to herself. Then she clapped her little hands and called out, 'Line up!'

Ellen stood on the porch in front of the saloon door; above her was the sign with the crooked wooden letters spelling 'Hotel International', to her left, the dusty window with the neon sign. She suddenly felt excited, almost exuberant. The others took their places next to her, in one row, Buddy, Felix, Annie. The fat ghost hunter pushed the only button on her camera, a little red light flickered on, she rushed out from behind the post, stumbled up onto the porch, and squeezed herself in between Felix and Buddy. She counted, 'Five, four, three, two, one,' and Ellen, who knew that she would never get to see this photograph and who suddenly thought in amazement that this would be one of thirty-six photographs on a roll otherwise full of ghosts, reached for Buddy's hand. She held it tight; he squeezed hers in return, and Ellen smiled and was sure she was beautiful, confident, and full of power and strength. And before she could think about anything else, there was a flash, the ghost hunter yelled, 'Photo!' and then everything was dark again.

The following morning they woke up late. Ellen had a headache; Felix claimed he'd had a headache every morning ever since they came to America. They packed

their things, loaded them into the pick-up, smoked cigarettes that made them feel ill on the stoop in front of
their room. The neon sign in the window of the Hotel
International was turned off, the saloon door was locked.
The Ford pick-up stood in front of the motel, the Chrysler
was gone. Lizards scurried over the walls, rustled in the
unreal stillness.

It occurred to Ellen that they hadn't paid for their
drinks yesterday, but when she went over to Annie's office
to make up for that, she found the door locked, the venetian blinds down. Someone had removed the 'Vacancy'
sign from the flagpole. They waited a while longer, but
no one came and nothing moved, and then they climbed
into their truck and drove off, westwards.

Today, when Felix and Ellen sit down to supper with their
child, Felix sometimes repeats the sentence, 'And when
we finish eating, we'll tell you how your parents got to
know each other.' It's a gag, a little joke, and Ellen has
to laugh at it too, has to laugh every time, even though
she thinks the joke is eerie and she doesn't really know
what she's laughing about. The child is still too little to
be told about it. Ellen wants to know what it will be like
when she can tell him about it. She's looking forward to
that time and she's afraid of it too. She'd like to tell her
child that in the decisive moments of her life she was
always sort of unconscious. She would like to say, 'You're
here because Buddy in Austin, Nevada, told us we didn't
know what it was like to buy sneakers for a child, a pair
of perfect tiny sneakers in a perfect little shoe box. He
was right – I didn't know and I wanted to know what it
was like. I really wanted to know.'

# Pimp

Johannes insisted I call it *Karlovy Vary*. Not Carlsbad. Under no circumstances Carlsbad. It was like a point of honour for him, a tribute to the past. *Carlsbad* – he stretched out the word, making it sound ugly, uglier than it really was – only people who didn't know any better would use it. I found it hard to say *Karlovy Vary*, but then finally I did say it. A city in a valley in the Czech Republic with a fountain of warm, salty, healing water.

Like me, Johannes lived in Berlin. He had studied painting, and without having created a great stir on the art scene he managed to get by on shows and the sale of his pictures. He liked living in Berlin, but left the city as often as possible to work in foreign, far-away places for half the year and then return to Berlin. He had looked after the house of a distant acquaintance in southern France, rented an apartment in a small town in America, lived for three months in a lighthouse in Scotland, and when he had no money, he was also content to stay in less spectacular places. That year he had settled on

153

Karlovy Vary. Somebody had put at his disposal an apartment big enough to use as a studio, for as long as he wanted, in any case till the end of the year. He had taken off in early August, and by the time I arrived, he had already been there for six weeks. He seemed to like the place.

I had known Johannes for a long time, whatever that may mean. I had known him for ten or twelve years. At the beginning I was very much in love with him, and when that stopped, he fell in love with me, and we tugged at each other for a while until we gave it up. After that, whenever I mentioned him to anyone, I referred to him as 'my best friend, Johannes'. Perhaps only so I wouldn't have to say, 'My friend, that is to say my *friend*, not my lover.' He had once asked me to write a text about one of his pictures for a catalogue; I made a stab at it, and he was satisfied with the result. Since then I have been writing for him on a regular basis. He pays me for these pieces.

The afternoon I handed him that very first text – two and a half pages about a picture in which an orchid or an open heart melted into a gleaming deep-black background – we met in a café. He was in a hurry and didn't even take off his coat; he drank an espresso, skimmed the text, said, 'Yes, yes, that'll do,' put the folded pages into his pocket, said goodbye, and left. I remained behind, feeling hurt and offended, furious, with tears in my eyes. Later I stopped being so sensitive. There were also texts that he discussed with me at length, surprised and happy about what I had seen in his work and thought I understood.

He had called me from Karlovy Vary and said, 'I've

finished a pretty large picture and need a text for the catalogue. You can have two weeks to do it. Could you come and look at it?' Actually, I had neither the inclination nor the time and expressed a halting objection, but he wasn't listening or really didn't understand me; he just kept saying, 'What? Whaaaat? Hello?' And I shouted, 'All right! I'll do it! I'll do it. I'll come.' Then we hung up.

I drove to Karlovy Vary. It took seven hours. On the map it hadn't looked that far. I left Berlin around noon; was stuck in a traffic jam at the Oberbaum Bridge for an hour, and for another hour in the afternoon in Dresden, but as I approached the Czech border the roads were less crowded. A boy and a girl holding hands were waiting at the border crossing, hoping for a ride. I tried to make my face look friendly and open, but they ignored me and got into a car with Czech number plates. At the checkpoint the official pored absent-mindedly and unnecessarily long over my passport; then he waved me through. I exchanged some money, bought a carton of cigarettes. The landscape was bleak, and a cold wind blew across the car parks in front of the duty-free shops. I took another look at the map. The road seemed to lead in a straight line direct to Karlovy Vary – Karlovy Vary, of which I knew nothing except that it was an old spa town with hot springs whose waters you could drink, and Johannes was now sitting there in an apartment 'high above the roofs of the town, I promise you' waiting for me. Waiting how, I wondered – bored? full of anticipation?

I drove on, lit a cigarette and turned on the heat. Small wooden shacks lined the sides of the road; they sold Coca-Cola and sweets and behind the floor-to-ceiling windows naked girls bathed in red light were dancing away under a disco ball. I wasn't prepared for this, was so flustered by the first wooden shack of this sort that I turned to look at it for such a long time I almost drove off the road. But then came more wooden shacks, car parks, bus stops; the naked girls – in platform shoes and wearing silver bows in their hair – were now dancing on the street, inured to cold and wind. I slowed down to look at them, speeding up only when I caught their eyes, their amused, ambiguous, knowing smiles, as though they knew something about me that I had never revealed to anyone. I thought Johannes should have prepared me for this stretch of road, and I was glad I was driving by myself and didn't have to resort to either an embarrassed silence or conversation.

The road became wider, went through villages and small towns; the girls danced in huts, in the windows of bars and cafés; they sat in front of blocks of flats in the evening sun, braiding each other's hair, while little boys played soccer on the street in front of them. I saw no men, no women, just these girls and little boys, and trucks stopping in the car parks in front of the bars. And coloured neon signs – *Love* and *Girls* and *Dance* and *GoGo* – flickering outside the dilapidated house facades. The sun set and for several minutes bathed all this in a heavy, golden light. I turned on the car radio and turned it off again. I thought of Johannes and for a moment I didn't want to see him or to get to Karlovy Vary. I drove straight ahead and on and on, saw one last girl by the side of the road, a tall girl in a silk nightgown, her red hair pinned up, standing in mud to her ankles, and then nothing more. Only level plains and gentle hills and lights in the distance. Later there were industrial plants, soft-

coal mines, gravel pits, abandoned factories. The moon
rose in the sky. Towards eight o'clock in the evening, I
arrived in Karlovy Vary, parked the car in a multi-storey
in the centre of the city, and walked the rest of the way,
following the directions Johannes had given me.

I had been to Paris, Bern, Bremerhaven and Zurich with
Johannes. In Paris and in Bern, I was invited to the open-
ings of his shows. I had written the texts for the cata-
logues and I stood next to the radiator for an hour with
a glass of champagne in my hand before returning to my
hotel and leaving again the following day to go home or
some other place. I had gone to see him in Bremerhaven,
where he lived in the early years. I went there to see him
again, and to finally tell him what I wanted to tell him,
and of course I told him nothing, confessed nothing, and
nothing at all happened. In Zurich I was the woman he
loved or thought he loved, and at night we lay next to
each other on a pull-out couch in a hotel room in the red
light district, and I turned my face to the wall and put
my arm over my head, and he began to cry and said,
'You're cruel'; but I wasn't. In Karlovy Vary I was nothing
to him and he was nothing to me, so finally we were
friends, and perhaps only now I would like to know
whether that's really what we wanted to be. That, or
something else after all.

I was standing outside his apartment door on the sixth
floor of an Art Nouveau building painted white on a
street that led uphill and at the end of which some cypress-
like trees seemed to be growing into the night sky. In the
stairwell it smelled of lemons, soap and floor wax. It was
quiet. I knocked three times on the green door with the
brass lion's head, pushed the hair out of my face with

my right hand, smoothed my coat. I wasn't thinking of Zurich. Or Bremerhaven. Perhaps I was thinking that I would gladly have drawn out this moment, the moment before someone would open the door and my face would take on an expression I know not of what, but I am sure that I wasn't thinking about that either. Johannes opened the door. He was wearing a pair of suit trousers, a plaid shirt, his hair shorter than ever, not that it made him look any different. He said, 'Come in.' He would have said it the same way anywhere in the world. And then we embraced.

'Karlovy Vary,' Johannes said, 'is the most famous spa in Europe. *Vary* means warm bath and *Karlovy Vary* means Karl's warm bath. That's because, while he was hunting around here, Emperor Charles the Fourth discovered the spring and found that its waters healed the wounds he had received in the battle of Crécy.' We were sitting on the floor, on a dark green oriental carpet at a low table. Johannes poured tea into cups of wafer-thin porcelain. He said, 'In the old days the spring waters were used primarily for baths, but now they're taken primarily as an internal remedy. You have to buy a cup with a spout and drink the spring water four or five times a day.' I said, 'What are you talking about?' and he smiled to himself in a way that seemed to indicate that I didn't yet know enough about all these things.

The room was large, lighted indirectly by several lamps. It led into another room, and then into another and on into a fourth and a fifth. I had rarely been in an apartment like this. All the walls were painted eggshell white in colour and had a dull sheen that reflected the light. The rooms were full of antiques: Empire desks and little rococo chairs, Chinese vases, wall hangings, pen-and-ink drawings in dark frames, brocade tablecloths on massive dining tables and deep velvet easy chairs in front of a fireplace, crystal vases full of wilted flowers standing on long-legged side tables, many pieces of Chinese or Asiatic furniture like the table at which we were sitting, a chaise longue in front of the window, and carved stools in front of cloudy mirrors. I walked through the hall with its many turns and corners and set my bag down beside the dismayingly large bed in the bedroom. Johannes had not offered me any other sleeping arrangement.

From far away he had called out admonitions: 'Take off your shoes, you're scratching the parquet floors with your high heels!' – 'The water in the bathroom is boiling hot' – 'Don't open the balcony door or I won't be able to close it again.' Sometimes his voice sounded closer, sometimes further away – mischievous, deliberately confusing. Walking back from the bedroom, I couldn't find him for a long time. All the rooms had two or three doors; whenever I entered a room he had just left it, until I grabbed his wrist in the kitchen and furiously hissed at him, 'Stop! Stand still!'

Now sitting at the low table, he pushed a pillow behind his back and said, 'Chronic nervous disorders, emotional disturbances, gout and psoriasis, hypochondria, weakness of the abdominal organs, dropsy, scurvy, syphilis . . .' Interrupting him, I asked, 'Is this a habit of yours, or something? A sort of quirk – not talking about what you should be talking about, but about something completely different, the exact opposite? Am I right?' Johannes didn't answer. I took a sip of tea; it tasted dusty; the little porcelain cup felt light and hot in the hollow of my hand. The last room had been cleared, all the little tables, chairs and chaise longues pushed against the wall. Through the open doors I could see Johannes's easel, a large, covered painting, palettes, spray cans. The apartment smelled of turpentine and paints and a perfume I wasn't familiar with.

I said, 'Where are we?' and Johannes said, 'In Karlovy Vary.' Then we both had to laugh. I told him about Berlin and my work and alluded to possible love affairs, encounters and nights. Then we talked about the art world and art galleries, about betrayal, pride, money and discipline. And then I was tired and wanted to go to bed. I wanted to go to bed before Johannes did, wanted to be asleep before he lay down next to me. I went over to the window and looked out. I said, 'So, to whom does the apartment actually belong?' And Johannes said, 'To a Chinese woman. The mother of the owner of my gallery.' I said, 'And where is she, this Chinese woman?' And Johannes said, 'The Chinese woman is dead. She is dead, died two months ago. Almine didn't want to give up the apartment, but she didn't want to leave it unoccupied either, so she proposed that I work here, for half a year perhaps.' I said, 'And what in the world was the Chinese woman doing here in Karlovy Vary?' Johannes replied, 'She drank the hot mineral water and longed for home – that surely must be what you want to hear.' I said, 'Good night,' and walked down the long, dark hallway to the bedroom.

I opened cupboards full of clothes, fur coats, hatboxes, shoes, stoles. In the mirrored cabinets in the bathroom there were little open rouge jars, perfume bottles, medicine, the Chinese woman's toothbrush in a crystal glass on the shelf above the porcelain sink. I touched everything, sniffed at all the things, and for a long time I stared at the imprint of a finger in a jar of night cream – her index finger? her little finger? – I washed my face, put on my nightgown and got into bed. The sheets were freshly ironed and smelled of laundry detergent. I turned off the light on the bedside table, turned over on my side, and looked through the open door down the hall. Light came from all the open doorways; I could hear Johannes walking back and forth; he coughed and the parquet floor creaked. I thought of the Chinese woman. I thought I was going to be sick but wasn't. A small golden clock ticked on the bedside table; the alarm hand pointed to six thirty.

Johannes had certain habits, rules by which he lived, back then when I first got to know him, and also later in Karlovy Vary. I'm sure that he'll never give up these habits. They'll change minimally; they're contingent on where he is living, on the people around him for a shorter or longer period of time. But basically they'll stay with him until he – do I want to say it? – until he gets old and forgets them. Ten years ago he was living in a three-room apartment in the Kreuzberg district of Berlin. The apartment was heated by a stove and had an outside toilet, the windows leaked, and the power kept going off. In the winter he would get up at eight in the morning, go into the kitchen, put the kettle on the range, and get back into bed until the water boiled and the kettle whistled. Then he would make tea, jasmine tea with sugar and cream, and drink the tea in bed, his back propped against the wall and looking out of the window at a bare locust tree in the morning light; there were umbrellas and empty bird-food nets hanging in its branches. At some point he would get up, take an ice-cold shower – he had read about that in Brecht – eat an apple, bite into half a lemon,

161

and start working. How do I know all that? Did I actually see it, or did he tell me about it?

Years later I saw the spa promenade of Karlovy Vary again on a package of Oblaten wafers, an awkward drawing, a suggestion of the colonnade, the small springs, the white benches by the river. On the brown wrapper it said 'Carlsbad Oblaten, a delicious memory'. I remembered Karlovy Vary, the white bench on which we sat, Johannes and I; the memory was shocking because it came so very suddenly, clear and detailed. Back then we would leave the house around noon and walk down to the river. The houses gleaming white against the blue late-summer sky. Fat old men in sleeveless vests standing on their balconies smoking cigars would then turn and disappear into shadowy rooms behind the curtains, carefully leaving the balcony doors slightly ajar.

The spa promenade was so dazzling in the midday sun that I had to shut my eyes, put on my sunglasses. 'What a silly affectation. You're not Russian,' Johannes said, striding erect and hurriedly along beside me. 'I'm going to show you a Klimt in the Spa Sanatorium; you won't recognize it.' It was a mural, a mosaic, I really did not recognize it as a Klimt, and can't remember a single detail of it any more. I do remember halls with linoleum floors, glimpses into tiled rooms with zinc bathtubs, massage tables, antiquated inhalation equipment, a nurse wearing a blue cap standing next to a table, bent over a newspaper, smoking. I remember the silence in the Sanatorium, framed photographs of Spa orchestra musicians hanging on the second-floor landing, the beautiful, serious-looking first violinist, the red-haired, sadly laughable clarinettist. 'For Spa guests only,' the woman selling tickets in the entrance hall said; she was eating plum cake and didn't even look up. 'Concert tickets for Spa guests only, and you want to know what they play – good gracious, Strauss, waltzes, all that nostalgia music.' At that Johannes was already back out on the street, the door closing heavily behind him.

At the first kiosk we came to I bought a cup with a spout, a traditional spa cup – it had a stag painted on it. Johannes claimed he had never bought one for himself, 'And I don't intend to now.' I said, 'I don't understand that. I really don't understand that,' repeating it several times.

Groups of German tourists. Old women leaning on canes, gold necklaces around their necks and bracelets on their wrists, fox furs draped over their stooped shoulders. Russians and Poles. The silhouettes of the pointed gables of the Art Nouveau houses, then the mountains and the forests that were already tinted with autumn colours, now and then a strange smell in the clear air. 'That's the sulphur,' Johannes said as though spelling it out. There were Germans sitting around a fountain with a golden tap; they were wearing windcheaters and tan trousers, their spa-contented faces turned to the sun; we sat down next to them.

At first I hesitated to fill my spouted cup with the mineral water, but then I did and, putting my head back, drank it. The water was warm and salty, nauseating; I drank cautiously, taking small sips. The Germans were discussing their weight and their digestion, diets, blood sugar levels, afternoon naps and supper, the curative effect of the mineral spring water. 'Listen to them,' Johannes said, quite superfluously. I refilled my spa cup with the water; the clock at the Spa Sanatorium struck the hour.

'Coffee time,' the Germans said, stood up and sauntered off. Johannes waited till I had drunk my water the way you wait for a child to finish its lemonade. He said, 'You're drinking it as if it were water from Lourdes.' I wanted to say, 'I'd like to be drinking the water from Lourdes.' But I felt it would be useless to say that; it wasn't Johannes's fault.

We walked along the colonnade, past countless fountains, wooden planters with palms growing in them; we walked slowly, everyone was walking slowly. The world had shrunk down to Karlovy Vary – nothing except warm mineral water, the southerly light, and the vague thought that perhaps basically nothing mattered to me, nothing at all, and for one brief moment maybe it really didn't.

In front of the big fountain of Karlovy Vary spring water at the end of the promenade – the fountain had been cordoned off and its waters had coated the slate stones of the street with a silvery verdigris layer – a children's choir was singing something that sounded like Schubert's 'Ave Maria'. Ignoring the signs saying 'No Smoking', I lit a cigarette. A group of elderly Polish men gratefully followed my example. Johannes vanished for half an hour, then he was suddenly standing next to me again, looking flushed.

The higher up the hill we climbed, the more broken down the houses, the more dilapidated the streets. Spiders' webs floated in the air, and mangy cats scurried over walls that had fallen into ruin. The street rose steeply and turned into a forest path. And there it lay, already behind us, below us: beautiful, bright Karlovy Vary. I said, 'Johannes, turn around, look how beautiful it is.' But Johannes hurried on up the forest path without looking back and gasped over his shoulder down to me, 'Once we reach the top, we can come back in the cable car.' I walked along behind him, my eyes fixed on his back, a familiar back, a once-familiar back.

Johannes was wearing his blue American army jacket, the jacket he always wore. In its innumerable pockets he used to keep all kinds of things: fish hooks, birds' feathers, nuts, a piece of twine, a small blue stone from the French Atlantic coast, a New York subway token, on a folded piece of paper the pattern for a tattoo he wanted to have done some day, a thumbnail-sized Chinese toothbrush and a torn armband. I knew every single item. A long time ago I had sat reverently before him and said, 'Show me what you have in your pockets.' Johannes had emptied them and put everything on the table in front of me. I didn't care to know which of these things were still left, what had been added, what had been lost. On the whole, I didn't want to know anything about Johannes, about the man he now was, the man he would continue to be from now on, but from when on, actually? I didn't want to commit myself.

High on top of the hill there was a tourist café, a hut of dark-stained wood with a set of antlers over the entrance, and a terrace where all the chairs had been tilted up against the tables, and the gravel was already covered with reddish leaves. Johannes took two chairs dripping with rainwater and brushed the leaves off the plastic table-cloth on one of the tables. A waiter came shuffling out of the wooden shack.

We ate beef roulade with dumplings and cabbage. Johannes drank white wine, and I had an ice-cold Coca-Cola. I was thirsty and hot and a little dizzy. The bubbles were tingly on my tongue. The wooden terrace railing was a tangle of spiders' webs, beyond it the forest descended steeply into the valley and to the Karlovy Vary suburbs, the blocks of flats and empty car parks. In one of the flats a small window was opened and flung a mirror of sunlight over the access road. I took off my sweater and sunglasses. Johannes ordered a second glass of white wine; the waiter stood irresolutely at our table, gazing down into the valley with us; then he turned away. Wasps hovered over my Coca-Cola glass, motionless as though suspended by threads. For some reason my heart contracted and then relaxed again, a brief awareness of the randomness of places, of light and circumstances; a beautiful life during which we're allowed to stop off in a place like this one. Or in others: a bridge across the Seine, an excursion boat off the coast of Sicily, a hotel room in Amsterdam with a view of the Red Light district, and Karlovy Vary, beef roulade and a dry white wine which I didn't want to drink. I rolled myself a cigarette and looked at Johannes's face, Johannes who after all knew better; I saw the indifference in it and a kind of pride. This sunlight, the red leaves and the last warmth were not dependent on anything, certainly not on us.

Johannes said, 'Look, a siskin,' and pointed into the forest; I saw nothing, no siskin. I said, 'Yes.' I wondered whom I should tell about this, someone for whom this would be beautiful, this noonday silence; if not for us, then someone I could tell about it for whom it would be. I said, 'Johannes, I'd like to meet someone whom I could tell things to. Someone to whom I could write a letter. I haven't written a letter to anyone for a long time.' Johannes frowned and said nothing.

Far down in the valley, an ambulance driver turned on

his blue light, heading in the direction of the old city; the penetrating wail of the siren reached all the way up to us. Johannes said, 'In fifteen minutes it will come up here, pick you up and drive you away because you're hopeless, damn it.' And I said, 'In fifteen minutes it'll be here to take you away because you refuse to understand anything.' We looked at each other angrily. An insect crawled across the plastic tablecloth. I was full, didn't want to eat any more of my roulade, and pushed the plate away. I put my sweater and my sunglasses on again. We paid and left.

We took the cable car down to the valley. I stared at the cable car driver's bleached-blonde hairline and once briefly past her and down into the abyss – imagining the speed at which we'd hurtle into the valley if the brakes were to fail, imagining how we would grab each other's hands, if we'd even get the chance . . . Johannes and I sat far apart in that small compartment, a ghost train compartment, turning our backs on each other. Not that this had any sort of significance.

'*There is a light coming into my window,*' Johannes sang that afternoon as he lay on the dead Chinese woman's big bed, his eyes closed; wasn't really singing, more humming, and whispering. Something was coming in through the half-closed blinds – light, but that's not what it was, it was something else. I lay on my side next to him and looked at him and found him still good-looking, just as back then, just as always, his peculiar, downy hair, his small chin, his rough skin. For all he cared about me, for all I cared about him, I could just as well have been lying next to a dead man, next to anyone, or even in an entirely different place. And yet we were so close. It pained me, surely not him.

I got up and left him, went through the hall into one of the other eggshell-coloured rooms. There I sat down on a chair against the wall and realized that I was already hungry again and would have liked to eat supper. It wasn't until later that I asked myself how it happened in the first place that we had been lying there together, next to each other, tired and lazy; how did it happen that we were sitting on the edge of the bed, had taken off our shoes, stretched out on our backs, turned towards each other – nothing more – while outside the light was fading and the wind slammed the blinds against the window panes. I couldn't remember.

Perhaps Johannes did have a grasp of something, something I couldn't grasp because I was too sentimental and holding on too tight, whereas he just resigned himself and turned his stubborn back on time. '*It's a long way to China,*' he repeated several times, mysteriously, as though it was supposed to mean something to me. He had a short-wave radio that he took with him on all his trips and which was now standing on the windowsill in the dead Chinese woman's kitchen. He fiddled with it until he found an Arab station. 'What sense is there in listening to Czech music when we're in the Czech Republic? You don't realize you're in the Czech Republic until you hear Arab music or, for all I care, Mongolian or Bengali music – in any case, something completely different.' I was standing next to him, no help at all, because he wouldn't let me peel carrots, clean the fish, or set the table, insisting, 'No, no, I'll do it myself.'

On the radio a man's high voice was singing cascading notes up and down, a heart-wrenching singsong, cooing and vibrating. It made me think of a distant place, of a desert moon outside the windows, of jackals, desert sands that would bury the Art Nouveau houses of Karlovy Vary and choke its springs, and then I didn't feel like thinking about it any more, and I remembered that Johannes had once sent a letter to me in Essaouira, Morocco.

I had gone to Morocco because he had been there some years earlier and perhaps he had said something like, 'If you want to give form to your peculiar longing, go to Morocco.' Whatever. I did go there, but my longing wasn't great enough to go there alone; I went with someone else, not with Johannes, with someone else. Johannes had given me addresses of hotels, pensions, restaurants he had liked, where he had stayed overnight or eaten. Most of them I ignored, but in Essaouira we took a room at the Hôtel du Tourisme. Johannes had recommended the hotel – it was near the sea, built into the walls of the old city, sun-bleached and dilapidated. Yellow birds flew around in the atrium, and sand and sea salt crunched between the sheets. We paid for our room in advance, filled out the registration forms, but when the receptionist saw our passports he suddenly stopped what he was doing, pulled a letter out of a drawer, and said it had arrived a week ago.

The humidity had soaked open the envelope, which was made of folded newspaper – Johannes never bought ready-made envelopes, always folded his own out of old paper. On the outside it had my name and Hôtel du Tourisme, Essaouira, Morocco. I didn't show my amazement, my happy surprise; I took the letter quite casually and calmly, as though I were a seasoned traveller, without ties, a person to whom people send letters into the unknown, into the wide world: maybe she'll get it and maybe she won't. And if she gets it, then it will mean something, be a sign that will effect a change.

We went up the stairs to our room; I held on tightly to the letter because I knew that the man I was with, in a fit of jealousy, would rip it from me if he had the chance, tear it into many little snippets, and throw them out of the window for the sea wind to carry off. I read the letter in the toilet, and for the rest of the trip I carried it under my shirt, close to my heart, hiding it at night before we went to sleep, always in different places. I've forgotten what it said, what Johannes had written.

In the kitchen in Karlovy Vary – Johannes was slicing onions, rubbing pepper between his hands, peppercorns, cardamom – I said, 'Do you remember the letter you once sent to me in Essaouira?' And Johannes quite honestly said, 'No.'

We sat down at the table in the eggshell-coloured room, ate fish with tomatoes and paprika, couscous and salad, drank wine with it. I didn't really want to know where in Karlovy Vary Johannes had managed to find these almost exotic food items. We ate from large porcelain plates and refilled our wine glasses from the carafe. A draught from somewhere made the candles flicker, and in the kitchen Arabs continued singing softly to themselves. My initial feeling of revulsion at the thought of eating and drinking from the dead Chinese woman's plates, cups and glasses had vanished. I ate her spices and drank her wine. The Chinese woman sat at the head of the table, her tiny hands folded on her stomach; she wore a red kimono and smiled at us, graciously it seemed. I asked Johannes, 'Weren't you afraid at first?' And he said, as though he also saw her, 'Oh yes, in the beginning I was. I thought it strange and also absurd, Almine's readiness to let me stay in her dead mother's apartment. I spent two or three uneasy nights, but then I stopped being afraid. If I'd been afraid, I wouldn't have been able to work.' He cut open the white belly of the second fish and carved it up. That last sentence was characteristic of him, this ability to decide to end something and then be done with it. It was a talent I would have given a lot for.

I would have liked to talk more with him about the dead Chinese woman, who had obviously been immensely rich and eccentric. I saw her walking along the promenade taking dainty little steps and drinking her medicinal water from a Chinese spa cup. What is a Chinese woman doing in Karlovy Vary – it sounds like the beginning of a joke. 'And where does her daughter Almine, the owner of your gallery, live?' 'In Paris,' Johannes said tersely; obviously he didn't want to talk to me about the dead Chinese woman.

So I leaned back and waited for him to decide what he did want to talk about. I thought we ought to talk about something; it wasn't late, we couldn't go to bed yet; we had to sit around together for a little while longer. Actually it didn't much matter to me, and I was grateful that it didn't. I thought how anxious and trembly I would have been if I still loved him, if I still wanted to show myself to him, still yearned for him. I had no yearning for him.

Johannes finished eating his fish unhurriedly, drank his wine, and wiped his mouth with a linen napkin. 'Would you like something else?'

'No thanks. I'm very full. It was good.'

He stacked the plates and pots, got up and disappeared into the kitchen. I exchanged a meaningful glance with the Chinese woman and made a face in the direction of the kitchen door. Johannes clattered with the dishes, called out, 'I'll be right back.' A polite, strange and handsome host with dark blue eyes and the lightest-coloured hair. I was ready for a fight. It was quite senseless. 'Do you want a gin and tonic?' I didn't answer him; I could hear him opening the refrigerator, could hear ice cubes dropping into a glass. He called out, 'Do you remember Miriam?' From the way he emphasized *you* I realized that this was supposed to be the counter-question to my question about the letter to Essaouira.

I said, 'Of course I remember Miriam.'

Johannes came back into the room, put the tonic water bottle and a glass on the table in front of him, sat down and said, 'And what was your first meeting with Miriam like?'

I said, 'Do you want to talk about her because you miss her so much or because you really want to know?'

Johannes looked at me indignantly and said, 'I want to know what it was like for you, no more and no less. You don't have to give me an answer.'

So I gave in. I said, 'How long has it been, three years? Four?'

And, sounding very sure, Johannes said, 'Four years.' His exact pinpointing of the time made me dizzy for a moment.

Four years. The summer after Morocco. Johannes had given me a ring, a large, silver ring, a ring he had designed and had someone make to order, with a stone in it that he had found on some Greek island. The ring was intended to be as symbolic as it looked, and I had accepted it. What had that been? A wedding? A promise? I took the ring and disappeared. I had work to do, no time to worry about anything. After I had been gone for a long enough time, Johannes telephoned and asked for the ring back with an earnestness that couldn't be contradicted. He was right. I was fed up. I went to Kreuzberg one morning in late summer, the ring in my right coat pocket; I had allowed myself ten minutes to talk.

The three-room apartment in the building in the rear courtyard, an outside toilet and a stove to provide heat, the locust tree with the umbrellas in its branches. Just as I walked into the rear building, a door slammed on one of the upper floors and someone came down the stairs. I knew at once what was going on. I walked up the steps, and she came down. We met on the third floor, walked past each other, touched elbows, looked at each other. Her eyes were dark brown, her face light and full of freckles, calm, with an expression of contentment, nothing insecure, one morning in late summer, then she was gone. When I looked out the window I could see her unlocking her bicycle from where it had been chained to Johannes's bike, push it across the courtyard, and disappear through the gateway. For the ten minutes I had scheduled to talk with Johannes, to offer him one last riddle and then to leave, I stood around in the twilight of the apartment block hallway, breathing in and out, trembling, astonished at the anger and sadness that welled up in me from God knows where. I ran up the stairs, two steps at a time, and then I was at his door pounding on it with my fists. The door wasn't locked properly and simply flew open, and I stumbled in, ridiculous and crying now, stumbled through the entrance hall into the little room where Johannes was sitting on the bed, his back against the wall, looking at the locust tree and balancing a cup of jasmine tea with sugar and cream on his knees. The window was open, it was still warm outside. I took the ring out of my coat pocket and laid it on the bedside table next to the empty wine glasses, the ashtray filled with cigarette butts, and an open book, Giuseppe Ungaretti, *Poems*. Johannes turned from staring at the tree and looked at me as though I weren't there at all. I turned round, walked back through the hall to the open apartment door and closed it behind me, carefully and quietly.

The Chinese woman in her eggshell-coloured room in a city in a valley in the Czech Republic – *it's a long way to China* – nodded several times, stood up and bowed gracefully; her kimono rustled, then she was gone. Johannes said, 'Actually, how did you know that it was Miriam; that is to say, how did you know that this woman, a stranger, who came out of my apartment, had been with me?' I replied, annoyed, 'I don't know, I just knew. You know something like that. It's obvious.' He said, affably, 'And what was it like?' I said nonchalantly, 'What was it supposed to have been like – it was awful. Awful.'

I didn't feel like talking about it with him this way. I wanted to think about it, that it was really awful and that now it wasn't any more – it *had been* awful – and how could we sit here together in the bilious aura of all our hurts and talk about it? I couldn't concentrate. I said, 'I know that she's still here. I mean Miriam. She's still here, and I know it; you don't have to tell me.' Johannes smiled and said, 'But I really would like to say it: "She is still here."' He didn't sound triumphant. He poured some tonic into his tumbler; we clinked glasses, drank, smoked, talked, and were silent, and when we were silent, I thought I could hear the fountains of the Karlovy Vary spring, its bubbling water, at the end of the promenade, running over the fish-scale paving stones. Do you hear it too? Yes, I hear it too. The Chinese woman, crouching in the dark hall, was folding tissue paper into dragons and releasing them into the air like butterflies.

'Do you still remember,' I asked, 'do you still remember at the opening of your show in Paris two years ago how beautiful you thought I was?' I was vain and probably sad, but Johannes was, too. He said, 'Of course I still remember that. You were very beautiful. You were wearing a fur coat and black, high-heeled shoes, and your face was luminous. You stood by the radiator for half an hour. You didn't talk with anyone. You were cold; then you left.'

At breakfast the following morning around ten o'clock in a hazy light – it had started to rain during the night and was still raining – Johannes burst out laughing and couldn't stop for a whole hour. He had got up before me. When I came into the kitchen he was already sitting at the table, eating his customary apple and a small slice of white bread. I said, 'I like this weather. I like it when it's grey and misty outside.' I said, 'I think I'm in a good mood.' And Johannes put the apple he had just cut in half back on his plate and burst out laughing. I waited politely. I thought he'd surely let me in on what had amused him so, but Johannes stopped laughing and said nothing. I said, 'What's so funny?' He looked at me and then at his apple and back at me and again began to laugh, harder, longer.

I sat down at the table across from him. Now I had to laugh too; I said casually, 'Listen, what are you laughing about?' Johannes shook his head, held his hand in front of his forehead, then in front of his eyes, laughed, calmed down, stopped laughing. I poured myself a cup of coffee. Cautiously I said, 'Johannes?' and he pushed himself away from the table with both hands, got up and went over to the sink, and stood there with his back to me; his shoulders were quaking. I stared at him. I said, 'Did I do anything, last night? Something I can't remember any more that could have been so outrageously funny?' And Johannes stretched out both hands in a defensive gesture. I said, 'I don't understand.' He flinched and bent over the sink; I said annoyed, 'Are you laughing at me or what? Dammit, what are you laughing at?' He left the kitchen. I could hear him in the hall. Suppressed snickering, catching his breath, ridiculous moaning, a renewed fit of laughter. I poured milk into my coffee. I thought, 'I'm bored.' I listened. Johannes came back to the kitchen, again sat down at the table, said, 'Excuse me,' and picked up his apple. I looked at him steadily until he looked at me, a few seconds. A slight blush coloured his face, I could see that he really was making an effort to control himself. But it didn't work; he started laughing again. He buried his face in his hands. I said as casually as I could, 'So you're not going to tell me what's so funny.' And he said, choking, 'Nothing. Nothing is funny. I can't tell you.' I gave up. I leaned back, warming my hands on the hot coffee cup and looked at him the way you look at a sick person or a prisoner or a witness. I waited, watching him. He was out of breath, his face had turned dark red, tears were running down his cheeks, the laughter shook him and seemed to be painful. From time to time, I laughed too. Johannes was no longer trying to repress the laughter, to stop for my sake; he simply let it roll over him like a wave, let himself go. I couldn't remember ever having laughed like that. He got up again and staggered out of the kitchen, walked through all the rooms and came back, stood out in the hall, took a deep breath, and surrendered to it again, enjoying it. I ignored him. I gazed out the window into the drizzle; the curtains in all the windows of the houses across the way were drawn. The wind blew through the branches of the plane trees. Johannes was now laughing behind the closed bathroom door, far away in the bedroom, and once briefly in the stairwell where the echo grotesquely doubled the sound of his laughter.

At some point it became quiet. I listened and couldn't hear anything any more; I waited a moment longer, then I got up and went through all the rooms looking for him. He was lying on a little chaise longue in the studio, his right hand on his stomach. I remained standing in the doorway and said, hesitantly, 'Is everything all right?' He said, quite serious, 'Yes, everything's all right.' I stood there and thought of repeating the question, but I didn't. I said, 'Don't you want to show me your picture, the one I'm supposed to write the text for?' And Johannes said, 'I think I've changed my mind. I don't need a text. The picture isn't finished yet. I'll show it to you some other time.'

I washed the dishes, had a second cup of coffee on the balcony in the drizzling rain, and then went back to bed. I read three pages of the foreword in an art catalogue Johannes had given me, maybe to show me how a real text for a picture ought to be written, then I fell asleep. Johannes woke me up an hour later. He said, 'You'll get depressed if you sleep too much in the daytime.' I said, 'Would you bring me a piece of chocolate and a ciga- rette?' That made Johannes happy. He brought me a box of Chinese ginger chocolates; I couldn't make out the expiry date, but I ate them all up anyway. Johannes sat on a chair next to the bed and watched me, then he got up and left.

I heard him moving things around in the studio. The short-wave radio was playing Mongolian music, Johannes was whistling softly to himself, then it sounded as if he was rinsing paint brushes in the kitchen. The rain was now drumming on the metal windowsill. It seemed strange for me to be spending so much time with someone when our relationship was so unclear and the distance between us so uncertain. I wasn't close enough to Johannes to follow him through all the rooms, blabbering, uninhibited and devoted; yet I was close enough to him to let him sit by my bed and watch me, sleepy-eyed, my hair dishevelled, consuming twenty ginger chocolates one after the other. I stayed in bed because I didn't know what else to do, with him, without him.

In the afternoon I got up; outside it was already getting dark. Johannes had gone out. He didn't tell me where he was going, nor did he ask me if I'd like to come along, which was all right. I wouldn't have wanted to go with him. I asked, 'Do you know anyone in Karlovy Vary?' He said, 'No. Nobody. I don't want to get to know anyone either; it would keep me from my work.' I was keeping him from his work too. I knew that. Of course he couldn't work while I was there; he really didn't want to have me write the text for his picture. It was time to leave. I would leave tomorrow morning. Standing in the kitchen, my right hand on my hip, I drank the rest of the tea in his cup, cold jasmine tea with cream and sugar; then I put the cup back on the table and went into his studio. Bluebeard's room. The seventh room.

The air around me seemed to vibrate; my skin felt

strange, and I had the feeling I couldn't hear properly. The blinds in the room had been raised; rainy light came in, and all the objects looked blurry and out-of-focus. The paintings were turned to the wall, draped with cloths; no painting on the easel, no finished picture hanging on the wall. Tacked up on the wall between the windows were pieces of paper on which Johannes had written notes to himself, cryptic phrases: *Jürgen Bartsch, resistance, skin resistance, empty cans*. On the desk, pencils, newspaper clippings, paper, a tobacco pouch and cigarette papers, the little case for grass that I had given him years before, drawing pins, lighters, empty coffee cups, Polaroid photos – Johannes with a black cloth over his eyes – a volume of poems by Nietzsche, postcards with a view of the Karlovy Vary promenade, an inkwell, tweezers, three spray cans of paint, a glass paperweight that had a Chinese bamboo pagoda inside.

What I was looking for was not on the desk but on the windowsill, carefully stacked into a pile – blue envelopes, rectangular blue envelopes addressed to Johannes in tiny handwriting. To Johannes in Karlovy Vary, in a town in a valley in the Czech Republic with a fountain of warm, salty, healing water. My heart had stopped beating. I could have turned on my heel, left, closed the door behind me, and gone on to do something else. I didn't. I took the first letter; it was very light, didn't weigh anything, didn't smell of anything either, no matter. I drew the square-ruled sheet of paper out of the envelope, unfolded it, and began to read. Spiders' webs, a mesh, an intricate pattern like a Chinese puzzle. I have never been afraid of reading other people's mail, their diaries, their private notes; rather, I have always been afraid and yet I did it frequently anyway because of some

179

reverse feeling of duty, to discover something I was not allowed to know and yet had to know in order to make a decision.

Miriam's letters were all obscene. Obscene, sexual, pornographic, unrestrained. She reminded Johannes of certain states of arousal, described nights with him still to come, lost herself in unbridled fantasies. I hadn't thought that Johannes even had sexuality, certainly not this kind – so, was it his sexuality or only Miriam's, her suggestions? It wasn't my sort of sexuality, and a voice whispering inside me regretted that. I read the third, the fourth, the fifth letter, then the sixth only to make sure that this was actually all that she had written to him: 'This longing deep within me, in my very darkest recesses'; I read the last letter because I thought: What if she were indeed to write a sentence like, 'This morning I finally went to the National Library to compile the material for my Masters Thesis'? But she didn't write any such sentence. I put the letters neatly back in their place, all the edges lined up. I thought of Miriam's light face and her brown eyes, of Johannes in the white bed, of the things on the bedside table: two wine glasses, an ashtray, a book. Was that suggestive? I remembered saying to Johannes in the tourist restaurant high up on the hill above Karlovy Vary, 'I'd like to meet someone again to whom I could write a letter,' and I would have given a lot to be able to take back that sentence; it seemed ridiculous to me now. I had said it in the wrong place and at the wrong time.

I left the studio, Bluebeard's room, the seventh room. I went back to the kitchen, opened the refrigerator, and took a big swig of gin directly from the bottle. I said aloud, 'I wish I had never seen her. I wish I hadn't read her letters. I wish I weren't here.' But I knew I was lying.

Johannes came back in the evening and nothing about him betrayed where he had been. During the hours I sat at the kitchen table waiting for him he had become a different person, a stranger who led a life I knew nothing about. The way I looked at him must have indicated this too, for he stopped close to me and said, 'Is something wrong?' I said, 'No. What should be wrong?' He changed his clothes, and then we went out, stumbling over the rain-wet cobblestone pavement of a nocturnal and dead Karlovy Vary. The fountains gurgled softly on the promenade. 'A last sip of mineral water?' 'No more mineral water, thanks very much.' We walked to the multi-storey where I had parked my car and took the lift to the top floor, bribed the doorman with an incredible amount of American dollars that Johannes pulled out of his coat pocket, and stepped into the Belle Etage, Karlovy Vary's only night club. It had been a long time since I had spent a night in a discotheque, and I had never ever been to a discotheque like this one.

Outside the huge windows lay Karlovy Vary, the dark, the beautiful, and not a soul was looking out; they had all turned their backs on the panoramic view as though they couldn't stand seeing it any more, and were concentrating on the centre of the room. I wondered whether they lowered the blinds in front of the windows when the sun came up over the mountains and the forests. I can't think of anything worse than the light of morning outside the windows of a pub where I'd been drinking all night long. Johannes said, 'At about three o'clock they close the blinds, and nobody even notices.'

181

The room was as large as the parking decks below us, as large as the fourth-floor parking deck where my car was – a room full of tables, sofas, cosy alcoves, lit by tiny golden lamps. In the middle of the room was the dance floor, above it a disco ball, a nineteen-seventies atmosphere, fluorescent blacklight and a laser show. It was full to bursting, waitresses moved between the tables with overflowing trays of cocktails and champagne bottles. Surprisingly the waitresses were all in their fifties, stout, determined, robust matrons who had the situation well in hand; they collected the money for drinks on the spot, and when asked – without any fuss – indicated the Czech prostitutes who were sitting next to each other in a row at the bar, sipping from champagne flutes and yawning.

On the dance floor Russians and Poles were behaving like lunatics, Germans held on to the tables, weaving back and forth with heavy drunken heads; the very elderly spa visitors, little old ladies with their fox furs and golden chains, were just about to leave. Young Czechs were standing at the door waiting to get in, impatiently stepping from one foot to the other, quite clearly inviting the old ladies, who were fussily putting on their fur hats, to go home and go to bed.

Johannes yelled into my ear, 'This is the only club in Karlovy Vary that stays open until early morning. Everyone comes here, really everyone, and the Russian Mafia is making a fortune!' I nodded idiotically; I felt unwell, watched by everybody. We were led to a table, seated with a married couple, brusquely asked what we wanted to drink, two gin and tonics with ice. I slid into the corner of the leather banquette, took off my coat, and pressed my knees together under the table. Every three minutes a prostitute pushed off from the bar and, as though pulled by a string, headed for a table and became submerged in the dimness under the little golden lamps. Another took her place at the bar. There was never a gap. The prostitutes wore white dresses that lit up spectrally in the fluorescent blacklight and were extinguished as soon as they sat down. Johannes followed my gaze and said, 'On the floor below us there are rooms, a kind of hotel where they rent rooms by the hour, the place is very popular.'

The waitress slammed our glasses of gin and tonic down on the table in front of us, collected our American dollars; she gave me a contemptuous look. The couple at our table introduced themselves. Rudi and Vlaska, maybe sixty years old, she Czech and he German, married for ten years, the umpteenth marriage for each of them. Vlaska was beautiful, Rudi obese and elegant in a white suit, a narrow tie lashed around his fat neck. Johannes leaned across the table, listening with an expression of extreme attentiveness to the most personal of stories the two were shouting at him from both sides. I drank my gin and tonic, aggressively caught the eye of the waitress, and simply ordered another. I would have liked to say, Please bring me three. I felt I couldn't cope with this situation sober.

Men sauntered casually past the bar, assessing the prostitutes; the prostitutes exhibited their bare shoulders and burst into hoarse laughter. At the till the stout waitresses put their heads together, became agitated like bees, then swarmed apart again, their full trays held high over their heads. A second lukewarm gin and tonic. Vlaska sang Johannes a Czech folksong; on the dance floor people became hysterical because of some popular tune. Rudi loosened his tie, offered me a cigarette, and touched my fingertips with his fat, sweaty hand. I smiled, he smiled back; we clinked glasses, he called out into the room, 'Next round!' The waitress was nowhere to be seen. Johannes leaned towards me and said, 'Are you all right?' I nodded and was just about to reach for his arm, but he had already turned back to Vlaska. I stared at the revolving disco ball, its blinking reflections, until I got dizzy. The prostitutes gleamed swan-white, the gin and tonic tasted like water, the Russians on the dance floor shouted, '*Every breath you take, every move you make,*' under the table Rudi put his hand on my knee, I was totally sober, it didn't help, nothing helped. Johannes sat next to me, a handsome stranger, a client or whatever; I'd like to have grabbed him by the shoulders and shaken him.

Vlaska got up and disappeared. Rudi took his hand off my knee, pointed at one of the prostitutes at the bar – who then immediately looked over in our direction – and began to describe an incident to Johannes that apparently was rather racy. I didn't want to hear any of it. I turned away and gazed out the window. The entire room was mirrored in the glass, outside the same as inside, no Karlovy Vary, no fountain, no dark forest.

Johannes said, 'Excuse me,' got up and left. Dumbfounded, I looked at Rudi's shiny face, which he immediately turned to me, without a second's hesitation. I thought it was outrageous that Johannes had left me alone with him. Rudi said, 'Are you together or something?' And I didn't answer, which didn't bother him. He waved again to the waitress, grinning at me. I wondered whether Johannes was at that moment together with Vlaska somewhere, whether they had agreed on some secret signal and were now at this very moment having sexual intercourse in one of the rooms on the floor below us. Actually I wondered, was Johannes just having it off with Vlaska, an expression I had read in Miriam's letters that totally threw me.

Vlaska did not come back, nor did Johannes. There was no opening in the ranks of the prostitutes; one couldn't tell whether one of them had taken off with Johannes, the one Rudi had talked about, or another one; they all looked alike. Rudi grabbed my hand, my wrist, my arm; he squeezed hard and it hurt; he said something I no longer understood. I felt ill and was tempted simply to get up, take him along and go to a room and there to let him teach me about something I knew nothing about, had only an inkling of, not even that much; I could have told Johannes about it later. I pulled my hand away and got up. I staggered along the passage; once the fluorescent blacklight made my shirt briefly light up, the cuticles of my fingernails, the seams of my jeans, snow-white. I staggered into the toilets and threw up into the sink; one last elderly Czech lady stood behind me and held my forehead with her cool hand.

Late that night, perhaps in the grey of dawn, maybe early in the morning at five, I was standing in front of the wardrobe in the hall of the dead Chinese woman's apartment. The doors of the wardrobe were open, the dresses suspended on hangers on a brass rod, silk dresses, velvet dresses, taffeta, lace and embroidery, furs and shimmering brocade. From the dresses rose a mild smell of mothballs, powder, perfume and something else that I didn't recognize, a smoky note. I was swaying a little, my head felt hot and feverish. I brushed my hand over the dresses on

their hangers and couldn't decide. I wished the Chinese
woman would come back and select a dress for me that
would fit me like a second skin. But the Chinese woman
was sitting in the kitchen at the big table putting countless rice kernels together in complicated geometric
patterns resembling frost flowers – she had better things
to do. With my eyes closed I took a dress off its hanger.
I opened my eyes again; the dress was of blue silk with
golden threads running through it and had a high collar.
It didn't fit me like a second skin and I couldn't close the
buttons at the back, but when I turned round and looked
in the mirror, my own face at least, red-cheeked, familiar,
flashed back at me above the high blue collar. I stood
there like that for a while and looked at myself. I didn't
know what I ought to do now, with the dress, with myself,
with Johannes, with everything. I didn't know if that was
sad or not or nothing. I went to the bedroom and stood
next to the bed. Johannes was asleep. I thought that this
wasn't right. But it wasn't wrong either. And then at last
Johannes opened his eyes, just like that, as though he
hadn't been sleeping at all. He looked at me and for a
moment I was afraid he wouldn't understand, but then
he reached out and pulled me down to him. He stroked
the blue, shiny material and said softly, 'That really feels
beautiful.' He lifted the covers and I lay down beside him.
I lay with my back to his stomach, and he put his arm
around me and held my hand until I finally no longer
had to think of him.

And all that counts for nothing. Karlovy Vary. I don't
know what it was, this visit of mine to Karlovy Vary –
a series of chance moments, one coincidence that causes
a change, perhaps that's what it was. I remember it the

way I remember the letter to Essaouira, and Miriam's face, and these memories are useless too. My memory of Karlovy Vary is overlaid by the memory of Miriam's letters, her unbridled sexual attacks, Rudi's saliva in my face. It's too bad, but probably it's always like that. It lies like a veil over something else. It is as if I were to close a box full of old, meaningless, wonderful stuff, and at the last moment think of something, a tiny little object at the very bottom of the box, and open the box again, take out everything, but be unable to find the little thing, the only proof of its existence being a hunch, nothing more.

I haven't seen Johannes since. If I were to meet him, I could tell him about the fog through which I drove when I left Karlovy Vary. A wall of fog, so unexpected that at first I had to stop to orient myself, and then I drove on at a crawl for a long time, almost an hour. I could only see as far as the end of the bonnet, no further; the rest of the world was white and had disappeared. It made me feel uneasy and I drove leaning far forward as though that way I could see better; there was nothing to see, and suddenly I felt that I was in a kind of twilight zone. I thought: And when the fog lifts there will be something else there, something strange and new, and in the midst of all my fear this thought made me happy. The fog lifted as suddenly as it had come. I couldn't even see it in the rearview mirror any more. In front of me were the barracks of the German–Czech border patrol and the customs officials and the passport inspectors and the sky. They waved me through and I drove on home.

# Where Are You Going?

We've reached the point where Jacob now comes to see me in the evening. He arrives around ten, knocks on the door, and carefully hangs his jacket, scarf and cap over the back of my kitchen chair – it's cold this winter and I like that. He always brings something to eat for himself, usually from the Chinese restaurant. Maybe he assumes that I wouldn't have any food in the house; he has never asked me whether I do.

We sit on the floor in the living room, eating rice with vegetables out of plastic containers. Jacob doesn't seem to have the slightest idea how embarrassed I am whenever I have to eat in the company of someone I'm in love with. He eats with gusto, I only pretend to do so. He cleans up whatever I leave. When he's finished, he stretches out on his stomach, lights a cigarette, and cradles his face in his left hand. He always takes off his shoes. Sometimes the telephone rings in the hall; I never answer it, but I do get up and turn off the answering machine. When I come back to the living room, Jacob looks at me.

We talk a lot. Mostly I stare at the wall while we do.

189

I once told him that it makes me weary to be telling the same old stories over and over again, about the past, my childhood, my first loves and the last, the decisive moments of my life, happiness, the things that make me what I am. How I am. I'm not sure he understood. I'm often not sure he understands me, but that doesn't change my enthusiasm for Jacob.

He says, 'Does my past bother you?' He means his affairs with women.

I say, 'Not really.' I'd like to say, 'Does my past bother you?' I'd really like to say, 'My past could bother you a lot.' But that would be arrogant and, besides, not true. So I don't say it.

Jacob's hands are large, soft and warm, rather unusual. He uses aftershave even though I've told him several times already that it isn't necessary. He has his hair cut too short and too often. Unlike me, he never gets really drunk. When he leaves, we embrace; he says, 'Can you still stand it?'

I say, 'Why do you ask me?'

He says reluctantly and insincerely, 'Are you sad?'

I say, 'No.' Then he leaves and I close the door behind him.

Although it makes me weary to always repeat the same old stories, I can't resist and tell them anyway. I am about to tell Jacob the last story. It is December, a few days before New Year. Jacob wants to know where I spent last New Year's Eve; he wants to know with whom. I tell him I went to Prague. I say: Back then, when I drove to Prague with Peter for New Year's Eve, I was, to put it simply, in love with Lukas. Lukas wasn't at all in love with me. But Peter was. He was Lukas's friend. If I couldn't see Lukas,

I saw Peter. I misused Peter because of my longing for Lukas. Peter put up with it. In December I hardly saw Lukas at all. He had withdrawn. When I called him, he wouldn't pick up the phone. If I stood outside his door, he wouldn't open it. The days were icy, clear and cold. I didn't try to force him. I wasn't really suffering. Being unhappily in love just seemed to be a condition of life.

Shortly before Christmas, I accidentally ran into him in the park. We stood facing each other like strangers. I said, 'And what are you doing for New Year's Eve?' I was still clinging to the idea of being with him as the old year ended, a symbol for the coming year in which everything had to turn out well just as in all the previous years.

Lukas said, 'Don't know. Probably hang out and see what happens.' And he stared past me up into the bare branches of the poplars.

I left him standing there and went to Grell Strasse to see Peter. I walked slowly; the town was deserted; everyone seemed to have left, to have gone back home. I knocked on Peter's door, and Peter opened it immediately. If he was surprised to see me, he didn't let on. He had the heating on and was watching television by candlelight. He seemed to be existing, even without me. I thought that amazing. I sat down next to him on the sofa and, without saying a word, we watched ski jumpers soaring through the air.

Peter took my hand and placed it on his knee. I left it there. I said, 'And are you still planning to drive to Prague with Micha and Sarah for New Year's Eve?'

Peter made an affirmative noise. He had long ago got out of the habit of using the clear word 'yes'.

I thought for a while, and then I said, 'I'd like to go with you. I'll go to Prague with you for New Year's Eve.'

191

Peter nodded, continued to watch television, didn't look at me. Presumably he was afraid I might dissolve into thin air if he were to look at me. He had no inkling that I was incapable of performing such tricks in those days.

Jacob keeps saying, 'I want to share everything I see with you; I want you to see what I see, and if that isn't possible, I want to tell you all the things that happen to me when you're not around.' He sounds convincing, and he also says, 'I suffer because I can't see the world twenty-four hours a day through my eyes and yours.'

I listen to him with rapt attention. I try to understand, and I say to myself – I suffer because of it, I suffer because of it. I think of Jacob all day long. I'm happy thinking of him, it is a feeling of joy that I know could be interrupted at any moment. It makes me happy to anticipate this interruption, to be afraid of it, and to long for it. I try to remember everything I see, try to share with him everything I see. I try hard:

The homeless man at the bus stop who asks a girl for a cigarette; the girl gives him what's left of the cigarette she's been smoking and gets on the bus; the homeless man finishes the cigarette. I want to know if Jacob finds that as intimate an act as I do. The woman at the supermarket till who opens the door for me and says in a very loud voice, 'Come in,' my soft, surprised 'Thanks', and my concern that she might not have heard me. The boy on the street, a baseball in his left hand, a packet of cornflakes in his right, who has turned round to look at me and continues looking for a long time, not interested in me, but angry. The sunlight streaming into the room through the slats of the venetian blinds at nine o'clock

in the morning. Ry Cooder's most recent music. The red
brake lights of cars at night, traffic lights, street lamps,
neon advertisements, their reflections on the rain-wet
asphalt. My friend Anna standing at the window in her
apartment – we had eaten together, had drunk some wine,
and told each other everything; she has her back to me
and says without turning round, 'I knew we'd be sitting
here like this when the summer was over.'

Sentences like that. And the smell of wetness, of rain,
and of coal in the stairwell. And that when autumn arrives
I never know whether it's warm or cold outside, whether
I'm feeling cold or whether I'm just tired. Another
sentence I heard in passing: 'Oh, that's nothing. I once
knew a woman who lived above a Chinese restaurant,
right above it,' and the absurd thought I have: I'd like to
be that woman. Can I tell Jacob all this?

The winter I decided to go to Prague with Peter for
New Year's Eve, Micha was in love with Sarah. Sarah
loved Micha. And Miroslav, who loved Sarah, was living
by himself in Prague, and the venetian blinds on all his
windows were always pulled down. I have him to thank
for the only Czech word I know: *smutna*. *Smutna* means
'sad'.

Miroslav had called Sarah and said, 'Wouldn't you like
to come to Prague for New Year's Eve? It's snowing and
the Moldau is frozen over. We could go up on the roof
and watch the fireworks.'

And Sarah had said, 'I'll come, but only if I can bring
Micha because I don't go anywhere any more without
Micha, and maybe there'll be some other people coming
with us too.'

And Miroslav said meekly, 'Bring anyone you want.'

193

Later Sarah said that his voice sounded far, far away, as if he were calling her from the moon – or Mongolia. She didn't seem to know which of the two she should prefer. Sara and Micha drove to Prague by themselves because Micha had bought a pistol and had to do target practice in each Czech forest they passed.

Peter and I took the train. We met in the late afternoon on December 30th at the Berlin Ostbahnhof. It was already dark; it never seemed to get really light any more. They were doing some reconstruction at the Ostbahnhof, and I wandered for what seemed to be an eternity through temporary underpasses, tunnels, and passageways until at last I found Peter queuing in the 'container' they had set up to sell tickets. He was wearing a ski cap and looked different and unusually confident, as if he knew exactly where to go.

Against my better judgement, I had said goodbye to Lukas outside the door to his apartment. He had opened the door only a crack. I said, 'I'm going to Prague for New Year's Eve, I just wanted to say goodbye.'

Lukas peered through the crack and said in a faint whisper, 'Well then, so long.'

I wanted to say something else, but he had already closed the door. So I left.

I joined the queue next to Peter and touched his arm briefly; he said, 'Hello,' and smiled a little – he looked sad, childlike and serious. We bought tickets, bottled water, some cans of beer, cigarettes and sweets and boarded the train. The carriage was not divided into compartments. Fluorescent tubes flickered on the ceiling, the seats were lilac-coloured. My face reflected in the window pane looked green and horrible, and so I looked through my reflection out at the winter-gloomy night-time city, at its streets, suburbs, highways, industrial areas, and then at last nothing, just fields, telegraph poles, occasional lights in the darkness.

Peter, sitting next to me, was reading the newspaper *Bild*; he'd been reading *Bild* for years with a kind of provocative mindlessness; from time to time he'd read me some totally amazing passage from it. Then I took his hand and put my head on his shoulder. After he had drunk all the beer, we went to the dining car. I felt people were staring at us: a woman in a brown coat with a fur collar, a man with long, uncombed hair already greying at the temples, wearing an old, second-hand windcheater, and holding his last can of beer in his right hand. Did we look lost?

It felt good being with Peter in that dining car, sitting at a table with a tablecloth. The cloth was spotted, the beer mats were limp and worn, the salt shaker was made of plastic and the salt in it a grey lump. We sat facing each other and didn't talk much. I drank tea; Peter had a beer. The waiter seemed drunk or maybe just apathetic. Soft music from a radio drifted out of the tiny kitchen. I still saw my face every time I looked out of the window.

'Give it up,' Peter said gently. 'Out there is Greenland or Kirghiz or the Steppes, whatever you desire.' Apart from that, he was what he himself liked to call down-to-earth. I asked him about Miroslav, Micha and Sarah. I found it difficult to picture the three of them celebrating New Year's Eve together. 'But that's what Miroslav wants, and after all it reflects the way things really are,' Peter said stubbornly, not wanting to understand. And then we were silent again, and I looked at him, and he looked around the dining car with his dark, narrow eyes, and thought his own thoughts.

I wanted to ask him, 'What are you thinking?' but I didn't. From time to time we smiled at each other.

The train crossed the German–Czech border at Schöna and made a brief stop in Decin. The tracks seemed to be covered with snow, and a yellow light came down from the arching street lamps; the conductors stood around on the platform, breathing into their cupped hands. No one asked to see our passports; the young woman sitting at the table next to us slowly painted her lips red; Peter hummed, drumming on the table top with a beer mat; the waiter was sitting in a corner. December 30th, 8.10 p.m. Still time enough to think about what kind of year it had been and what the coming one would be like. Lots of time actually.

Suddenly my head felt very heavy and I wanted to put it down on the stained tablecloth. The waiter got up, disappeared into the kitchen, came back, and put another lukewarm cup of tea in front of me even though I hadn't asked for it. He didn't return my smile. There was a jolt, and the train began to roll again. Without warning, the young woman at the next table burst out laughing.

'We'll see what happens,' Peter said, as though he were answering a question I had asked. I thought of New Year's Eve last year. I couldn't for the life of me remember where I had been then – at a party? at the beach? at home alone? in a taxi on the way somewhere? New Year's Eve was the one time of the year when I would definitely be unhappy, in a different way each year and yet every year the same. I would have liked to say something about it to Peter, but his face was like the moon – you had to look past it to really see it. Lukas was sitting in his green armchair by the stove waiting for something to happen. Peter wasn't waiting for anything any more, and I had not yet decided.

At 10.48 p.m. the train arrived at the main railway

station in Prague. We took a taxi to Miroslav's place; the fare consumed half our Czech money in one fell swoop. Peter cursed; I didn't care. Micha and Sarah were standing outside the apartment block where Miroslav lived, and they looked happy. The first, premature rockets flew into the night sky; the Moldau was pitch black and not frozen over at all.

'It's nice that you're here,' Sarah said, and I, at a loss for words, replied, 'Yes. Nice that we could come.'

Jacob is very tall. He seems to think he is too tall and walks slightly stooped, usually holding his head tilted to one side as though that would make him look shorter. Maybe it does. When he is sitting down, you can't tell how tall he is. He says he was thin once; he isn't thin any more. His body has become softer and broader. For a long time I was afraid of seeing him naked for the first time. His skin is white, the sort of white I might find unpleasant. Would his body feel like his hands? Jacob isn't good-looking, but it doesn't matter to me whether he is good-looking or not.

I saw him naked for the first time at Hellsee, a lake outside Berlin. It was evening, summertime. That afternoon, talking to him on the phone, I had suggested we go swimming; I was nervous because I knew that I would probably see him naked for the first time, and he, me. Still, that's precisely why I wanted to go to the lake, so as to finally put all this behind me. Surprisingly, Jacob immediately and gleefully agreed. He said, 'That's a great idea.'

Towards evening we drove to Hellsee; that had been his suggestion – he had no idea that I was very familiar with Hellsee. It was Lukas's favourite lake. We parked off the road. I would have parked at the old brick works, but Jacob didn't seem to know about that option. Hellsee is located deep in the woods; you have to walk quite a way to get to the water. There aren't any really good spots for swimming, but if you follow the shore long enough, you come to a bridge that leads to a small island. And on this island there are some lovely places from which to go swimming. Jacob knew about the island.

We followed each other along the forest path, which was too narrow for walking side by side unless one went arm in arm, snuggling up to each other. We didn't do that. I walked behind him. I had to force him to let me walk behind him. Not for anything in the world would I have walked along in front of him with his eyes on the back of my neck or elsewhere. I was dizzy with nervousness, unable to say another word.

It was humid and felt almost as if a thunderstorm were coming; I'd had a headache all day, but now the pain was letting up. I knew it would disappear in the cold water of the lake. When we got to the island, the bridge was gone. Jacob said it had still been there three years ago. I didn't say that it had also still been there a year ago. Only a narrow strip of water separated the island from the shore; it was about nine feet wide and looked muddy and slimy, not particularly deep. Voices could be heard coming from the island.

Jacob said, 'They must have got there somehow'; he had trouble hiding his disappointment about other people being on the island. I took off my shoes, put my right foot into the water to test it, and stepped on a layer of mud and leaves that yielded under my foot. I couldn't decide how deep the water actually was. I pulled my foot back. Jacob was watching me. I walked hesitantly along the shore. It looked as if one could get to the other side by taking one big step. I hated situations like this. Jacob started to pull large branches out of the undergrowth and dropped them again, as if undecided; he looked incompetent.

I said, 'Maybe you could go first.'

He said, 'Of course,' and I suppose it was his cynical, disparaging, that's-exactly-what-you'd-expect-from-a-woman tone of voice that made me just go ahead and do it. Jacob stood where he was, waiting. I put my right foot into the water again. The ground yielded. I lifted my skirt, holding my shoes in my right hand and my sunglasses and cigarettes in my left, and moved away from the shore. I took a big step that almost got me to the other shore, and then the ground under my left foot gave way; that is to say, it was simply not there any more. My foot stepped into nothing but ooze and slime, and I sank amazingly fast into it. I sank up to my chest and kicked and flailed about me; I flung my shoes, sunglasses and cigarettes on to the island shore and took a deep breath; I was making panicky swimming movements.

Behind me I could hear Jacob frantically coming into the water. I turned round halfway and yelled, 'Don't get too close to me' – a sentence he'd later be repeating endlessly amid uncontrollable laughter – I thought having him pull me out of the mud would be even more degrading than drowning in the mire before his eyes. I tugged on the branches and vines floating on the surface of the water; everything gave way, sank, disappeared with a sucking sound; so I just let myself sink in up to my neck and swam the last stretch to the shore of the island.

When I climbed out of the water, I was covered from head to foot with black ooze and rotten leaves. I wiped the dirt from my face with the back of my hand, then turned around towards Jacob. He was standing on the other shore, and I was surprised to see that he had taken off his trousers. He looked ridiculous; I have no idea what I looked like. Simultaneously we burst into wild laughter. He yelled, 'I'm going to swim out into the lake and then to the island! I'll throw you my things!'

And then he undressed and knotted his shirt around his trousers and shoes. I had no chance to think about how he looked. He threw his things over to me but with such poor aim that they fell into the water and immediately sank. So I had to go in again, swearing at the top of my voice. Jacob didn't react but ran along the forest path till I could no longer see him.

The voices we had heard from the other shore were coming closer now; I tried to hide but was too slow. And there they were, standing in front of me, two astonished girls staring at me with undisguised curiosity. I straightened up, said hello and walked past them. But when I was far enough away, I turned round and watched them. Holding on to each other and supporting themselves with branches, they safely reached the other shore at a seemingly shallow spot further down. I walked to the swimming area.

Now there was no one else on the island. I could make out Jacob's head far out in the lake, gallantly far out. He waved, I didn't wave back. My cigarettes were unusable. I took off my wet clothes and rinsed the dirt off with lake water, Jacob's things too. Then I hung everything up on some tree branches, which was pretty futile because the sun was already setting behind the trees on the other side of the lake. Nothing would dry now.

I walked into the water and swam out towards the

middle; the water was warm, Jacob swam over to meet me. His face above his naked shoulders looked funny; his hair was wet, he was laughing. I swam away from him; I had to laugh too; laughing and swimming at the same time wasn't easy. For a while we just played around in the water; he mimicked my, 'Don't get too close to me!' and almost burst a gut laughing. We were nervous, I think, happy and bewildered. At some point I swam back, got out of the water and sat down in the grass, drawing my knees up to my chest; briefly I felt cold, then no longer, I would have liked a cigarette; I was naked; that couldn't be changed.

Jacob came out a little later; now I could see him, his naked body looked just as I had imagined it. It wasn't awful. He sat down next to me and put his arm around my shoulders; his teeth were chattering. I looked out at the lake, at the water; a light layer of dust seemed to be suspended over it. On the opposite shore a fisherman was throwing out his nets; night was falling. Now and then we laughed softly.

He began to kiss me, my shoulders, my arms, my neck. I could smell him; he smelled sweetish. He embraced me and I embraced him; my eyes were almost closed but through the narrow slits I could see his penis, watch it get big; it scared me. Jacob pushed my shoulders till I was lying on my back and then he lay down on top of me, looked into my face. Close up his face seemed totally strange. I could look past him up into the treetops; it wasn't the first time I had seen them from this perspective on the island in the Hellsee. Jacob looked at me as if he wanted to ask something, and I closed my eyes. He tried to make love to me, but it didn't work. I hadn't seen his penis getting smaller and tiny again; I would have liked to; it would have calmed me. He lay on top of me like this for quite a while.

Eventually it grew completely dark and then cold. We got up, packed up our wet things and crossed the water at the same place the girls had, hours earlier. We walked naked through the woods, back to the car without meeting anyone; we were now walking hand in hand, close together. Jacob got a raincoat and an old shirt out of the boot; he gave me the shirt; then we drove back to town. I didn't want to let go of his hand during the entire trip. The moon was a sickle. We stopped briefly at Anna's. Through the door she handed me a pair of trousers and a sweater without asking any questions. Then we drove to Jacob's friend Sasha, where Jacob disappeared into the bathroom for two hours, drying his things with a hair dryer while I waited with Sasha in the kitchen and drank a great deal of red wine very fast.

Several times Sasha impatiently asked me, 'Why doesn't he simply wear one of my shirts?' I didn't answer him. Then, at last, Jacob came out of the bathroom, looking as though nothing had happened. We drank some more wine, and that caused me to say to Jacob, 'I'd like to spend the rest of my life with you.' He said my name. When it got light, we left.

Peter said, 'Once we get to Miroslav's house, we have to walk up one thousand five hundred stairs, but from there you have the most beautiful view of the Moldau.' The stairs were stone steps, and maybe there were more than one thousand five hundred. When we finally arrived at the top, I was out of breath and no longer wanted to see the Moldau, which Peter – more regretfully than triumphantly – wanted to point out to me from the window at the top of the staircase. Countless doors led off from the stairwell, and at one of these stood Miroslav, a short man. He bowed to us, didn't quite want to get out of the doorway, and said in a gentle, barely audible voice, 'Welcome.'

Sarah pushed past him. The apartment was surprisingly large – five rooms, all of them almost empty and unused except for the living room where a huge couch and five easy chairs were crowded in front of a television set. The air was stale and stuffy; there were candles burning; the television was on but with the sound turned off. Miroslav dropped down on the sofa and immediately closed his eyes. There was a thick layer of stuff on the floor around the sofa; later I identified it as the shells of pumpkin and sunflower seeds, pistachios and peanuts.

Sarah appropriated all the rooms, including the kitchen by dropping jackets, shoes, hats and bags full of New Year firecrackers here, there and everywhere. She ignored Miroslav, ardently kissing Micha whenever she happened to pass by him. Micha kept breaking into cool, ironic laughter; he seemed either drunk or stoned. I went over to the window; now I did want to see the Moldau and Prague, the golden city. I wanted to reassure myself that coming here, being here with Peter, leaving Lukas alone, had been the right thing to do. I knew very well that Lukas liked being alone; at least he liked being away from me.

The blinds had all been lowered; Sarah raised them, one by one, forcefully, brutally. Very far down, very far away, the Moldau was black and shiny. On the horizon, factory chimneys were sending up smoke. I could hear Miroslav's heavy, exhausted breathing. Peter touched my arm; I turned round and followed him through all the rooms to the last one. It had a bed, a small lamp on the floor, nothing else. 'Would you like to sleep here?' Peter asked, not looking at me. The bed was too narrow for two.

Gratefully I said, 'Yes.' He put my bag down at the foot of the bed, and when I hugged him, he put his head on my shoulder. Then he said softly, 'But Miroslav is sadder than I am.'

Miroslav had poured himself some schnapps, a large water-glass full. He got up again and stared at the still-muted TV screen on which a wolf was walking through a snowy landscape. Sarah was sitting on Micha's lap.

Miroslav looked away from the TV and into my eyes and said, 'My name is Miroslav. Would you like some schnapps?'

I said very distinctly, 'No, thank you,' and he shrugged and turned away again. I sat down in one of the dusty easy chairs; for some reason I didn't feel like taking my coat off yet. Peter brought me a glass of bitter black tea. For a while he walked around, apparently putting things away; then he sat down next to me. Sarah was talking into Micha's ear; now and then she turned to Miroslav and shouted something at him. Miroslav did not react.

Very far away firecrackers were exploding. The whole room smelled of Becherovka liqueur, hashish and ciga-rette smoke. Eventually everyone was drunk and rowdy, even Miroslav and Peter, but Peter was getting abusive and insulting. So I took his hand, and we sat there like that, hurt but together; I steadfastly returned Miroslav's drunken stare. When it grew light, when Miroslav switched off the TV and put on some Czech records to which Sarah and Micha danced – closely entwined, forming a single silhouette against the shiny grey windows

– I went to bed. I walked through all the rooms, not closing any of the doors behind me; taking off only my shoes and coat, I lay down on my back on the narrow bed and listened to the music, Sarah's laughter, Peter's eager, imploring voice, Micha's singing.

Jacob isn't shy about starting brief conversations about love, again and again. He likes talking about love, about our love and love in general. He never says anything he might regret later; he doesn't regret things. He insists that nobody will ever say about us, 'Love was their undoing.' He really gets a kick out of saying that. I wonder . . . up to now I've never thought about failing. Jacob is sure we have time, lots of time, all the time in the world. He knows that the things that upset us about each other, that we can't express, that we question in vain, all the things that remain incomprehensible and hurtful, that these are already the first stage of love. He knows more than I do. He says, 'I'd like to grow old with you.' Then he turns around and leaves. It's the best he can do.

I no longer remember how long I slept in Prague the night before the last night of the year. When I awoke, the sun was shining brightly into the room, the windows were open, and someone had covered me with a blanket while I was asleep. Micha, Miroslav, Sarah and Peter were sitting in the living room as if they'd never gone to sleep. On the table in front of them were used breakfast dishes, coffee mugs, egg cups. Micha said, 'Good morning.' It was the first thing he had said to me since we arrived. I half waved and quickly went into the bathroom, locked the door behind me, and sat down on the rim of the bath. I had no idea what I looked like. I listened. I found being together with Sarah, Peter, Micha and Miroslav difficult. I turned the tap on, then off again.

Peter knocked on the door and asked, 'Coffee, tea or juice?' For a moment I was happy to hear his voice, glad he was here.

For breakfast I had three dusty Czech rolls, bananas and cornflakes, and drank four cups of coffee as well as some water. It seemed as if I couldn't stop eating. The TV was already on again. Miroslav lay on the couch, his eyes half closed. Micha was watching TV, Sarah was sorting firecrackers; from time to time she spoke softly to Miroslav, who then smiled absent-mindedly. Peter was sitting next to me, smoking cigarettes, not talking.

I knew that we wouldn't be going into the city. We wouldn't be walking across the Charles Bridge and into Josefov, wouldn't be crossing Wenceslas Square, wouldn't be going to see Hradcany Castle, wouldn't sit in the Café Slavia drinking hot chocolate with whipped cream and gazing at the Moldau. We wouldn't stand at Kafka's grave and wouldn't go up the hill in the cable car. Ridiculous to do that. Never mind that we were in Prague. We could just as well have been in Moscow or Zagreb or Cairo.

And wherever we would have been, Peter would now have opened his first bottle of beer, taken a swig, sighed, put it down again, and rolled himself a cigarette. Once he said, 'Mexico is the only place where I'd like to sit and drink schnapps by the side of a dusty country road in the midday heat, because in Mexico you can fall off a chair and never have to get up, never.' I might have thought that offensive, but I didn't. I understood it, in a certain way I understood it.

Miroslav didn't seem to have understood it, not yet. He sat up, ran his fingers through his hair, yawned, opened his eyes wide several times and said, 'Well now, what would you like to do?' He spoke German with a muted Czech accent. I had been afraid for his sake that we would arrive at this point.

Micha and Peter did not react at all, but Sarah looked up from her firecrackers and said, 'Eat some roast pork with *Knoedel*. That's what we'd really like to do.'

But Miroslav didn't quite understand and said, 'In the Old Town?'

And Sarah said, 'No, not in the Old Town, no way. Where I'd most like to go is to that place in the Vietnamese market right around the corner.'

Micha snickered. Peter got up and left the room. Miroslav stared at Sarah and said, 'I think I don't quite understand you. You're in Prague and you want to eat at the Vietnamese market round the corner; you don't want to see anything, you don't want to see my city?'

And Sarah said calmly, 'No. I don't. I don't think the others want to either.'

And then with his left hand Miroslav pushed all the dishes off the table. Micha said, 'C'mon now, really.'

Sarah began to yell.

I got up and went to look for Peter who was sitting on the windowsill in the dark little kitchen, staring at the firewall of the building in the rear courtyard. He said, 'I'm sorry about that. I should have told you what it would be like.' He didn't look at me. I leaned against the wall next to him and looked out too. The firewall was grey and smooth. I said, 'Don't feel bad; I would have come along anyway.' Peter laughed as if he didn't believe me.

In the living room, Sarah and Miroslav were shouting at each other. Miroslav was shouting in Czech. The TV sound had been turned up again, presumably by Micha. Peter and I waited in the kitchen without speaking. The gas water heater above the sink went on with a hiss and then off again. Bags of pistachios and peanuts were piled up on the kitchen shelf next to countless bottles of schnapps. The apartment door slammed shut; Peter and I were still waiting, polite, lethargic. Then Sarah was standing in the hall; she said, 'We can go now.' We walked down the one thousand five hundred steps. Miroslav had disappeared. Actually it was as if he had never been there.

Outside it was cold and sunny. The grey smoke from the factory chimneys was rising straight up into the air. I walked behind Sarah, Micha and Peter. Cars droned past us. Freighters moved on the Moldau. I knew the Old Town was behind me – a panorama of bridges and church steeples, Hradcany Castle way up on the hill. I didn't turn around.

The Vietnamese market was one block away, a muddy car park on which draughty shacks were sinking into the dirt; the snow Miroslav had told Sarah about had turned to filthy packed ice. Some Vietnamese stood in tight groups around metal barrels in which fires smouldered, acting as if they didn't have the slightest connection with the garish stuff that hung from the plastic awnings of their stalls – kitchen brushes, images of the Virgin Mary, sweaters, indoor fountains, cans of food, children's pyjamas. A gust of wind blowing across the square slammed the awnings against each other and set the plastic hangers clattering; the fires in the barrels blazed up. Sarah walked ahead of us through the alleyways between the stalls, her hands deep in the pockets of her army jacket. Micha followed her, a proud triumphant expression on his face. The Vietnamese paid no attention to us.

In a dark shack we ordered wild boar goulash with *Knoedel*, and without asking us they immediately put four glasses of Becherovka on our table. I slid mine over to Peter, who tossed it down without hesitating. Oriental-eyed teenagers hunkered down at the counter. We said little to one another, pushed the beer mats around on the chequered tablecloth. I rolled a cigarette, took a drag and passed it on. The waiter set our food down at one end of the table, and we handed round the plates. Soft meat in brown gravy and something resembling slices of dry white bread. 'This is bread,' Micha said. 'No,' Peter said, 'these are *Knoedel*, slices of big Czech dumpling, and this is the way they're supposed to be.' I ate and had the absurd thought, 'Nothing is missing. Nothing at all is missing. It's all just the way it's supposed to be. Everything is simply grand.' I had to stop eating because suddenly I was shaking with laughter, but no one joined in.

Outside dirty rain was falling. The waiter cleared the table and said, 'The food was very good.' Then he poured more Becherovka, stubborn and insistent. We sat there for another hour or two, paid and left. It had grown darker; the Vietnamese were packing up their stuff. I asked Peter whether they also celebrated New Year's Eve, and he answered patiently, 'Fireworks come from Vietnam. New Year's Eve comes from Vietnam. Of course they celebrate New Year's Eve, but at a different time and probably also in a different way. They carry around dragons. And in the meantime they watch us.' I hooked my arm under his and wished he would go on talking like that.

Sarah bought two cheap metal rings at a jewellery stand. Micha bought some rockets and small firework cannons from a Vietnamese man with a childlike Eskimo face; he was wrapped in furs. The rain-soaked firecrackers were done up in red parchment paper. Far away, bells were ringing. Green and red lights blinked on in the shack where we'd eaten. The market square now stood empty, muddy and desolate. Micha ran down a long alley, threw his cannon into the air and gave a yell. The Vietnamese ducked and ran round the corner. Golden rain, silver rain, pyramids of stars, reddish sheaves of fire, Micha's crazy, hoarse voice, very far away.

Peter, running, dragged me from one alley to the next. I didn't care why he was suddenly running; I ran too. We ran through a labyrinth of plastic awnings and wooden structures, an ancient woman wearing a turban on her head was bent over a kettle, dogs were tearing at rubbish bins, no daylight at all now, huge puddles, a feeling in my stomach as if I were dreaming, and then back to the main street, the Moldau, the traffic, the light of the street lamps along the river. The sky now black, a small moon near the factory chimneys. Prague, December 31st, seven o'clock in the evening.

I have known Jacob for almost a year. I don't think about whether that's a long time or not. Jacob says we'll be together for ever. This makes me uneasy because even now everything between him and me seems to consist only of memories. I once went to an exhibition with Jacob. The exhibition was in a castle on the shore of a lake in an area where he had lived as a child. We went there by car. He showed me 'his' special places; as we were crossing a river, he proudly said, 'And this is the Spree.' I was aware of the meaning of this excursion.

In the evening we arrived at the castle. The castle grounds were deserted. Not a single car in the car park; on the lawn by the lake a man was ponderously setting up a projector for an outdoor movie. We seemed to be the only visitors; the young woman at the ticket office was startled when we entered the hall and she issued the admission tickets to us as if she were doing it for the very first time.

Jacob had been saying all day long that there was supposed to be one good picture among the fifty bad ones at this exhibition. But we couldn't find the good picture. All the pictures were dreadful; so were the installations, video projections and sculptures. We walked through the rooms hand in hand, opened drawers of built-in cupboards, concealed doors and casement windows with views of the lake. The castle was beautiful, dilapidated, run down; the cupboards empty; behind the concealed doors were plastic pails, disinfectant and brooms; the brocade wallpaper had been painted brown; and grey linoleum covered the parquet floors. Sometimes we stopped and embraced awkwardly; Jacob seemed to be in a good mood, and I was too, although the strange perfection of the day had made me taciturn, dull, not expecting anything. We would stop to hug, then let go of each other and walk on; we didn't talk about what we saw; we were of one mind.

The last installation in the last room, in front of which hung a black felt curtain, was entitled *Wohin des Wegs?* – Where are you going? I drew back the curtain and we entered a room whose walls were completely covered with wooden slats. They reached almost all the way to the ceiling, letting in only a narrow sliver of light. It was quite dark; what light there was seemed to float just under the ceiling, milky and dusty, except on the right wall; there the evening sun was casting a very small, glowing, golden rectangle of light. The room was warm, a little stuffy, somewhat like an attic in the summertime; it was the sort of warmth that enters your body and robs it of resistance. We stood there a while, gazing at the rectangle of light, then Jacob went outside and I followed him.

Later, driving home through the night, we talked about it. Jacob said, 'The artist can't have known about that strange spot of light. So that can't have been the point; it's just a meaningless installation except that we happened to enter the room at just the moment when the evening sun projected this admittedly very beautiful effect on the wall.' He actually used the words *effect* and *admittedly*, but that wasn't why I later thought that at that moment we were going in different directions. It was the significant difference in our perception, in what we believed in or were ready to believe. I was sure that the whole point of the installation was precisely this golden rectangle of light. The evening sun, a clear sky, a certain incidence of light and a brief instant, he and I, the walk through the castle, and the moment we accidentally entered the room, not too late and not too soon, and the question *Wohin des Wegs?* – Where are you going? I would have known my answer. Jacob didn't believe me, and he hadn't even thought about what his answer would be.

Later, too, when we told someone else about it, they said that there had already been shrines in the pyramids, built in such a way that at certain times of the day they were, so to speak, blessed by light, but Jacob refused to be persuaded. He did not believe it.

We drove back to town, sunflowers on the back seat and the car ashtray full of nervously smoked cigarettes. The knowledge that we had spent a day together, had endured it, and had even been happy made us content, lethargic and dull. Towards midnight we were back in

Berlin, went to have some wine, and argued. Jacob said, 'We should have stayed; we should have stayed there in the country.' Maybe. But we didn't. This I remember. From time to time.

Back at the apartment, Miroslav was washing dishes in the kitchen one thousand five hundred steps above the Moldau. The TV was on, and the layer of peanut shells around the sofa seemed to have grown even deeper. Micha and Sarah were standing in front of the kitchen shelf as if they were at a supermarket; after some reflection they put two bottles of schnapps into their jacket pockets and disappeared again. I knew they intended to get engaged before the end of the year: 'Down by the river under the highway bridge,' Sarah had said in a tone of voice that brooked no argument. I didn't know whether Miroslav knew about their plans. Peter opened all the windows, lowered the volume on the TV, lay down on the sofa and closed his eyes. Outside, the traffic rumbled by. The peanut shells rustled; I sat on the edge of the sofa, undecided. Then I went to join Miroslav in the kitchen.

He was still washing dishes – Sarah's, Micha's, Peter's and mine. I took a teatowel off the chair and began to dry. I expected him to say, 'You don't have to do that.' He was slowly, deliberately washing a saucer; he cleared his throat, turned to me and said, 'You don't have to do that.' I smiled politely and said, 'I know.' I didn't say, 'I know, but I feel sorry for you. This whole business is regrettable, and I think I ought to dry the dishes now to keep you from thinking you're a complete chump. So let me dry, let me do it.' We looked at each other in the dim light cast by a lamp clamped above the sink, then he turned away. He was using too much detergent. We were

213

silent for quite a while, then he cleared his throat again and said, 'You're not doing so well.' I immediately and defiantly said, 'Yes, but you're not doing much better.' He gave a short laugh and made a birdlike movement with his head.

I no longer remember whether I wanted to talk to him. He was now handing me the washed plates and cups, each time making an apologetic sound. Close up I could see how old and tired his face was. He said, 'And Peter – is he your boyfriend?'

I was surprised that he seemed to be concerned about us. I said as matter-of-factly as possible, 'No. He's not.'

And he considerately said nothing more for a long time. When I had finished drying the dishes, he wiped off the table, swept the palm of his hand over the chair seat and invited me to sit down. I shook my head. He smiled a forced smile. I twisted the teatowel, I felt I had done enough for him, but he didn't want to let me go. He sat down, got up again, pulled open the kitchen cabinet, and said, 'Are you hungry? Let's have supper together, fish fingers, bread and wine. How about it?' I didn't answer.

He dragged a frying pan out of the cabinet, tore open the package of fish fingers, sliced some bread. I could hear Peter sigh in the living room. It sounded as if he were sighing in his sleep. Miroslav turned on the radio. The oil in the pan sizzled, the water heater rumbled, he was making a lot of noise, and when it was finally noisy enough, he asked, almost singing the words, 'Then who is your boyfriend?'

I said, 'Lukas. You don't know him, and he isn't really my boyfriend. I only wish he were.' I had the feeling that I wasn't talking about myself at all, but rather about Lukas.

Miroslav dropped the frozen fish into the pan, jumped

aside as the oil splattered, and said, 'You are beautiful. You're not stupid. What's wrong with him that he doesn't want to be your boyfriend?'

I said almost in a whisper, 'Miroslav, that's really a foolish question. He doesn't want to be my boyfriend because he doesn't love me. That's all.' Miroslav shook his head like a clown. The radio was playing Czech folk music.

Now I did sit down after all, not because I wanted to go on with this conversation but because I suddenly felt quite ill. I thought of Micha and Sarah under some road bridge by the water, of the little metal rings, the traffic roaring overhead, the brackish smell of the river, Sarah's face. I wondered whether they would make some sort of promise to each other when they exchanged rings. What do you promise each other when you get engaged? Maybe I could ask Miroslav, he might know. I looked at him. He was standing by the stove, turning the fish, slicing tomatoes, sprinkling salt and pepper over them, and then he interrupted my train of thought and said, 'You could come here. You could simply come here. You could live here with me. You could give it a try. We would learn to make it work. I have money and a job; you'd be secure; we'd learn to love each other – it's possible to learn to do that.'

I said, 'Yes. I could. But I won't.' My heartbeat seemed to be slowing down. He looked at me. I looked past him, out of the window at the firewall in the rear courtyard, which was no longer distinguishable from the sky. I thought about his proposition. I sat there and thought about it and imagined something as precisely and painfully as possible. That was the end of our conversation.

\*　　\*　　\*

Early in the year when I first met Jacob and probably already loved him – loved him instantly and on the spot – he avoided me, and I spent nights waiting for him in pubs. I left things to chance, going to any old pub where I knew he had sometimes gone to have a drink. I would sit down at the bar, order a glass of wine, and wait for him. I would look out into the street through the steamed-up windows, and if someone came walking by who had his shape, his posture, who perhaps slowed down, stopped, pushed open the door and came in, my heart would skip a beat. Sometimes it was he, sometimes not. Now, since I don't have to wait for Jacob any more because he no longer avoids me, there are nights when I sit next to him in a bar and someone walks past outside the window, slows down, looks in through a steamed-up pane, then turns and keeps going. That's when my heart misses a beat in a sort of habitual shock, and only at that moment do I realize it can't have been Jacob. There are nights when I think quite clearly and lucidly, 'I'll call Jacob, ask him whether he wouldn't like to go out; the night is so warm, we could have a drink together, just a little glass of wine.' And then I turn to him; I don't have to ask him; he's already here.

Towards nine in the evening, Peter and I left Miroslav by himself in his apartment. Sarah and Micha had not returned, and Miroslav told us he didn't intend to clink glasses at midnight with anybody to welcome in the New Year; there was nothing he wanted to wish anyone, and as for himself, he didn't want to be on the receiving end of any good wishes either; we were free to go. We sat with him till he had eaten all his fish fingers, the tomato and onion sandwiches; we sat there, one of us on his right and the other on his left, and said nothing. Then we set off, leaving him sitting on the sofa; he was wearing slippers, a cardigan, and a scarf around his neck. He looked like an old ghost. *Janáčkovo nábřeží, Smetanovo nábřeží, Masarykovo nábřeží.*

We walked along the Moldau, holding hands, and I remember Peter saying, 'These Czechs can really manage to accommodate the most consonants in the most beautiful way in their language.' He said, 'I love Prague.'

That surprised me. I said, 'Why do you love Prague?'

He said, 'What are you asking me?'

I held his hand very tight. I think in those days we didn't trust words; we wanted something else to speak for us – but what? The Moldau, the river, the wintry cold, the halos around the street lamps if you squeezed your eyes almost shut. All those things, and all the questions without answers, the observations without questions. We were together, tomorrow that would no longer be the case; there was nothing else to say. That is what I believed. I'm not sure – do I still believe that today?

We wandered through the streets until it got too cold, had a beer and some tea in a Czech restaurant. Coming back from the toilet, I couldn't find Peter and our table for a long time – he didn't look much different from the other people there. The Czechs sat together; they were rather quiet, didn't seem to attach much importance to New Year's Eve. It wasn't until eleven thirty that it got a little noisy. Some people paid and left; I would have liked to know where they were going.

Shortly before midnight, we were standing on a bridge over the Moldau; we didn't have any champagne or fire-crackers, not even a watch. We were betwixt and between two years, unanchored, somewhere; then fireworks exploded over the Hradcany, and everyone around us embraced; we embraced too. 'Happy New Year, Peter. All good wishes. It will all turn out for the best, it just takes time, and don't be sad, I'm sad enough already.' 'All good wishes to you,' Peter said.

Around one o'clock we walked back. The coloured paper in which the now burnt-out firecrackers had been wrapped turned the snow at the kerbs red and blue. My hands were cold, my feet were too. I was exhausted; I knew that tomorrow I would be going home. New Year's Eve was over, I had survived it.

The apartment was too hot; Miroslav lay in the bath; Micha was sitting on the sofa, a little paper hat on his head, staring at the TV. Sarah wasn't there. There was dirty confetti on the floor. We sat down with Micha and poured some schnapps and clinked glasses: 'Happy New Year.' I sipped a tiny bit and it burned my tongue for a long time. Miroslav was splashing around in the bathroom; on TV the Czech Television Ballet was dancing before a dilapidated beach setting. Micha hummed a little to himself, indifferent, indestructible. The little metal ring glittered on his left hand. 'Where's Sarah?' Peter asked.

'Outside, she's setting off her firecrackers,' Micha said, 'and where were you?' Just then Miroslav walked past us in an embarrassing bathrobe. Outside, rockets exploded in the night sky, sporadically and far apart. Peter, Micha and I sat on the sofa, watching TV. Now and then Micha said something like, 'Well, an hour has gone by already.' We were eating peanuts, crisps, bananas, caramels and sour pickles, and then I got up and said, 'Good night.'

The last time I drove out to the country with Jacob, we stopped at a petrol station on a country road because I

had to use the toilet. I climbed out of the car and asked
Jacob if he wanted me to get him something. He said,
'Yes, a bar of chocolate.' I went in; the fat woman attendant didn't say hello but charged me a mark to use the
toilet. She said, 'Doesn't he have to go too?' which amused
me.

I said, 'No, he doesn't.' I bought the bar of chocolate.
When I came back from the toilet, the fat attendant was
standing next to the one and only petrol pump, close-
mouthed, arms crossed. Jacob had driven the car as far
as the exit, had got out, and was now leaning against the
open car door looking across the road. I walked towards
him and sensed the attendant's eyes on my back. I saw
what she saw: a car with its doors open, a man waiting,
a woman; the woman gets in on the passenger side; the
man gets in too; the doors slam shut; he starts the engine;
they drive off; the car moves away and is soon out of
sight. This, when all is said and done, was the only time
I had a sense of myself and Jacob – through the eyes of
a female petrol station attendant at a dilapidated station
on a country road.

I woke up in Prague in the early hours of the new year. I
woke up and for a moment didn't know where I was.
The room was dark; I could hear someone else's breathing,
deep and calm. Outside the window the sky was black,
no stars, no moon. I sat up. Peter was lying in a sleeping
bag on the floor next to my bed, curled up like a child,
his head on his folded hands. From far away came the
sounds of soft voices and music. I got up; the floor was
cold; the floorboards creaked. I didn't want to wake Peter,
not for anything – if I did, wouldn't I then have to ask
him to lie down with me on that narrow bed because the

floor was much too cold? I tiptoed through the empty rooms; the doors were all open except for the last one, the door to Miroslav's room was closed. Through the crack at the bottom came a green light.

In the kitchen I drank a glass of water from the tap; the water tasted metallic and bitter; I was thirsty and drank too fast; my stomach contracted. I thought, Maybe I'm homesick, maybe I'm yearning for something, maybe I had a bad dream, and then I remembered that Lukas, who never wanted to talk about love, did say something about it, but just once – Love was abuse, one way or the other.

I put the glass in the sink and walked down the hall and carefully opened the door to Miroslav's room. The green light was coming from the television set, the voices and the music too. Miroslav was sitting in an easy chair surrounded by peanut shells. He was awake and looked at me as though he had been waiting for me. He was alone. Sarah and Micha seemed to have vanished, and maybe Peter wasn't really lying on the floor next to the bed at the other end of the apartment. I stood there on the threshold, taking deep breaths as though I wanted to commit a smell to memory, and with the smell the present state of affairs – that room, as green as an aquarium, full of smoke and unreality, the meaningless things drifting around in it, a sofa, a table, a bookshelf, glasses and bottles, stones from the Giant Mountains, framed photographs, dried plants, Miroslav in his armchair, a figure without bones, toneless, and somewhere there was me. I was also there somewhere, in some other night, and the look that passed between us, between Miroslav and me, a look from him to me and from me to him; and we would be sitting there like that always and for ever.

'Would you like to know,' Miroslav now said, and his voice sounded amazingly clear, 'would you like to know the word for "sad" in Czech?'

'Yes,' I said, 'of course I'd like to know.'

'Well,' Miroslav said, and although he didn't move an inch, the distance between us seemed to shrink, 'it's *smutna. Smutna* is the word for "sad".'

Jacob said, 'And then?' It's eleven o'clock at night; we've finished the Chinese food. I ate only a little but talked a lot instead. Jacob didn't notice. He lights a cigarette and hands it to me, a gesture that is supposed to be very meaningful. He says, 'And then? What happened then?' I take the cigarette and pour myself another cup of tea; we're still sitting on the floor, a position that will later make it easier to kiss and to touch each other. It is warm in the room; outside it's cold, two more weeks till New Year's Eve. I say, 'Nothing happened then. The next morning I went back to Berlin. Peter brought me to the train. He stayed on in Prague and came back by car two days later with Sarah and Micha.' Jacob smiles knowingly. For a while he is silent, thinking about what I told him. I know that he'll soon ask me what Peter is doing today, where he is and how he is, how Micha and Sarah are, and if they're still engaged. And what shall I say in reply? Peter lives on Grell Strasse in a beautiful room that looks out on horse chestnut and plane trees; there's always beer and a bottle of schnapps in the refrigerator. Whenever I come to see him, he opens the door, and then I sit down next to him on the sofa, hold his hand, and put my head on his shoulder. I think: You ought to stay – but I don't.

Sarah and Micha separated six months after that New Year's Eve. Sarah now lives with a lawyer on Kurfürstendam.

221

In June, Micha fell out of the window of a third floor apartment and barely survived the fall. Since then he's been a different person and says he is through with this world and doesn't have much time left, not that it makes him sad. And then there's the other story, also true, about the morning in May when Sarah and Micha held up the Reinickendorf branch of the Deutsche Bank, and then didn't leave their house for three months, not until September when they went to South America with Peter. From there they write letters and send packages containing coffee, liquor and sugar cane. Now I have to laugh.

Jacob looks at me and says amiably, 'What are you laughing about? What are they doing now – Peter, Sarah and Micha?'

I raise my eyebrows, try to look enigmatic. I'd like to say, 'Every story has an ending.' I'd like to say that our story will have an ending too, and that I know what that ending will be. I want to ask him whether he'd like to know, I would really like to tell him about it.

He straightens his legs and changes his position slightly, moving closer to me. In about three and a half minutes he will touch me. Maybe he'll say, 'Tell me.' Maybe I'll say, 'I can't help trying to imagine the future, Jacob. I can't stop thinking that sometime or other and maybe quite soon I'll be telling someone the next story, a story about you.' He sighs and shrugs. Then he looks at me with his brown eyes – which are a bit too large – both direct and doubting. He is going to ask me one of those questions for which I never have an answer, a question that turns him on, puts him in the mood – 'Which do you prefer, a kiss on the back of your neck or a bite into your Adam's apple?' I wish he wouldn't do that. I wish he'd leave. And he does leave, only not yet.

# Love for Ari Oskarsson

*Some enchanted evening*
*you may see a stranger,*
*you may see a stranger*
*across a crowded room*

It was in October that Owen and I left town to make the journey to Tromsø. During the summer we had applied for gigs at music festivals all over Europe, sending off a silly little CD full of love songs. We didn't get a single invitation, and there wasn't any positive response from elsewhere either, and so when I found an invitation to the Northern Lights Festival in Norway in my mailbox in September, I assumed it was a gag. Owen tore open the envelope and waved air and bus tickets in front of my face. He said, 'It's not a joke.' The Northern Lights Festival had invited us to spend a week in Tromsø. I had to search through the atlas for a long time before I even found Tromsø. A concert in a small club. No fee. But free room and board and a one hundred per cent probability of getting to see the Northern Lights. 'What is a

Northern Light?' I asked Owen, and Owen said, 'Matter. Matter flung out into space, a lot of hot electrons, exploded stars, how do I know.'

One of the songs on our CD was called, 'I'm off to Paris'. 'I'm off to Paris, to Tokyo, Lisbon and Berne, to Antwerp and Rome. I'm going around the world, *and I'm just lookin' for you*, believe me, I'm just lookin' for you.' It was out-and-out silly. Owen sang it sort of to himself in a tired, childish voice, plucking at a string on his guitar, and I accompanied him with high notes on the piano; it was silly, but it had a sort of foolish charm, especially, I suppose, for people who didn't understand the words.

Owen and I actually had fun working on pointless things. We liked spending time together. We liked talking about what we could do, would do if we had the money, if we were different, lived different lives. Owen had his friends, and I had mine. We didn't have a life together; we weren't in love with each other; we could have gone our separate ways without missing any of it. We had recorded this CD and burned it ourselves; it was our third joint production. We gave it to our friends, took it around to the Off-Off and Fringe festivals, and by the time Tromsø sent us the invitation, I had already decided to stop making music.

Owen hadn't decided anything. Sometimes he did one thing and sometimes another, but he didn't intend to make any decisions. He could actually do quite a lot of things, he could sing and dance and was a passably good actor, and he could lay floor tiles, install plumbing, drive a truck and baby-sit. Owen was looking forward to Tromsø. He said, 'C'mon, be happy, it's a chance to take a trip, a trip somewhere. Is that something, or isn't it?' and I said, 'Yes, that is something.'

We would fly to Oslo and from there go on by bus. In those days Owen was having an affair with a singer. She sang with a fairly well-known band, sang songs with the same sort of words as our 'I'm off to Paris', singing them, admittedly, with an amazing earnestness. She was very beautiful and yet always looked a little the worse for wear. She drove us to the airport and seemed to be having difficulty coping with the fact that Owen was going away for a week. We stopped at a multi-storey car park just before the airport.

Above us the planes coming in to land roared by so low that you could see the faces of the passengers at the tiny windows. We took the lift to the roof of the multi-storey. Under her fur coat the singer wore a strapless evening gown and net stockings. She took off the fur coat, and that impressed me because it was pretty cold. At the edge of the roof she struck a pose, throwing back her head and gracefully extending her long, beautiful arms towards the sky. When one of the planes took off just above our heads, she went up on tiptoe so that it seemed as if she could take hold of the lowered landing gear and fly away with it.

I whispered, 'What's that supposed to mean?'

And Owen said theatrically, 'She's saying goodbye, man. That's goodbye. That's what it looks like. I'm not supposed to forget her. That's what it means.' The singer looked at Owen and draped the fur coat over her bare shoulders. We left the multi-storey and drove on to the airport. Owen seemed preoccupied. He suffered from an extreme fear of flying and was busy performing a lot of therapeutic coping routines, breathing techniques, reciting poems and doing stretch exercises. He took a swig from a bottle containing some sort of marsh marigold preparation. Then he scribbled something on a little piece of paper and balled it up in his fist. The singer tried to wrench the paper out of his hand. Owen wouldn't open his fist. The SAS ticket agent became impatient and said, 'Window seat or aisle?' and Owen almost shouted at him, 'Aisle, man!' – he couldn't possibly sit by the window.

Then he dutifully kissed the singer hard on the lips innumerable times; I looked at the ticket agent apologetically. Our baggage rumbled away on the conveyor belt. The singer held on to Owen's neck and said plaintively, 'What does it say on that slip of paper, Owen? What does it say?'

I knew that what it said was 'Daddy loves you, Paulie'. Paul was Owen's son. Before every flight Owen would write this message on a slip of paper and hold it in his hand for the entire flight. He imagined that after the plane crashed, when they found him dead yet miraculously unscathed, they would pry open his clenched fist, and the world would know of whom Owen was thinking during the last minutes of his life. It was an improbable notion but seemed to calm him. Owen snapped, 'None of your business.'

The singer stayed behind the glass partition of the departure lounge. I turned off my mobile phone. Looking through the large windows, I could see the propeller plane that would fly us to Oslo. I turned away.

Tromsø was bleak. I can't remember ever having seen a city in the North that wasn't bleak except maybe Stockholm. But Tromsø was exceptionally bleak. In all those cities and towns it always looks as if the harbour had been there first, then a few fishermen's houses went up around it, then a small fish factory and more houses, and then a bigger factory, a road into town, a road out of town, a shopping centre, a 'downtown', and a suburb that seemed to spread out indiscriminately according to no plan, spoiling the landscape, until it petered out.

Nobody picked us up at the small bus station, and no one answered the phone at the office of the Northern Lights Festival. 'What a miserable, rotten place,' Owen said. We were standing outside the bus station at a ramshackle stand, drinking lukewarm coffee from flimsy plastic cups. The wind was decidedly colder than at home. When I called the Northern Lights Festival again an hour later, the phone was answered by a woman who sounded as if she were a hundred years old. She didn't understand my questions but then, in English, she huffishly blurted out the address of a guesthouse in the centre of town. '*Gunnarshus. See if you can stay there.*'

I shouted into the telephone, '*Festival! Music Festival, you know! Northern Lights!* And we are invited, dammit!'

And she shouted back in impressively accent-free German, 'The festival has been cancelled!' Then she hung up.

I walked over to Owen, who was feeding the remnants of his frankfurter to a wretched-looking dog. He looked unreal with his guitar slung over his shoulder. I said, 'The festival has been cancelled,' took my backpack and went back inside the bus station. Had the bus to Oslo been standing there ready to depart, I would have climbed aboard and gone back at once, but of course the last bus to Oslo had already left. Owen didn't follow me. I studied the departure schedules, the incomprehensible Norwegian words, the advertisements for liquorice sticks and orange juice. Then I went outside again. Owen was still standing at the hot dog stand; he now had a bottle of light beer in one hand. I said, hesitantly, 'We could give Gunnar's Guesthouse a try.'

Owen said, 'All right then,' and we set out.


The Gunnarshus was on a small street downtown. Anyway, it was in a district that seemed to be more or less the centre of Tromsø. Surprisingly there were many little shops and quite a few pubs and taverns, two big supermarkets, several hot dog stands and a McDonald's. The guesthouse was dark except for two lit-up windows on the second floor. It looked deserted and run-down. Owen hit the door with the palm of his hand, the door swung open. The hallway smelled damp and stuffy. We stood there on the threshold, at a loss. Owen called into the darkness, 'Hello.'

Somewhere, far at the back, a light went on and someone came shuffling down the hall. The door closed and then was opened again, just a crack. A shiny white, narrow Norwegian face peered out at us through the crack. 'Northern Lights Festival,' Owen said, sweetly.

'Been cancelled,' the face said. The door opened wide, and the beam of what looked like a kind of anti-aircraft searchlight hit us. We put up our hands to shield our eyes. 'Welcome. Late guests are my favourites.'


Except for us, no band had accepted the invitation to the Northern Lights Festival. No one had come. Evidently all of the others – like me at first – had assumed the invitation was a joke. 'So, what are we supposed to do now?' Owen asked. We were sitting at a table in Gunnar's kitchen drinking black tea with milk; it made me think of English orphanages. The kitchen was warm and cosy. Gunnar, smoking a cigarette, sat in a rocking chair by the window. He wore a Norwegian sweater and felt slippers; I would have been disappointed if he had looked any different.

The light outside the window was blue. I took off my jacket and hung it over the back of my chair. I wanted to stay in Tromsø. To never leave Tromsø. Norway. Fjords and waterfalls, and roads going through forests where you had to switch on your headlights even in the middle of the day.

'Now that you're here,' Gunnar said, 'you might as well stay.' But it didn't seem to interest him much, one way or the other. 'It's October. Anyway, nobody comes to Tromsø now, no tourists, nobody. You would have stayed here if you'd played the festival. Well, you can stay here now, a week if you like. Would you like to?'

Owen looked around the kitchen as though he had to think about it first. An old cast iron stove. Small shelves full of mugs and chipped plates. Seven chairs around the wooden table. On the wall over the sink a set of rules for guests written on wrapping paper in a childish scrawl: 'Always write down any beer and wine you take out of the refrigerator. Always wash your dishes. If you're planning to get smashed, do it in your room. Breakfast served until ten a.m.'

'What is this place?' Owen asked. 'A youth hostel? A home for rock 'n' rollers?'

Gunnar said, 'It's a guesthouse. I rent rooms to tourists in the summer, and in the winter the musicians who come to the festival live here, as well as a few other people; you'll be seeing them. Just now there are two others here, Germans like you.'

Owen looked at me. I looked at Owen. His face showed the expectant bliss that I knew and liked. I didn't say anything and Owen said, 'Well – I guess we'll stay.'

The room in Tromsø reminded me of rooms in cheap hotels in New York where I'd stayed. A wide American-style bed, a sink with a mirror above it, a plywood wardrobe and a white-painted radiator in which water was gurgling. The window looked out on a small street, but such was the room that on the other side of the window might just as well have been Soho, or Little Italy, or First Avenue in the East Village. A room that seemed bigger than it was and where you could lie around on the bed and do what you do when you're in love – imagine something, surrender to your pounding heart, open the door to anyone, and always long to be on the go.

Owen was quite beside himself. 'Can't we simply stay here for ever?' he asked. 'Let's simply stay here in Tromsø, in Norway. Not a soul back home knows where we are.'

'I don't know where I am, either,' I said. We were standing next to each other at the window, smoking and looking out. Reflections of the lights of a passing car flitted across Owen's face, the room was warm, far away a door slammed shut, someone walked slowly down the hallway. 'When I was little I wanted to be a fighter pilot,' Owen said. 'Did I ever tell you that I wanted to be a pilot?'

'No, you didn't,' I said. 'Tell me about it now.'

I never again saw any of the people I met on my trips abroad if they were just travelling, like me. That includes Martin and Caroline, whom we met at the Gunnarshus. I'll never see them again, and that isn't bad because I won't ever forget them. Martin had come to Tromsø for a year, Caroline for half a year. Martin was studying Scandinavian literature in Bonn and was here in Norway to write his PhD dissertation, a complicated treatise about ancient Norwegian manuscripts. 'Tromsø,' Martin said, 'has the biggest archive of Norwegian manuscripts.' I didn't believe him and it seemed to me that he was on the lookout for something quite different here, but I didn't want to force him to tell me about it.

Caroline had come to Tromsø as an au pair. She was very young and was studying German language and literature in Tübingen. She seemed shy, had a serious and easily influenced outlook on the world and yet a capacity for enthusiasm, and she was amazingly fearless. The Tromsø family she was supposed to work for as an au pair was in a shambles; the father drank too much, beat his wife and children, and kept drunkenly grabbing Caroline under her skirt. That caused her to quit the job, but not to leave Tromsø. Instead she got a job at McDonald's and then after closing time she pushed supermarket shopping trolleys together. She said it was nice in Tromsø and nice in Norway. Even without the au pair job she would stay as long as she had originally intended, maybe even longer. Later Owen said, 'There's something so comforting about Caroline,' which was exactly how I felt too.

We had that first conversation about the reasons for coming to Tromsø, and the pros and cons of beginnings and goodbyes, in the kitchen the next morning. Caroline, in her coat, was leaning against the radiator by the window, holding a cup of tea; she was about to leave for McDonald's. Martin had spread a pile of papers on the table and was working. Gunnar was nowhere in sight. Both Martin and Caroline's reactions to our arrival at the Gunnarshus had been pleasant but casual; two Germans in Tromsø, nothing surprising about that. They went on with their usual morning chores, on close friendly terms with each other and polite towards us. They didn't fall over themselves to express interest in our music or the foundered festival.

Later I realized that I also behaved like that when I was travelling and staying in a strange place for an extended time and somebody arrived later, an excited novice who immediately wanted to know all there was to know about the best bars and the cheapest stores and the most beautiful places to hike to in the area. I tell them about this and that, then point out that time was passing, and go back to doing my own things. Not out of arrogance, it was more insecurity on my part because the stranger – amidst all the excitement and uncertainty of being a stranger – reminded me of my own foreignness.

Martin said, 'Café Barinn, if you want a good cup of coffee,' and Caroline said, 'We could cook supper together this evening.' Then she left, closing the door softly behind her the way only people who are always considerate of others do.

I stayed indoors in Tromsø. Almost all the time. I had decided to think of this room in the Gunnarshus as a place I had moved into without there being any end in sight to my stay there. A place, moreover, where I could see the world passing by on the other side of my window. I could have been anywhere; what was going on outside was of no importance. I lay on the bed and read Caroline's books – Hofmannsthal, Inger Christensen, Thomas Mann;

and Martin's books – Stephen Frears, Alex Garland and Heimito von Doderer. I felt that coincidence had swept me up and dropped me into this room so that I would find out something about myself, about how things were supposed to proceed from here on, with me and with everything else – a long pause before something would happen, presumably something big, without my knowing what it would be. Sometimes I walked down Tromsø's short main street and back again, gazing at my reflection in the plate-glass shop windows. Then, returning to the house, I lay down on the bed and looked out of the window. 'Are you happy?' Owen asked. And I said, 'I am.'

Owen, on the other hand, went out all the time. He explored Tromsø as though he were doing a research project. Within forty-eight hours he had found out what was beautiful, odd, disgusting or unusual in Tromsø. Then he would come back, sit down next to me on the edge of the bed, and tell me about it, but his stories didn't make me want to see any of the things he had seen. He kept his hat on, didn't take off his anorak, smoked a cigarette, and rushed out again, banging the door shut behind him. From the window I could see him running by.

In the evening, when Caroline came home from the supermarket and Martin returned from his mysterious archive of Norwegian manuscripts, we would sit in the kitchen, eat together, drink a bottle of wine. Sometimes Gunnar joined us, never saying anything and quickly withdrawing again. Owen made noodles with shrimp, noodles with tomatoes, noodles with salmon. For dessert we had chocolate and green bananas. Caroline and Martin abandoned their reserve and polite disinterest. Because we were strangers and had come together like this by accident and only for a short time, we got around rather quickly to talking intimately about the most private things: our origins, our parents, the stories of our lives, and about love.

Owen said he had turned into a nervous wreck after the break-up of his last relationship. Martin said he was gay, which briefly made Owen feel embarrassed. Caroline said, hesitantly, that so far she had not really been in love. At that Owen, of all people, burst out laughing. I didn't tell them much of anything, there was nothing to tell. I told them about a love affair I'd had a hundred and twenty years ago. I also had the feeling that, for Caroline's sake, I should get a grip on myself – with regard to my confessions, my preferences, even my drinking; it was not an unpleasant feeling.

Looking at me strangely, Martin said, 'Norwegian men are quite good-looking. I can recommend them.' That went right by me. I was far from falling in love. Sometimes I thought I ought to fall in love with Owen, but I couldn't; it was absolutely impossible. Still, I would have liked to fall in love with him. Owen was the one who talked the most. Martin also talked quite a lot. Whenever Owen got too loud, too passionate, or too excited about something, Martin would leave the kitchen and would not come back until Owen had stopped talking. Caroline said the least. Most of the time I had to ask her to talk and then make sure that Owen listened to her too. Owen tended to ignore her.

I liked Caroline. I liked the girlish, reserved way she sat there until close to one o'clock at night, dead tired, listening wide-eyed to Owen and Martin's discussions about sex and the pros and cons of one-night stands. She was worn out and visibly exhausted, but in spite of that she never went to bed until the rest of us did. In the morning I liked being alone with her in the kitchen. She made tea and I would talk with her like someone I was not – someone sensible, wise, sentimental and serious.

I wanted her to tell me about her life, and when we were alone together she did: her childhood in a village, her sisters and brothers, the half-timbered house in which she grew up and that was later torn down. Thinking of it in the Gunnarshus kitchen still made her burst into tears. When she was twenty she went to Ghana for a year to work in a home for the handicapped. That whole year she slept under the open sky, surviving malaria, travelling through West Africa, and filtering her drinking water through the fabric of her T-shirts. Now she lived in a commune in Tübingen with ten other students. She had a girlfriend but no boyfriend. She was thinking about perhaps continuing her studies in England. She didn't smoke, drank hardly at all, and she'd certainly never had anything to do with drugs, not even once.

She talked about herself, and I listened, and something about her reminded me of myself ten years ago, even though ten years ago I was totally different. I wanted to take her under my wing, to protect her, without knowing from what. On the windowsill in her room, which was next to ours, she had arranged photographs of her parents and sisters and brothers in a row and, in among them, incense sticks and bead necklaces from Ghana. When she left for McDonald's in the morning, to spend eight hours pushing hamburgers and French fries over the counter, I wished I could have changed places with her.

When she came out of her shell in the evenings and even dared to say something in front of Martin and Owen, Owen acted inconsiderate and arrogant. Once we were talking about travelling and all the coincidences that throw people together and then separate them again, and Caroline said there was a saying that she liked a lot: Life is a box of chocolates; when you reach in to take one, you never know what you're going to get, but it's always something sweet. And when Owen threw up his hands and said he hadn't heard anything so idiotic in a long time, I stamped on his foot as hard as I could under the table.

Of course it was an idiotic saying, but it was also optimistic and even in all its inanity it was totally understandable. I didn't want to begrudge Caroline her saying, and for a moment I hated Owen for not going along with it, for having to act out his fucked-up coolness even here. Martin was more diplomatic. Like me he seemed drawn to Caroline; he often spoke to her and asked her questions, giving her a chance to answer, but soon he was again bogged down in long-drawn-out discussions with Owen about basic principles.

We would sit together like that, while it rained outside most of the time. Occasionally Gunnar would appear, pour himself a glass of wine, listen long enough to get the gist of the conversation, and then immediately leave the kitchen again. It seemed as if we hadn't yet hit on a topic that would make him stay – perhaps we would never find one. I was tense and on my guard. I didn't want anything to shatter this togetherness among strangers in the far North. I kept count of the days we'd been there; after the third day I lost track, and time began to rush by. I began to think seriously about staying longer.

We did stay longer. We couldn't leave Tromsø after the week was over, we just couldn't. We spoke to Gunnar, and he offered us an accceptable weekly rate for the room, and so we extended our stay for seven days. I asked Owen whether he intended to call anyone back home to tell them we were staying longer. I said, 'What's the story with your singer friend?' Owen didn't answer. I stayed in the house and Owen went out. When he came back, he sat down and told me things; sometimes he would stop talking and look at me warily until I asked, 'What's the matter?'

He asked, 'Are you sick?' And I said, 'No, I'm not.' And he said, 'All right then, which chocolate do I like best and what kind of car would I drive if I had the money and what's my favourite love story?' He was afraid that I might pull away from him, forget him. I said, 'Peppermint chocolate. Mercedes-Benz. Your own.' That reassured him and he left again.

I still didn't want to see anything on the outside. I just wanted to lie there and think, to be by myself and have tea with Caroline in the mornings and eat supper with the others in the evenings. It was as if I were a little sick, as if I'd been sick and was now recuperating. I didn't distance myself from Owen. I was just perplexed about myself, and in a strange way I was content to be in this state of perplexity. We spent the evenings together. Sometimes Martin would arrive later or he would leave the house again at midnight without asking us to go with him. I was sure he was out on a date and would end up in bed with someone. It was amazing to see him leave and to know that he was going off to have sex. He never brought anyone back to the Gunnarshus. One evening, and just that once, Owen said too much – 'I'm not gay,' he said.

That night, as we were lying next to each other in the

bed, he moved towards me and whispered in my ear, 'Martin looked at me today.'

I whispered, 'How?'

And Owen said in a loud voice, 'Well, sexually, man.'

I didn't believe that. I knew that the only reason we could be together so pleasantly in this impersonal yet personal way was that there was no danger any of us would fall in love with one of the others – Caroline would not fall for Owen, and Owen would not fall for Martin; I wouldn't fall in love with Owen, nor Owen with me. It was a big relief to know this, and at the same time it was also sad. It was sad that for the first time in my life I found the absence of love, the absence of even the possibility of love, comforting and a relief.

Saturday night, our seventh night in Tromsø, we all went out together. We put our coats on in the hall and left the house. As I stepped out into the cold nocturnal street, I felt as though I hadn't been out in the fresh air for months. It occurred to me that by now we ought to have been back home in Berlin or at least we should have arrived at the airport in Oslo on our way back. I was glad we had decided to stay. Gunnar had invited us to go with him to a party of Tromsø artists – musicians, record producers, writers and students, as well as the people from the Northern Lights Festival; Owen said he wanted to punch them in the mouth. We all went in Gunnar's car.

The party was in the suburbs, at the home of a Norwegian writer, a low building from the fifties in a deserted neighbourhood. A lot of people were already there when we arrived; they all knew one another. We stood around awkwardly by the coat rack till Gunnar simply pushed us into the large living room.

I whispered, 'Don't introduce me to anyone, please, certainly not to anyone from the Northern Lights Festival.' Gunnar laughed at that and said, 'It's unavoidable.' The guests at the party looked just the way I had imagined Norwegian party guests would look, dressed in warm clothes, inebriated, with hot, flushed faces. The host didn't seem interested in greeting each of his guests. I asked Gunnar several times where he was, and Gunnar always said, 'Nowhere in sight.'

There were bottles of beer and wine, funny-looking crisps, and bowls filled with salsa on a long table. A fire was burning in the fireplace, and the more prominent of the Tromsø artists were gathered around it – a group of eccentric-looking people clearly disassociating themselves from the rest of the guests standing around the salsa bowls. I leaned against the wall next to the door. Caroline brought me a glass of wine. I felt that if she were to stand next to me, I would never get to meet anyone. She stood next to me. Martin was openly looking for gays and within five minutes he had discovered all of them. Owen, with remarkable self-assurance, forced his way into the group by the fireplace and began talking with a tall woman who was wrapped in a bearskin.

Caroline smiled at me. She smiled the way she smiled at me mornings in the kitchen when she was making tea in her calm and deliberate way and I was mentally formulating my first question to her, 'When did you begin studying German literature?' But we weren't in the Gunnarshus kitchen now. We were at a pretty dull, boring party in the Norwegian sticks, and yet I became restless. I put down my glass of wine; I didn't want to drink anything.

Martin was talking to a young fellow who looked like an English boarding-school pupil. He whispered something into the boy's ear that caused him to blush violently. Owen touched the tall woman's bearskin, the tall woman pulled Owen's cap off his head. Nothing happened. Caroline said something and I heard Martin laugh in a totally new way.

A short man was standing by the fireplace. His ears stuck out and he had a kind of Iroquois haircut. He looked Polish and was quite handsome. He seemed not the least bit interested in anything that was happening beyond the group of people standing by the fireplace, and for that reason I didn't like him.

Gunnar came over and introduced us to a publisher who had just published a very successful book about yoga for young children. I didn't know what to say. But Caroline did and ended up asking the publisher about the book, and he promptly began to demonstrate the various yoga exercises: the snake, the rhinoceros, the bear and the cat. When it came to showing the fish, he went down on the floor and, lying on his back, writhed around our feet.

Owen glanced over at us from where he was standing by the fireplace; I returned his look, opening my eyes as wide as possible. He turned away again. The short man lit a cigar. The publisher got up, brushed the dust off his trousers and said, 'Don't you find it's a bit lonely here in our Tromsø?' His German was so correct I didn't have the slightest desire to ask him where he had learned to speak the language.

I looked at him, took a deep breath and said, 'I quite like the solitude.' I was about to capitulate, to expand on this topic of conversation and then go on to another and eventually a final one about culinary specialities and the midnight sun in Norway. And after that we'd go back to the Gunnarshus. I had been lying around on my bed in that room too long and I felt an aching homesickness. I was about to simply give up.

But just at that moment the short man with the Iroquois haircut took hold of my arm and brazenly drew me away. He shook my hand – for such a long time that I wished he would never stop. And then he said in German, 'I'm off to Paris, yes? To Tokyo, Lisbon, Bern, Amsterdam.' He had a dreadful accent and did not seem to understand the words he was pronouncing. He giggled. He let go of my hand. He said his name was Ari Oskarsson.

And I said in English, '*Nice to meet you.*' I felt funny and turned towards Owen, who was expecting my look and rolled his eyes. The short man was the director of the Northern Lights Festival. Speaking English, he apologized for the cancellation of the concert and any inconvenience. He said he had liked our CD very much. I looked at him; I couldn't really listen to him, but that didn't seem to matter. He had a nervous tic and kept squeezing his left eye shut; the expression around his eyes was one of curiosity and irony. He was standing very close to me; he smelled good and was wearing a wrinkled black suit and a cheap silver ring on the little finger of his right hand. I picked up my wine glass. Caroline didn't seem to be bored with the publisher. Gunnar looked over at us from the other side of the room; his expression was indecipherable. The short man caught his look and said something about the reputation of Gunnar's Guesthouse, that it was known far beyond the city of Tromsø, that countless world-famous musicians had slept in Gunnar's beds.

Out of the blue, I suddenly said that I actually didn't want to go on being a musician. I hadn't really meant to say it, but I did. My face felt flushed. I said I had been lying around in my room at Gunnar's house for a week, recovering from some inner hurt of which I hadn't even known. I said I certainly wouldn't be leaving Tromsø in the near future. I stopped talking, and the short man, assuming an encouraging, amused expression, nodded. I said other things I hadn't actually wanted to say. I said I liked lying around, waiting for the door to open and for someone to come in.

He said, 'Who?'

I said, 'Just anybody.' In English, I said, '*You look so Polish.*'

He said, '*Do I?*' and smiled. He seemed about to reply, when a woman walked by. She wore thick sixties glasses, a woollen scarf around her neck, and she had wild hair. The short man said, '*Excuse me,*' grabbed her by the wrist and pulled her over. '*Excuse me. That's Sikka, my wife.*'

Shortly before midnight, Owen asked the publisher if he knew who that far-out, stunning, long-legged blonde was who had been sitting motionless on the stairs all evening, not speaking with anyone. The publisher didn't answer, but ten minutes later he left with the blonde on his arm after first saying goodbye to us and briefly introducing her: 'By the way, this is my wife.'

For a long while Owen couldn't get over it. The Norwegians at this party all had wives and at least three children. Sikka was Ari Oskarsson's wife; she didn't look as if she were his wife, but she was. She was odd-looking but had a sense of humour that I would have found amusing if she weren't already pretty tipsy. When Ari Oskarsson introduced her to me, it took me half an hour to recover from the shock. I was struck dumb and couldn't say a word till Owen came over and called Ari Oskarsson a 'prick' to his face. Ari Oskarsson ignored him. Caroline was talking with a woman who could have been her mother. Martin was eating crisps and seemed to be relaxing; the English-looking boy had stretched out on a couch and fallen asleep.

The party was breaking up. Glasses clinked in the kitchen; someone threw open all the windows; the woman in the bearskin left without saying goodbye to Owen. Owen said, 'Man, you always go for the same types.'

I said angrily, 'So do you.'

In the hall near the front door, Ari Oskarsson made me write my name in the guest book. Sikka had disappeared, and we were standing next to each other in front of the chest of drawers on which the guest book lay, overshadowed by a large bouquet of red flowers. Ari Oscarsson turned to a blank page, pulled a pen from his jacket pocket, and began to write the date, taking an amazingly long time. He seemed unsure of both the month and the year. Then he solemnly handed me the pen, and I bent over the guest book and wrote my name under the date and the funny-looking word, Tromsø. He wrote his name under mine, so close to mine that the letters touched and intertwined. It looked as though from now on we were wedded to each other. He straightened up, closed the book, and said we absolutely had to drive into town together, to another party. The party here was over. He smiled at me. He didn't seem to be all there.

Outside, standing by the front door in the cold, I remembered that I hadn't come here alone. I remembered that Martin, Caroline and Owen were here too. I was reminded of it when Caroline pushed her arm into mine and Owen hissed at me, 'Don't do something foolish.' It was too late. I was already awake.

Our host, who had remained anonymous to the very end, quickly locked the door from inside as though he were afraid we might change our minds. Ari Oskarsson decided that Caroline and I would drive into town with him and Sikka, and that Caroline should drive. He realized instinctively that she was the only one still able to drive; I hadn't had much to drink, but I had no driving licence. He decided that Martin and Owen were to go with Gunnar in his car. He gave Gunnar directions to the party, an artists' party in some pub. Gunnar wasn't listening and looked up and down the street, bored. He told Martin he'd drop them off at the pub and then go home. Martin was amused and seemed to find Ari Oskarsson as attractive as I did. Owen seemed irritated, bristling at Ari Oskarsson's bossy tone, but then he got into Gunnar's car anyway, first pinching me hard on the arm.

They drove off and I watched them go while Sikka, quite drunk, tried to explain to Caroline how to get there. Behind me Ari Oskarsson was noisily peeing into a hedge. I thought that I didn't give a fig whether I'd ever see Owen and Martin again. We drove off, Caroline at the wheel, Sikka sitting next to her, and Ari Oskarsson next to me in the back seat. He took my hand and said, '*I love the Germans. I hate the Germans. For sure, I hate the Germans.*'

Sikka turned round, looked at us and yelled, '*Christmas music!*' A kind of department store music was rattling from the car radio. I pulled my hand away and looked past Ari Oskarsson's face into the pitch-black Tromsø night. Then I looked at him. Sikka said, '*Left. Right. No-no-no-no-no, left, excuse me.*'

And Caroline said, in a surprisingly calm tone of voice, *'Don't worry,'* as though she drove extremely drunk people through this area all the time. For a while we seemed to be driving through a forest. Then along the water and again through a forest and then into a city. Downtown, strings of lights, horn-blowing drivers in queues of cars. It might be Tromsø, but it could just as well have been any other city. I didn't even want to know.

Owen had told me about the Captains' Quarter, a district of colourful old wooden houses on narrow streets with gardens at the front. He had said if he ever wanted to live anywhere in Tromsø, it would be here. The street where Sikka now yelled *'Sto-o-o-p!'* into Caroline's ear – so loud that Caroline stepped on the brake hard enough to cause the car to go into a skid – might have been a street in the Captains' Quarter. It was a narrow street and the houses were small two-storey buildings that looked cosy and comfortable as if the people who lived here might have come to terms with their lives and were content. Sikka tumbled out of the car and stumbled into one of the front gardens. Signalling us to follow her, she disappeared into the house.

Caroline parked the car with meticulous accuracy in front of the garden gate. We got out and followed Sikka. Ari Oskarsson was walking behind me; there was no way to get away from him. We entered the house, the door closed heavily behind us. It was pitch black and I heard Caroline gasp; then a light came on. We were standing in a kitchen without a table, only a kind of steel counter and a row of empty kitchen cabinets. The kitchen led into a room in which the only signs of someone living there seemed to be a shelf full of books and CDs. The table and the designer chairs around it looked absolutely unused. On the table lay a copy of *The Times*. In the next room, a white sofa standing in front of a huge TV blended into a white wall. In the last room, the stand-by signal on a computer was blinking in the darkness. The room where Ari Oskarsson and his wife Sikka spent their nights was nowhere in sight. I could see no stairs that would have led to the second floor.

Ari Oskarsson put his hand on my back and forced me to sit down at the ice-cold table. He sat down across from me and had Caroline sit next to him. Sikka found a bottle of white wine and filled three glasses to the brim. There was no glass for Ari Oskarsson, so he just drank from the bottle.

Caroline was pale. She said, '*Party? What about this party, and where are Martin and Owen?*'

And Sikka said, '*Feel free, feel free,*' got up and turned on the stereo.

Ari Oskarsson smiled at me across the table. I sat there prepared to cope with whatever was going to happen. From the stereo came space music with muted bass and a voice producing an incomprehensible gibberish at an unbearable pitch. I said to Caroline that things like this always happen in strange places and especially when you are going to be leaving soon. I didn't know whether this was really true. Caroline didn't answer. She made some signs with her index finger but I couldn't figure out what she was trying to say; she looked awfully frightened.

Ari Oskarsson again said he had liked our CD very much. He had liked the cover photo in which Owen and I were hanging out under a plastic palm in the rear court-yard of Owen's apartment block. Ari Oskarsson said he had known I'd look the way I did, even though in the photo I didn't look that way. I didn't know what to make of that. I thought I looked rather beautiful in the photo. Was he trying to tell me that I wasn't beautiful?

It seemed as though Sikka couldn't make up her mind as to what sort of music was appropriate for the occasion. She kept switching CDs. Nodding towards her husband, she said into the pile of CDs, 'He loves you.'

I got up and went into the bathroom next to the kitchen. It looked like a bathroom in a hotel, the towels were machine folded, small samples of shower gel and shampoo were lined up on the rim of the bath, Sikka's expensive cosmetics were lying next to the sink. I snapped open a powder compact and closed it again. Sikka didn't look made up. I wondered why people lived in apartments that looked like hotel suites, and then I left the bathroom.

In the living room I had to pass Sikka, and she held on to me and indicated she wanted to dance by pressing her bony hip against mine. She was still wearing the woollen scarf and looked as though she had a cold. I refused; I said I was sorry but I couldn't dance with her; it wasn't her fault; I could never dance that way. I sat down again on the chair I had been assigned and gazed at Ari Oscarsson, and he gazed back at me with that amused, chummy expression on his face.

He had taken off his jacket and I could see a tattoo on his left forearm, an H and a B superimposed, precise, black capital letters on his white skin. I decided that if I ever had the chance to touch the tattoo, I wouldn't ask him for the story behind it. Never.

Caroline, holding on to the edge of the table, was staring at the headline in *The Times*. Next to me, Sikka was now dancing to the muffled, low sounds of a German band Ari Oskarsson told me was called 'The Leave'. I had never heard of The Leave. I leaned back and felt that I could stay here, just stay, here or somewhere else; the music was quite nice, and Sikka kept her distance. Ari Oskarsson was now holding our CD in his hand and kept looking from the photo to me and back to the photo. I hoped that it wouldn't occur to him to play the CD now; I would have found it unbearable to listen to Owen's high childish voice and my piano playing. Evidently it hadn't occurred to him. And everything would have stayed like that if Caroline hadn't suddenly jumped up and cried out, 'Couldn't we leave now? Please, couldn't we simply leave now and pick up Martin and Owen?' Her voice trembled and she sounded as if we had been kidnapped.

Sikka stopped dancing. Ari Oskarsson got up and turned off the music. They had obviously understood what Caroline had said. We all put our coats on and just walked out, out of the house and into the cold street. We were walking next to each other, and nothing happened until we arrived at the Café Barinn.

The Café Barinn reminded me of a pub back home, a dive I'd been going to for years and which then closed at the high point of its fame – just at the right time. I wasn't sure I wanted to be reminded of it. The Café Barinn was a small place in an alley off the main street – a room full of old leather sofas and tables surrounded by broken chairs. The heating system seemed to have broken down. The room was cram-full of people but, in spite of that, cold. All had their coats and hats on. Punk music blared from the loudspeakers. We had to order our drinks at the bar and pay for them on the spot. I treated Sikka, Caroline and Ari Oskarsson.

Martin and Owen were nowhere to be seen. I was surprised to see Gunnar sitting at the bar. Caroline wandered through the room searching for Martin and Owen, then came over to me and said in dismay, 'They're not here.' To ask Sikka and Ari Oskarsson about them would have been senseless; when it came to Martin and Owen, Sikka and Ari Oskarsson didn't understand English. Another thing entirely seemed to have left Gunnar speechless. Caroline looked at him the way one looks at a traitor. It was all the same to me. I stood around next to Sikka, then Ari Oskarsson, then Caroline and Gunnar.

It was cold and nice and wild in this pub, as if the windows were broken and the roof in need of repair. It was obvious that as a group, the five of us didn't know what to talk about. Sikka turned to Gunnar. Ari Oskarsson went to the bar and ordered a hot chocolate with whipped cream for Caroline.

I waited. I was waiting but didn't have to wait long at all, and then he was standing in front of me and put his arms around me and staggered around with me and said puzzling things, and I tried to fend him off even though I didn't really want to. I was trying to fend him off for Caroline's sake, for Sikka's sake. But I wasn't serious enough about it. I pulled away from him, and everything about me felt so soft, and he grabbed me and drew me to him. He said something in Norwegian and something in English and something in Chinese. I didn't understand any of it. Except that he wanted to know how I had spent the last few years. He said he so much would have liked to have spent the last few years with me, as if he knew that the last few years had been horrible, although I realized that only now. I didn't know how I had spent the last few years.

249

I didn't know how I could get rid of him, how I was to keep him from touching me, when I really didn't want to keep him from touching me. I saw Sikka's back. I saw Gunnar. I saw Caroline. Ari Oskarsson held on to my hand and put his arm on my back as though we were dancing. I felt dizzy. I looked at Caroline and made a face, trying to imitate the facial expression of someone who's being assaulted, who submits, who lets herself be abused against her will. I must have got the expression all too accurately. Caroline was able to put up with it for five minutes, if that.

It was Caroline who pulled us apart, not Sikka, and it was for Caroline's sake that I let Ari Oskarsson go. Ari Oskarsson let me go. In a firm voice that I wouldn't have thought her capable of she said – and she sounded like someone who would stop at nothing – that she wanted to know right now where Owen and Martin were; she wanted to know now, right now. And Ari Oskarsson said, politely and suddenly sober, that he would go and get them, and he went out and disappeared.

I stood beside Caroline, close to tears. I didn't know if anything would have been different without Caroline, or whether things were like this because Caroline was there, because she was preventing something from happening, causing me to act out a part and turning me into someone with whom Ari Oskarsson would have liked to have spent the past few years; how many – actually, all of them.

I stood there with Caroline, and we stared into space and were jostled and pushed against each other and then the door opened again, and Ari Oskarsson came in and Martin and Owen were with him.

\*      \*      \*

Owen knows me. He knows me well. He came rushing into the Café Barinn and immediately started pushing me around, shouting, 'You make me puke with your shitty attempts at going it alone. Really. It really makes me sick.' It was futile to explain the situation to him, he didn't want to know. For a while longer he ranted on about the pub where Gunnar, supposedly on the way home, had dumped him and Martin, a heavy-drinking joint to get blotto in – no place for a party, a lousy, rotten place; in his whole life he'd never felt so duped and sidelined. Martin seemed to be taking it all rather casually.

They had sat around in that pub waiting for us and at some point or other they both realized we weren't coming, whatever the reason. Martin had said, 'Ari Oskarsson wants to have the girls to himself.' And then Ari Oskarsson walked in and told them the party was somewhere else. 'And so we went with him,' Owen said. 'Yeah, we simply went along with this prick, we had no choice. I should have beaten him up right outside that shitty joint.' He shoved me aside again, went over to the bar and ordered a beer. I knew he wouldn't stay angry for long. I decided to be patient. I hadn't felt this patient and calculating in a long time.

Sikka was talking to Gunnar, who seemed a little afraid of Owen, and she wasn't paying attention to us or to Ari Oskarsson. Her glasses were steamed up, but she didn't take them off. Owen took his beer over to where Martin and Caroline were standing and they started a conversation that, for all I knew, could have been about the lecture schedule at the University of Tübingen. I stood around in the middle of the room and was patient and calculating, and then Ari Oskarsson sat down at a table by the wall and motioned to me and I went over and sat down.

We sat across from each other, and there was nothing to say, and I no longer knew whether it was Tromsø that allowed me to feel like this or the room in the Gunnarshus or the last bus to Oslo that had already left seven days ago, or even before that, something entirely different. I no longer knew nor did I have the slightest interest in finding out. I looked at him and I could see that he was absolutely imperturbable, unmoved, empty – not just towards me, but towards everything. It wasn't unpleasant to see that. Before he kissed me, he gave me time to ask him whether all this wasn't difficult. He gave me time to ask, *'Isn't it a problem, because of your wife?'* And very convincingly he said, *'No. It's no problem. For sure.'* And then he kissed me. And somewhere far away I saw Caroline's thunderstruck face, and Martin's face and Sikka's face. Sikka looked at us, and Owen looked at us and said something to Sikka that made her laugh. I again thought briefly about being different, but I wasn't, and then I kissed Ari Oskarsson.

The Café Barinn closed abruptly. And without a lengthy debate we all went back to the house in the Captains' Quarter. I hooked my arm under Owen's. I was glad that now he'd also have the benefit of seeing their place, its coldness and barrenness, the hotel bath, and the steel countertop in the kitchen; glad that he, too, would be able to hear The Leave and join Ari Oskarsson in drinking white wine from a bottle. I was glad I could share this with him. I knew that we were really quite alike, and now Owen seemed to be glad too, even though he couldn't help telling me that I was impossible. He said, 'You go and kiss a married man in front of his wife; that's really the last straw, absolutely impossible.' And I squeezed his arm and said, 'I asked him first if it might be a problem, and he said it wasn't. So leave me alone, Owen, just let me be.'

Caroline was walking beside Martin; she seemed to be holding on to him. Martin walked determinedly and rapidly; he looked like a member of an interesting expedition going into an unexplored land. Ari Oskarsson walked next to me. Sikka and Gunnar walked behind us; I could hear Sikka's voice; it didn't sound tense or strained. At the apartment they switched on the lights, turned on the music, put the white wine on the table, just as they had done hours earlier. Gunnar put out some coffee cups into which he poured cognac. I didn't drink anything. I sat down in the same chair. I felt at home here. I was an obvious intruder with certain intentions. I wasn't going to justify myself, neither to myself nor to anyone else. Caroline and Martin sat down across from me; Ari Oskarsson sat down next to me, took my hand and held it in his lap. Sikka and Owen were standing around in front of the stereo putting CDs on, and Gunnar went from person to person, and it seemed his sole purpose was to make sure that everyone was all right. I wondered whether he knew the evening would end this way, whether this was his way of introducing us to Tromsø society, whether every weekend he would allow new arrivals to walk into the Ari-and-Sikka-Oskarsson trap. He avoided looking at me. Caroline and Martin were talking about the customs declarations you had to fill out at airports. Evidently they had decided to act as if everything was all right. Perhaps they really thought everything was all right.

Sikka and Owen began to dance together. I knew that this would happen, yet for a second I thought it astonishing. They danced together, at first some distance apart, then closer, and finally very close. Owen held Sikka very tight, undid her wool scarf and kissed her neck. He moved his backside the way he always does, in a way that Martin must surely have liked. Martin was watching them. We all were, even Ari Oskarsson and I, and then we looked at each other again. I had to smile, he smiled too. What was going on here wasn't about me, it was about Ari Oskarsson and his wife. They had invited these guests so that they could see each other. Sikka could watch Ari Oskarsson kissing a strange woman; Ari Oskarsson could watch Sikka dancing with a strange man; they could look at each other and see each other anew. I figured I had my own reasons for being here and it occurred to me that I might also be mistaken about it, all of it.

The light above the ice-cold table was very bright, much brighter than the light at the Café Barinn had been. Caroline and Martin had to sit together in this light at a table with people who were kissing each other, but I didn't really care. Owen kissed Sikka, and Ari Oskarsson kissed me. Owen took off Sikka's glasses and shouted, 'Look how beautiful she is!' Sikka blinked with that out-of-focus look near-sighted people have, then she took the glasses away from Owen and put them back on. From time to time she came over to where Ari Oskarsson and I were sitting and said, '*Stop that.*' Nothing more, then she went back to Owen. She no longer said, '*Feel free.*'

Martin was watching Owen. Caroline was watching me as if I were strange and weird; I could no longer prevent that. At some point Gunnar left the house without anyone really noticing; his task seemed to have been accomplished. When Owen thrust his hand into Sikka's trousers, Martin and Caroline also got up. Before leaving, Caroline stood next to me for a moment and asked me for the key to our room. I could have told her that the evening here wasn't going to end the way it might seem. I was certain of that; but I didn't say it. I gave her the key; I knew what she wanted; she didn't want to sleep alone; I understood that, and maybe she also wanted to know if we were coming home, and how.

Late that night, Sikka and Owen disappeared into a small bedroom that was hidden behind the bathroom. Eventually I followed them and looked in. The room was dark and silent; Sikka was lying in the bed and Owen was sitting on the edge of it.

I went back into the large living room and asked Ari Oskarsson whether we could take a drive sometime, into the woods, to the rivers, the waterfalls and the fjords outside Tromsø – to a spot he thought was beautiful and would like to show me. I told him I was planning to move out of the Gunnarshus but intended to stay in Tromsø. And he said, 'No.' I thought that perhaps he hadn't quite understood my question. I repeated it, and he again said, 'No.' And then he looked at me thoughtfully and said, *'Are you talking about sex?'*

I shook my head. I was confused by the question. Was I talking about sex when I asked whether we could take a drive out of Tromsø? Maybe. Maybe not. We were standing in the kitchen at the steel counter, facing each other and holding hands. The nervous tic in his left eye had stopped. Ari Oskarsson was calm. I was calm too. Maybe Sikka and Owen were sleeping together just then, and maybe not. That didn't seem to be the point. We embraced the way you embrace when you won't be seeing each other for a long time.

And then someone pushed me away from Ari Oskarsson, and Owen was standing there looking tired, and Sikka was outside the bathroom, yelling. She was naked and I was surprised to see she was wearing a garter belt. She was yelling something in Norwegian and came running up to me and shoved me against Owen. She said, '*You have to go. Both of you,*' as if I could ever have assumed that one of us would be allowed to stay. She pulled open the front door. Owen gently took my arm. I didn't look at Ari Oskarsson again. We went home.

Towards noon the following day, I woke up with a pounding headache. I was lying in my bed in the Gunnarshus room and Caroline lay beside me, and next to Caroline was Owen. I got up and washed my face with cold water. I looked through the window at the grey street, and then I went back to bed. Caroline and Owen woke up at the same moment. We couldn't get up for a long time. We lay there next to each other in that bed, exhausted, hung over and happy.

Caroline seemed to be disconcerted but at the same time more open; she was looking at us in a different way than she had before. No longer as if she never wanted to see us again. She said, 'How did it all turn out?' and sat up, pulling the covers to her chin. Her sleepy face was very soft.

Owen burrowed into the pillows, then raised himself and said, 'I don't even remember what she looked like. What did she look like, this Sikka? I mean, I had my hand inside her trousers and I don't even know what she looked like. That's really awful.'

I couldn't help laughing, Caroline laughed too. We went over the previous evening, hour by hour, asking each other about every detail. It was as if the night had been something very precious, irretrievably over, but wonderful. I said, 'What was it like when we kissed, Ari Oskarsson and I?'

And Caroline and Owen shrieked and clapped their hands and shook their heads, 'Impossible. Really. You kissing this character in front of all those people.'

I curled up at the foot of the bed and couldn't stop laughing.

'I said to that woman, "*Let's fuck together*,"' Owen said. He looked astonished.

Caroline said, 'Oh.'

And Owen said, 'It's true. In that bedroom I said to her, "*Let's fuck together*"; she was lying in bed, and I was sitting on the edge of the bed.'

'Where was I when that happened?' I asked, and Owen said that Ari Oskarsson and I had been kissing for an extremely long time, all the time.

'And what did she say?' Caroline asked, all excited like a schoolgirl.

'She said, "*No*,"' Owen said. 'She said, "*No, I love my husband*," and I said, "*Your husband is a prick*," and she said, "*But I love him*."' He doubled up and let out a shout. 'Man! Her skin was so soft, and she looked so beautiful without glasses, and I really wanted to fuck her, and she said, "*I love my husband!*" Imagine that!'

We couldn't imagine it.

After a while Caroline got up and made tea and came back to bed, and we drank the tea. The day turned into afternoon; dusk began to fall. My headache got better; I was hungry. I wished it would just go on like this: the lassitude, the happiness and the excitement; we couldn't stop talking about it. 'There should always be nights like that,' Owen said. 'All of life should be like that one night,' and Caroline said she didn't know if she could bear it.

\*    \*    \*

When it grew dark, Martin knocked on our door. I had been waiting for him, and it was almost as though I missed him. He looked in through the crack in the door and seemed not at all surprised to find us in bed together. He acted as if he were used to such nights; it amused him to see how exhausted we were, as if we were beginners in a world that had been familiar to him for a long time already. He sat down with us and said he had enjoyed the evening very much. He said it was nice to see Caroline's reaction to what I had been doing with Ari Oskarsson. It was nice to watch Sikka and Owen dancing together. He didn't really have to know how the night ended. The night was over for him. He seemed to have known for a long time: Nights like this pass, leaving no trace; other nights come along later, eventually. He said he was going to use Gunnar's car to drive to a reception at the town hall. The reception was being given by German ship captains who were erecting a memorial to the fishermen who lost their lives in Norwegian waters. We should come along; there would be free food and drinks.

We finally got up, still wobbly and dazed, got dressed with the doors to our rooms ajar and talking to each other across the hall. Gunnar didn't show up; he had disappeared, and maybe he wasn't in the house any more, had given up his role as house master – after all, we had 'arrived'. We drove in his car to the town hall. There the German ship captains were standing around a monolith of German granite. The mayor of Tromsø made an incomprehensible speech, and Norwegian girls sang Norwegian songs. I ate little sausages with mustard and pickles and little salmon rolls and drank Coca-Cola. I had goose bumps, I longed for home. I thought I would never go back home, but that I would stay in Tromsø together with Martin and Caroline and Owen. I thought I could stop time, that I could hide for ever. I was very serious. I thought of Ari Oskarsson, and whenever I thought of him something inside me contracted, and I had a great longing to kiss him one more time.

Owen stood next to me, went away, came back, and said, 'I asked them how much you can make here working in the fish factory.' Caroline and Martin were talking to the German captains. We tried hard not to lose sight of one another, but then at some point we did. Caroline was gone, and Martin was gone, but Owen was still there; he had the keys to Gunnar's car in his hand. He said, 'I'm going to show you the island now; it's the most beautiful spot in Tromsø,' and we left the town hall, climbed into Gunnar's car and drove off.

We didn't say anything about driving out to see Sikka and Ari Oskarsson again. What I mean is, we didn't talk about doing it but simply did it, without agreeing to do it beforehand. We drove to the Captains' Quarter in Gunnar's car and parked right across the street from Sikka and Ari Oskarsson's house. Owen switched off the engine but left the radio on, playing softly. I unbuckled my seat belt and lit my first cigarette of the day. The bright light was on in the large living room, but the curtains were drawn. We could see the blue flicker of the TV in the back room. Now and then a shadow moved through the room and into the kitchen and back again. It looked peaceful, and I assumed that Sikka and Ari Oskarsson had headaches and were tired.

We sat in the car outside the house for a long time. I wanted to go in. I wanted to knock and say, '*Excuse me,*' if Sikka had opened the door, and then we could have gone in and sat down in front of the TV with Sikka and Ari Oskarsson. They would have had to let us come in. They really would have. But I didn't knock on the door, and Owen didn't either. We just sat in the car and gazed at the brightly lit window, and then Owen started the engine and we drove on towards the island.

The island wasn't far from Tromsø, a small island with a lighthouse and two abandoned houses, nothing else, a rocky island one could reach when the tide went out by walking along the jetty that extended from the mainland. Owen loved the island. He couldn't stop talking about it and the fabulous view of Tromsø you got from there. He had been going to the island every day; at high tide he would remain on the mainland and look yearningly across to the lighthouse.

The tide was out when we arrived at the beach. We got out of the car and climbed over some small boulders and then we walked on the jetty over to the island. The lighthouse stood out brightly against the night sky. Every three minutes its green beam swung in an arc above us. Turning round, I could see Tromsø. Owen walked confidently along in front of me; he seemed to be familiar with the path over the jetty. I stumbled frequently, my shoes got wet; I was glad we were going to the island just then.

The island shore was steep and rocky. Owen took my hand and helped me up; the wind was more biting on the island than on the mainland; the sky above us was black and clear. Owen said he wasn't sure when the tide would come in, how long we could stay on the island. If the tide came in too quickly, we would have to spend the night there and wouldn't be able to go back until six hours later. I didn't care, I wasn't afraid.

We stood next to each other looking up at the lighthouse, over to Tromsø and up into the sky. Owen said, 'I said "*I love you*" to Sikka.'

I was silent. Then I said, 'When?'

And he said, 'When you kissed Ari Oskarsson in the Café Barinn. I walked over to her and said, "*I love you*," and then I said it again later.'

I said, 'And why did you say it?'

And Owen thought about it, and then he said, 'Just like that, for fun. She laughed, too.'

We were silent a while, stepping from one foot to the other; the wind was pretty cold and it whistled around the lighthouse. The windows of the two abandoned houses were boarded up. I said, 'Ari Oskarsson said, "*I love you*" to me, maybe just before you said it to Sikka.' I thought it was outrageous that I should be able to say this. I recalled that moment at the table by the wall when I saw that Ari Oskarsson was empty, imperturbable and unmoved, and it was precisely at that moment that he said it. He didn't lean towards me, and his facial expression didn't change; he simply said it, '*I love you*.' I recalled the moment.

Owen was staring at me. 'He didn't say that.'

'Yes,' I said, 'he really said it.'

'And how did you answer him?' Owen walked away from me and round the lighthouse; I ran after him. I had to laugh. Owen started to laugh too, he shook his head and said, 'You didn't, did you? Please tell me you didn't say it, please. You can't seriously tell me that you said it,' he shouted, even though I hadn't answered him yet. He called back over his shoulder, 'You didn't say it.'

And I called out, 'Of course I said it. I simply said, "*I love you, too.*" I said, "*I love you, too.*" And I was totally serious.' Owen stopped so abruptly that I ran into him. We giggled.

'*I love you, too,*' Owen said. '*I love you, too.*' He couldn't calm down; he thought it was so funny, and I did too, terribly funny, and yet there was something about it all that was utterly sad. And before I could get hold of it, this sadness below the pleasure of laughing about it, Owen threw his arms up into the air and yelled, and I looked up at the sky and what I thought had been a green cloud suddenly began to dissolve. It dissolved and trembled and became brighter and brighter and was a great swirl across the sky in all colours, glowing and beautiful.

I whispered, 'What is it?'

And Owen yelled, 'The Northern Lights, man, it's the Northern Lights. I can't believe it,' and we looked up and gazed at the Northern Lights – *Matter flung out into space, a lot of hot electrons, exploded stars, how do I know*. 'And are you happy now?' Owen said breathlessly, and I said, 'Very.'